Stories by Contemporary Irish Women

RICHARD FALLIS, SERIES EDITOR

STORIES BY CONTEMPORARY IRISH WOMEN

Edited by

DANIEL J. CASEY

and

LINDA M. CASEY

SYRACUSE UNIVERSITY PRESS

Copyright © 1990 by Syracuse University Press
Syracuse, New York 13244-5160

ALL RIGHTS RESERVED

First Edition 1990
95 94 93 92 91 90   6 5 4 3 2

The paper used in this publication meets the minimum requirements of American National Standard for Information Sciences — Permanence of Paper for Printed Library Materials, ANSI Z39.48-1984. ∞™

Library of Congress Cataloging-in-Publication Data

Stories by contemporary Irish women / edited by Daniel J. Casey and
    Linda M. Casey. — 1st ed.
          p.   cm. — (Irish studies)
      Includes bibliographical references.
      ISBN 0-8156-2489-1. — ISBN 0-8156-0249-9 (pbk.)
      1. Short stories, English — Irish authors. 2. Short stories,
English — Women authors. 3. English fiction — 20th century. 4. Women
and literature — Ireland. 5. Northern Ireland — Fiction. 6. Ireland —
Fiction. I. Casey, Daniel J., 1937-   . II. Casey, Linda M.
III. Series: Irish studies (Syracuse, N.Y.)
PR8876.2.W65S7   1990
823'.01089287 — dc20   89-29523
                                                  CIP

MANUFACTURED IN THE UNITED STATES OF AMERICA

With love to Conor

IRISH STUDIES

Irish Studies presents a wide range of books interpreting aspects of Irish life and culture to scholarly and general audiences. Irish literature is a special concern in the series, but works from the perspectives of the fine arts, history, and the social sciences are also welcome, as are studies which take multidisciplinary approaches.

Contents

Acknowledgments

The editors gratefully acknowledge the following: "The Empty Ceiling" from *Captives* by F. D. Sheridan (Dublin: Co-Op Books, Ltd., 1980); "Housekeeper's Cut" from *A Nail on the Head* by Clare Boylan (Harmondsworth, Middlesex, England: Penguin Books, 1985), copyright (c) 1981 by Clare Boylan. Reprinted by permission of Viking Penguin, Inc.; "Lilacs" from *The Stories of Mary Lavin*, vol. 3 (London: Constable and Company, Ltd., 1985); "The Cobweb Curtain" from *The Whispering Arch and Other Stories* by Rita Kelly (Dublin: Arlen House Press, 1986); "The Shaking Trees" by Lucile Redmond from *Paddy No More*, edited by William Vorm (Dublin: Wolfhound Press, 1978), (c) Lucile Redmond 1975; "The Quibbler" from *The Dark Hole Days* by Una Woods (Belfast: Blackstaff Press, 1984); and "A Scandalous Woman" from *A Scandalous Woman — Stories* by Edna O'Brien (London: Weidenfeld and Nicolson, 1974). Reprinted by permission of the author and Weidenfeld and Nicolson.

"Five Notes After a Visit" by Anne Devlin and "The Wall Reader" by Fiona Barr are reprinted by permission of the authors from *The Female Line*, edited by Ruth Hooley (Belfast: Northern Ireland Women's Rights Movement, 1985). "Saints and Scholars" from *A Belfast Woman* by Mary Beckett. Copyright (c) 1980 by Mary Beckett. Reprinted by permission of William Morrow & Co., Inc.

The remaining titles appeared in paperback from Poolbeg Press (Swords, Co. Dublin) between 1976 and 1980. The editors acknowledge, with thanks, the following: "A Season for Mothers" from *A Season for Mothers* by Helen Lucy Burke, 1980; "Aimez-vous Colette" from *The Lady with the Red Shoes* by Ita Daly, 1980; "A Minor Incident" from *Sixpence in Her Shoe* by Maura Treacy, 1977; "A Pot of Soothing Herbs" from *Melancholy Baby and Other Stories* by Julia O'Faolain, 1978; "Losing" from *A Gift Horse and Other Stories* by Kate Cruise O'Brien, 1978;

"The Sentimentalist" from *A Life of Her Own* by Maeve Kelly, copyright (c) 1976 by Maeve Kelly; and "Winter Break" from *Female Forms* by Emma Cooke, 1980. All are reprinted here with the permission of the authors.

Introduction

DANIEL J. CASEY and LINDA M. CASEY

Since the mid-1960s Irish women have participated in a cataclysmic political, economic, and social upheaval—a violent civil war in the North, an unsettling European economic alliance, and a traumatic clash of traditionalism and modernism. They have, so to speak, been wrenched from the security of marriage and family and the "God's-in-his-heaven" mentality into a complex world fraught with enormous psychic stresses and strains. They have survived that passage and, in surviving, they have begun to define a new social order.

The conflicts of this upheaval have not been lost on the younger Irish women writers who, although no more imaginative than those who preceded them, explore themes that have never before been addressed in Irish literature. They evolve female characters who challenge orthodoxy and characters who reflect strictly female experiences. They are intrigued by "what disturbs, questions, offends, angers, or may even be morally and culturally subversive."[1]

Gone is the nineteenth-century image of a mist-shrouded isle with peasants dancing on Big House lawns and thatched cabins with hens roosting on open half-doors. The modern writer more likely inhabits a world of computerized offices, chic boutiques, fashionable lounges, and fast cars—it is the world of her fiction. She portrays a society in flux, a society whose very traditions and values are in question. Di-

DANIEL J. CASEY is Vice President for Academic Affairs and Academic Dean, College of Our Lady of the Elms, and coeditor of *Modern Irish-American Fiction: A Reader* (Syracuse University Press, 1989).

LINDA M. CASEY has studied and taught English as a second language in Finland, Ireland, and Italy.

1

vorce and contraception, once generally denounced, are now shrugged
off by many as consequences of modernism and urbanization. The
revolution of thirty years has shattered stereotypes and wrought pro-
found social changes.

Yet as late as 1983 in a highly provocative, critical essay entitled
"Irish Women and Writing in Modern Ireland," journalist Nuala
O'Faolain said that there has not been a great Irish woman writer.[2]
According to O'Faolain, Irish women writers have produced nothing
comparable to the masterpieces of their male counterparts and nothing comparable to the works of contemporary feminist writers elsewhere. There are no Marilyn Frenches, Marge Piercys, or Mary Gor-
dons writing in Athlone or Mullingar.

While O'Faolain credits Edna O'Brien with a measure of com-
mercial success, she dismisses a long line of recognized women of talent who, she believes, may earn high marks for virtuosity but fail as
modern feminists. But are there Irish women writers the like of Yeats
and Joyce? Is there a developing feminist tradition in Ireland worthy
of serious critical attention?

Few will dispute the record, the contributions of Maria Edgeworth, Augusta Gregory, Edith Somerville and Martin Ross, Elizabeth
Bowen, or Kate O'Brien to the canon of Irish literature. Each has provided a significant body of drama or fiction, and each has interpreted
the Irish experience from a woman's point of view. *Castle Rackrent* (1800),
Spreading the News (1909), *The Real Charlotte* (1894), *The Death of the Heart*
(1935), and *Mary Lavelle* (1936) stand as articulate testimony to a su-
perb but neglected "second tradition" in the national literature.[3]

Because there are no acknowledged "great" works of prose, drama,
or poetry by women against which to gauge the works of this "second
tradition," the works of the best women writers have often gone un-
appreciated. They are typically cited in a note or in a paragraph or
two in the literary histories. Iris Murdoch, herself a Dubliner, says,
"I think being a woman is like being Irish . . . everyone says you're
important and nice but you take second place all the same."[4] What
then of Irish women writers? Nuala O'Faolain answers: "Women don't
count for much in contemporary Ireland, and neither does woman's
writing."[5] But is the situation really that bleak?

In a sense the women writers from Maria Edgeworth to Kate
O'Brien were favored. They were university educated or Ascendancy

class, writers of literary sophistication and social respectability. They were thoroughly professional, but they did not write with the urgency of those less favored. They often lived by literary conventions that restricted range and inhibited style,[6] although Kate O'Brien's *Mary Lavelle* did incur the wrath of the censors by flaunting "liberal values."

Elaine Showalter, in *A Literature of Their Own: British Women Novelists from Bronte to Lessing,*[7] goes further when she states that Irish women writers not only affirmed limitations set by critics and censors, but they also reflected a nearly casual approach to the art and, in so doing, accepted or appeared to accept second-class status. Still, beginning with Elizabeth Bowen and Kate O'Brien, Irish women have contributed an exceptional body of literature. In the vanguard of the successful contemporaries are Mary Lavin, Edna O'Brien, and Julia O'Faolain, who bridge the gap between those who wrote on more traditional themes and those whose works reflect more recent attitudes. Their works measure up critically to the best of Edgeworth, Gregory, Somerville and Ross, Bowen, and Kate O'Brien.

Lavin, an established writer now ranked among the "masters," owes her reputation more to the *New Yorker* than to the Irish publishers. O'Brien, who has received international kudos, has, until recent years, been without honor among the Irish critics. And Julia O'Faolain, in the 1980s, broke from her father's shadow to achieve prominence in contemporary fiction. These three writers lend outstanding selections to this volume and thus anchor the collection both by reputation and by contribution. "Lilacs," Mary Lavin's exemplary study of traditional life and traditional relationships centers on a conflict between a dealer in dung and his wife and daughters. Phelim Mulloy has made his living as a collector and seller of dung for plant fertilizer, and he has used his earnings to provide for his family and give his two daughters a convent-school education. Now his daughters, home from convent school, have convinced their mother to do their bidding to have the offensive dunghill removed. The outraged father stands his ground. Soon after the argument, he dies.

Lavin's narrative focuses on the widow and daughters left to face uncertain reality. Suddenly Ros Mulloy turns on her daughters. She echoes Synge's Maurya in "Riders to the Sea": "Did it never occur to you that it might not be easy for us, three women with no man about the place, to keep going, to put food on the table and keep a fire on the hearth, to say nothing at all about finery and fal-lals." Reality comes crashing down on the women in their struggle to survive.

In some respects, Lavin's story is old-fashioned. It draws on country life — courting, a wedding, wake, burial — yet there is at the heart of it psychological conflict and dramatic dialogue that reveal character fully. The dream of the lilacs provides a final irony. In her early stories Lavin ushers in a new realism in fiction that places women, frequently widows with dependent children, in survival situations. Not surprisingly Lavin's women survive.

In a 1976 essay published in the *Sewanee Review,* Edna O'Brien sums up her quarrel with Ireland this way:

> I had thought of how it had warped me, and those around me, and their parents before them, all stooped by a variety of fears — fear of Church, fear of gombeenism, fear of phantoms, fear of ridicule, fear of hunger, fear of annihilation, and fear of their own deeply ingrained aggression that can only strike a blow at one another, not having the innate authority to strike at those who are higher. Pity arose too, pity for a land so often denuded, pity for a people reluctant to admit that there is anything wrong. That is why we leave. Because we beg to differ. Because we dread the psychological choke.[8]

In 1959 Edna O'Brien left Dublin for London. Between 1960 and 1964, she produced a controversial trilogy — *The Country Girls, The Lonely Girl (Girl with the Green Eyes),* and *Girls in Their Married Bliss* — that struck a blow for a new candor in women's writing and established O'Brien as an iconoclast with a smart sense of style. Though still discounted by some academic critics, O'Brien's subsequent works, *A Pagan Place* (1970), *Night* (1972), and the later fiction, have secured her reputation.[9]

"A Scandalous Woman," one of her finest pieces, is set in the Clare countryside of her childhood and uses an observant child commentator to move the story. It is the story of Eily Hogan, a local beauty savaged by rural Irish life. Brought up in poverty by a backward mother and tyrannical father, the spirited Eily looks for adventure and romance in secret assignations with a Protestant bank clerk.

But morality in rural Clare is determined by a parish priest with a big stick and hellfire-and-brimstone-preaching Redemptorists who retard normality. The story is also cast with a leering schoolmaster who remarks how Eily "strips a fine woman" and a giddy schoolmistress who, in company, hikes her dress to receive the full benefit of the open fire. Ignorance is not bliss, though. Eily's shotgun wedding to the reluctant banker is full of absurdities and pretenses. She moves away, and she grows old and strange, trapped in a loveless marriage. The narrator remarks, on seeing Eily afterward, how she was coarser now, how the spark had gone out of her.

For Edna O'Brien Ireland is a mix of "richness and unquenchable grief,"[10] a Godridden country that has repressed and victimized women to preserve fanatical, errant traditions. The narrator of "A Scandalous Woman," older and wiser, reflects on Eily Hogan's fate and leaves the reader with: "I thought ours indeed was a land of shame, a land of murder and a strange land of sacrificial women." In that final line O'Brien makes her case.

The third of the established writers, Julia O'Faolain, is the daughter of Eileen O'Faolain, distinguished writer of children's stories, and Sean O'Faolain, *doyen* of Irish letters. Though her early works, like *We Might See the Sights* (1968), *Godded and Codded* (1970), and *Women on the Wall* (1975), use international settings and play on the "innocents abroad" theme, the novel, *No Country for Young Men* (published in Britain in 1980 and the U.S. in 1987) is her fictional tour de force.[11] O'Faolain has also written a history of women, *Not in God's Image: Women in History from the Greeks to the Victorians* (1973) with Lauro Martines, her husband.

O'Faolain's short fiction often ridicules Irish sexual inhibitions and hypocrisies. Set in bohemian Dublin in the 1950s, "A Pot of Soothing Herbs" catches the Irish in compromising positions—an adventurous but cautious virgin finishes up, after a night of revelry, in bed with two young men. The ructions that follow underscore the puritanical obsession with sex that haunts the Irish into the 1990s. O'Faolain tempers harsh criticisms of male-dominated Irish society with doses of humor, though she admits to harboring bitterness when she considers the oppression of women "at home."

Women writers following Mary Lavin, Edna O'Brien, and Julia O'Faolain write with conviction against the background of 1960–1990 Ireland. They are feminists, experimentalists, and stylists; political and social reformers; and, as Irish writers, accomplished storytellers.

F. D. Sheridan's "Empty Ceiling," a powerful mood piece, is existential in concept and lyrical in rendering. The narrator, a fifty-eight-year-old woman, has, she confesses, lost her grip on reality and retreated deep into the recesses of a cocoon after witnessing the horror of a boy's decapitation by an incendiary. And, Lucile Redmond, in "The Shaking Trees," hones symbols and images—Tarots and talismans—to psychic sharpness. Hers is a tale of tragic loss and drug-induced madness. Redmond's character slips from consciousness and slides into the silence of the forest. Both writers play out agonizing mindgames, seeking an end to the tunnel; both trace convoluted mental processes in a developing narrative. In the Irish context, the work of Sheridan and Redmond is highly experimental.

The modern Northern writers use Belfast and the border country for setting, and three of their stories center on sectarian fears and hatreds born of the recent Troubles. The Northern writers cannot be oblivious to the siege mentality that pervades life in the Six Counties. Their stories are, however, more than tales of women caught in the crossfire.

"Saints and Scholars," Mary Beckett's contribution, relies on extended dramatic dialogue between wife and mother-in-law to carry the narrative. The wife, an educated woman, has grown resentful. Trapped in a spite marriage to a spoiled "half-grown boy of forty," she harbors quiet rage, as her mother-in-law admonishes her to suffer silently and do the will of God. In the final dialogue the wife plays her trump card as the curtain descends.

"The Quibbler," Una Woods's Belfast story, concerns a university student's rejection in love. Malcolm Maguire, called "the quibbler" by his sweetheart, Sheila, because he continually dissects the meaning of words and finds fault with ideas expressed in any conversation, is another spoiled boy who has had his way too long. Immature and insecure, he mistreats a devoted mother, turns up drunk at Sheila's home, and finally destroys his relationship with her.

Threats and reprisals are the quotidian realities of the Belfast of Anne Devlin and Fiona Barr. Devlin's "Five Notes After a Visit" is a well-crafted story of two Belfast exiles—Catholic and Protestant lovers—home from London. In spite of their resolves, they find the complications of the ghetto mentality and the intolerance of divorce too much for them. Devlin's diarist, now alone and back in her London flat, pens this final entry: "I keep myself awake all night so I am ready when they come." Barr's "wall-reader" (she tells us, "Respectable housewives don't read walls") is also a victim of that ignorance and intolerance. Alone and lonely each day while her husband works, the housewife wheels a pram through Belfast streets confronting fantasy-provoking graffiti at every turning. An innocent exchange with an English voice in a gun-turret breaks the monotony of housework and nappies; however, this frequent, casual conversation leads to fear and trembling and eventually to exile.

Although, strictly speaking, Maura Treacy is not a Northerner (having grown up near Dundalk), she is nonetheless regarded as a distinguished Northern Irish writer. She sets "A Minor Incident" along the South Armagh border, where she portrays a single horrifying act of violence and cruelty by British troops against helpless women and children. It is a story that never makes the headlines.

Four of the selections look at male-female relationships in the context of the sexual revolution and the shifting sense of Irish morality. Ita Daly's "Aimez-vous Colette" is a charming story told by a shy, retiring provincial spinster schoolmistress "on the wrong side of forty" who leads two lives. She remembers, for the reader, her university days in Dublin and Humphrey Ozookwe, a gentle African boyfriend and the blackest man she had ever seen. She remembers, too, small-minded Irish prejudices that cost her that life. She retreats, she tells us, to a country hermitage and a convent school run by the French nuns. Her other life she now lives vicariously through the smouldering novels of Colette.

"Losing," set against Yuppie Grafton Street, is Kate Cruise O'Brien's story of an affair of the heart. In it a successful middle-aged antique dealer keeps his young mistress in hand with promises of shared commissions on sales and a partnership in a computerized dating service. When, out of boredom, she decides to pursue a life of her own, her lover shows his selfishness and egotism by telling her to leave, completely unable to understand that she could have interests outside of his.

Clare Boylan's "Housekeeper's Cut" and Emma Cooke's "Winter Break" would have been censored not many years ago. They are stories of women's extramarital affairs, stories of married women, sick with ennui, seeking reckless alliances and one-night stands. Boylan's tale is seriocomic. She tells us that Edward, who looks on love as a seasonal pleasure, used to meet Susan between meals and that he wanted her to look after him. Clearly their expectations are at odds.

When Susan telephones to say that she is coming up to London for two days, Edward immediately provisions the kitchen; creates an inspired still life with roast, vegetables, and garnishes; and buys a frilly apron. Once arrived, the impatient Susan slouches petulantly in an armchair, "her white skirt bunched under her thighs" while he imagines she should be in the kitchen doing something with the roast. Theaters, restaurants, Madame Tussaud's, broken only by passionate sexual interludes, figure into Susan's two-day London package. Edward's thoughts are nearer home—he puts the meat into the oven. Disappointments lead to tears and recriminations.

"Winter Break" treats of infidelity more seriously. Cooke begins, "Connie had been a child bride—back in the early fifties when it really meant something." She tells us how Connie and Tim returned to Tenerife at the start of their twenty-fifth year of marriage, Connie seeking love and excitement, Tim a bottle and a bed. The honeymoon is over. Connie strikes out on her own to see the sights of Tenerife and chances on an American tourist. They form an easy alliance—a visit to the botanical gardens, cocktails at an airy cafe, a stroll through the markets—and finish with a sexual liaison. She is a little surprised that she experiences no guilt.

Our last stories focus on unique characters who challenge modern life and mores. In "The Cobweb Curtain," by Rita Kelly, Julie Scott is a free spirit—she thumbs rides, drinks stout, and lives in England. But every year she returns to the Clondelara of her childhood, to a rough cabin with an open cooking fire and with hens roosting in the kitchen. She returns for an obligatory week-long stay with an aged mother. But Julie Scott, unlike so many others, has put the poverty and deprivation of rural Ireland behind her. She has resolved never to disturb the cobweb curtains of the past. Maeve Kelly's "The Sentimentalist" is a story told by an eccentric. The narrator, at eighty, recalls her English cousin Liza, who threw herself into the Irish Movement with a convert's zeal. Liza lost a husband to the Black and Tans and devoted her life to running an Irish school for fifty summers. She was, the narrator confides, an idealist living a useless dream, a singular woman fighting for "the ennoblement of womankind."

"A Season for Mothers" by Helen Lucy Burke, begins this collection because it is a brilliantly orchestrated tale by a gifted storyteller. Burke has not only captured the quintessential Irish mother-daughter relationship, she has captured it against the backdrop of the Holy City. The mother, Mrs. MacMahon, travels to Rome to visit her daughter, Martha, who works there at the United Nations. Mrs. MacMahon, a study in Irish piety, makes good on a vow at her husband's deathbed to pray for his soul at St. Peter's.

While abroad, Martha's mother runs in odd company. She meets an arrogant prince of the Church who virtually ignores her and a parasitic Irish whiskey priest who wheedles her money for drink and for whom she steals whiskey from her daughter. Although appalled by her mother's behavior, Martha pretends to know nothing about it and attempts to forgive all. For the duration of this role-reversal, Martha MacMahon hardly sees her lover, Giorgio, because she does not want her mother to know that she is having an affair—with a married Italian.

The newer writers are breaking fresh ground, ridding themselves of worn stylistic restraints and wornout story lines. They are capturing the attention of the nation and occasionally the attention of the world. Never before have so many Irish women written for publication; never before have so many published fiction of quality. [12]

Stories by Contemporary Irish Women is offered to showcase examples of the best in short fiction by women whose works should appear beside those of Benedict Kiely, Brian Moore, William Trevor, John McGahern, Bernard McLaverty, and other respected contemporaries in the tradition.

Our decision to include only short fiction in this collection precludes notice of important contemporary novelists like Jennifer Johnston and Molly Keane. Yet short fiction is the obvious choice here, for it is not only a modern genre that offers the reader variety in theme and style, it is also a distinctly Irish genre that springs from the *seanchas,* or *sean-sgéal,* traditional tale-forms embedded in the Irish psyche. Frank O'Connor, in his introduction to *The Lonely Voice*[13] says the modern Irish story derives directly from these sources. Where O'Connor goes wrong is in suggesting that a proper story will echo "with the sound of a *man's* voice speaking."

Until the 1960s publishing in Ireland was a man's preserve. In spite of token listings which cite the tradition of women in Irish literature from the Nun of Beare up through Edna O'Brien, Nuala O'Faolain is right in saying women have been left out. A glance at the contents of the Irish anthologies is evidence enough that the national literature has largely ignored women; a sad truth of modern Irish literature over the years is that second-rate male writers have too often eclipsed the better women writers.

The climate is, however, changing. The Irish Women's Movement has made inroads, and inside forces in publishing are responding to inequities. David Marcus, a novelist and former literary editor of the *Irish Press*, has promoted women of talent since the 1960s, especially through "New Irish Writing" and his edited anthologies. Poolbeg Press, through the 1970s, produced a dozen good paperback story collections by contemporary women. More recently Catherine Rose at Arlen House, a feminist press in Dublin, has issued a number of important titles — *Irish Women: Image and Achievement,* edited by Eiléen Ní Chuilleanáin, and *Woman's Part,* a collection of short fiction covering 1890 through 1960, edited by Janet Madden-Simpson.[14] Blackstaff in Belfast has also added titles. The women themselves — poets, playwrights, journalists, critics, and writers of fiction — have also become more self-assertive and for the first time, the Irish reading public has the opportunity to pass judgment on the work of women through the critical process.

The collection before you represents a sampling of some of the best English-language short stories of the past half century. The stories are modern masterpieces by prize-winning Irish women, who have by their works signaled the start of a single tradition in the national literature.

NOTES

1. Francis Stuart observes this in "The Soft Centre of Irish Writing," in *Paddy No More,* edited by William Vorm (Dublin: Longship Press, 1982), 5–9.

2. Nuala O'Failain (O'Faolain) reiterates this thesis in "Irish Women & Writing in Modern Ireland." She proposed it earlier in "Women, Writing, and Ireland Now," in *Ireland and the Arts,* ed. Tim Pat Coogan (London: The Literary Review, 1983), 88–91.

3. There are, of course, many other writers in the tradition. The above works should, however, be required readings on any Anglo-Irish survey.

4. In *The Red and the Green,* 20.

5. O'Faolain in "Women, Writing, and Ireland Now," 88.

6. Elizabeth Bowen has perhaps shown more "professionalism" than the others, though her novels tend to follow the conventions.

7. London: Virago, 1979. Patricia Meyer Spacks, *The Female Imagination* (London: Allen and Unwin, 1976) also makes this argument.

8. In "Mother Ireland," 84 (1976), 34.

9. The American feminist anthologies, like the *Norton,* edited by Sandra M. Gilbert and Susan Gubar (New York, 1985), feature O'Brien.

10. "Mother Ireland," 35.

11. New York: Carroll & Graf, 1987. Julian Moynahan writing in the *New York Times Book Review,* 1 February 1989, 7, calls this novel "a stunning performance."

12. Caroline Walsh provides a survey in "The Female Fiction Explosion," in the *Irish Times,* 18 October 1985, 13.

13. London: Macmillan & Co., Ltd., 1963, 13-45.

14. Arlen House, a feminist press in Dublin until 1988, published a line of scholarly and trade titles in addition to those cited. Janet Madden-Simpson's collection *Woman's Part* (1984) is an excellent sampler covering fiction from 1890-1960.

A Season for Mothers

HELEN LUCY BURKE

Spring brought to Rome the first of the wild asparagus and the baby new potatoes from the South of Italy. It also brought the first and heaviest crop of mothers. Considerable bargaining about them went on between the girls. "I'll drive yours to Castel Gandolfo if you have mine twice to dinner," and "I'm giving a party for mine, and you can bring yours if you introduce mine to the Cardinal."

Mrs. MacMahon arrived by charter-flight at Fiumicino on the Monday after Easter, in all the black glory of her recent widowhood. Martha blinked at the enveloping sootiness, which included a sort of raven's wing attachment on her hat. It was her mother's first visit to Rome, and her first airplane trip.

"Never again," cried Mrs. MacMahon. She touched significantly the Rosary beads which hung over her wrist. "I prayed, and here I am. But never again. Not if I have to spend the rest of my life here."

"There was a little bit of bumpiness over the Alps, and we all felt it, I'm sure," interjected an Englishwoman who stood close by. Martha recognized her from previous years as Mrs. Whiteside, whose daughter Olive worked with her; they had made a lunch arrangement for their mothers. "Your mother sat it out in the loo. Only one loo for the whole plane too, dear. Doesn't seem right, does it?"

HELEN LUCY BURKE was born in Dublin, where she works as a senior civil servant in local government. In addition to writing fiction, she is a freelance journalist with an eye for everything from cooking to politics. Ms. Burke published a novel, *Close Connections,* in 1979; and a story collection, *A Season for Mothers,* in 1980. She won the coveted Irish PEN Award for her story "Trio" in 1970.

13

"What a horrible woman," said Mrs. MacMahon, not waiting until they were out of earshot. "Common. She told me she had been 'in service' if you please. I didn't think that sort of person would be coming out here." In the car she blinked eagerly at the dry countryside defaced with hoardings, and demanded where St. Peter's was.

"There," said Martha, taking her hand off the steering-wheel and waving it largely at the horizon. Mrs. MacMahon immediately crossed herself and bowed her great feathered casque, as would a Moslem towards Mecca. For the rest of the journey she kept turning her head like a compass-needle in the direction Martha had given, while her lips moved. When she suggested going straight to St. Peter's to offer thanks for her safe landing, Martha told her it was locked up for the night.

"Locked? Surely not. What about the Monday Night Novena?"

"I don't think there is a Monday Night Novena in Rome."

Mrs. MacMahon set her chin obstinately and informed her that the Holy Father himself had praised Ireland for its devotion to the Mother of God and its attendance at the Novena. "You just want to keep me away from it, that's all." In her mind's eye she saw a tall slim figure in white leading the responses, while her own voice joined in, humbly (but audibly), and the tall slim figure in white would become aware of the reverent old Irish voice. . . .

Martha's elegant flat received tepid approval.

"Well, you certainly live in style. In style," nodding a grim condemnatory head. "Far too grand for the likes of me." For the latter comment she adopted a meek little voice and sat forward on the edge of her chair, to show that she thought that Martha thought that the furniture was too good for her to sit on. Her temper improved with dinner, which was excellent. She even consented to sip at the chilled Frascati, making wry little mouths to show it was being drunk medicinally, when Martha told her it was the opinion of a Cardinal, whom she would be meeting, that more tourists were killed in Rome by the water than by anything else. There was enough lingering heat in the air to let them step out on the terrace afterwards and identify the huge domes of Maria Maggiore and John Lateran, which heaved themselves out of the jumble of ochre roofs. St. Peter's in the far distance was shrouded in mist. Just opposite and below was the modest facade of the local orphanage church.

"I'll get six o'clock mass there tomorrow morning," said Mrs. MacMahon.

"Six o'clock?" cried Martha. "Couldn't you wait until later?"

But it turned out that later would not be the same at all. In Mrs. MacMahon's view Masses fell into the same category as mushrooms and deteriorated as the day went on. "Just wake me up—you needn't bother to get up yourself. Once I know where it is I can find my own way." She assumed an air of chivalrous reckless bravery as if Captain Oates were setting out once more into the Antarctic blizzard.

"You know that we have the United Nations Conference for the next ten days," Martha reminded her. "You just sit out here on the terrace and take things easy. I'll leave you some money and an Italian phrase-book, and if you like to go shopping there's a good—"

Mrs. MacMahon cut her short. "No! I'm not going to trouble anyone. You won't know I'm here. You'll have your own friends coming here, and what would an old woman do with herself, roasting in the sun at my age, or buying things in the shops to titivate. To pray, that's why I came here. You just drop me at St. Peter's on your way to work and collect me in the evenings. I'll be there all day praying. Just praying and thinking."

Martha's mouth opened and shut again without uttering a sound. It was miles through heavy traffic to St. Peter's and more miles in the opposite direction to her office. Besides, it would be as absurd to try and pray in St. Peter's as it would be in a railway station. Still, there was nothing for it but to let her mother find these things out for herself. The old lady went to bed, telling Martha not to go to any trouble for her with one of those fol-de-rol continental breakfasts. Just a plain Irish breakfast would do her: fried egg and rasher, and a bit of thin toast. "None of that pasta for I won't have it."

"You wouldn't like to just take things easy for tomorrow, and rest yourself after the trip? Cardinal Marconi says more tourists fall ill by overdoing things on their first days than—"

But it turned out that Mrs. MacMahon had made a vow, and horrid proof of its potency was provided the following morning when Martha decanted her from the car in the square before St. Peter's. Once emerged, she sank first to her knees and then, dreadfully, lay full length on the ground kissing the stones which were wet from the spray of the fountains. "For his soul, Lord," she groaned as she reared herself up on her forearms. The posture, combined with her long black dress, gave her the appearance of a seal on a rock. Any idea Martha might have had of escorting her inside and getting her settled, vanished in a twinkling. "Remember, Lord of mercy, for his sake," wailed the votary again, sinking down on her flippers, and horrified Martha crying, "Half-past five at the end of the colonnade" sprang back into the safety of the car. She had provided her mother with 4,000 lire spending money and an Italian phrase-book: what more could she do?

She could have stayed to see me safely into the church, thought Mrs. MacMahon. She could have introduced me to the priest in charge. She could have told them I was Irish. She could have taken the day off if she wanted to, and stayed with her mother. From behind the pillars on her right came loud noises of a motorcycle revving, and the clanking of a tram. She opened her eyes and looked at the pavement from which steam was beginning to rise in little curls as the heat of the sun hit the damp stone. She kissed the hallowed ground, cried out "For his soul," and marched on the Basilica, heavy-footed, awed, reverential, as one of the early Goths.

The air inside struck against her face with the cool dampness of a cave. She noticed a sweetish smell, like an attic with dry-rot. Once more she prostrated herself and kissed, as if it were flesh, the hallowed pavement. St. Peter himself had walked here, and St. Paul. She planned to visit the church where their dried skulls hung in a basket, as a salutary *memento mori*. What we all come to sooner or later, the worms and the judgment of God before the throne, she had told her husband when he was dying, for he had never been the devout kind that can go with confidence and it was better for him to face up to what must be. His staring terror-filled eyes still troubled her sleep, and called to her for prayers.

"Vietato, vietato," shouted an Italian voice. A rough hand hauled her from the floor. An official arm waved her on: the other arm gestured at the door behind her where a resentful queue was forming.

"Would you not even leave a widow to her prayers?" she cried at the uniformed back which was hastening in the direction of a group with a movie-camera. "Oh, great Catholics. Great Catholics indeed, moryah! that don't remember who it is that pays you."

But sure was it any wonder that they would be lacking in reverence and not a Blessed Martin or an Infant of Prague within sight?

No, not a Sacred Heart itself in all the long walk to the top altar, but only a collection of statues which were no fit sight for modest eyes anywhere let alone in a church, and paintings of bold rossies with hardly more than a ribbon to save their decency.

A ballroom is what it is like, she thought. Then she felt guilt for passing such a judgment on the Pope's own church, and for a penance she shuffled to the nearest column which bore an edifying statue. At least the statue had wings and a halo, and it carried a lily in its stony hand, and its dress, though closely fitting enough to show the projection of two large nipples, covered it from throat to ankle. Kneeling, she wondered if it could be the Angel Gabriel, for she had always thought of Gabriel as a male angel; and besides (if he wasn't) he would surely have had the decency to wear a brassiere when making the Annunciation.

"For his sake, Lord, and forgive me for criticizing Your church."

When finally she reached the top of the great basilica, she was surprised to find no Mass going on. In her fancy she had imagined the Pope himself at the altar, a cardinal or two ringing the bells. Even the altar itself was hidden behind a kind of four-poster bed with twisted barley-sugar pillars. But still it *was* St. Peter's, the Holy Place, and as she lowered herself again to the marble pavement, making groaning noises like a laden camel, she felt as does a child who has come home. She was at the heart and center of the mystery.

Worldly and all as some people might think the church, was there not good reason for it? Christ's Vicar on earth must be held in respect by people to whom worldly trappings were all. He himself must think little of it: an austere simple holy man: simple white clothes: the thin nose of him and the bags under his eyes: they couldn't be looking after him properly.

Shifting from one knee to the other she thought of how she would come here day after day, a humble old Irishwoman who trusted in her God, and how the grand people who looked after the church would speak contemptuously of her in their pagan Italian way and laugh at her piety and snigger about her to the Pope. "We would see her. Take her to Us." Then the slender white figure raising her from the ground, the dark sad eyes smiling into hers. "Your faith edifies Us, daughter." A little conversation then about how she was only a simple Irish widow who had never stirred away from her kitchen until her husband died. "You can cook, daughter? We have need of you." An offer of a post as the Papal housekeeper. Feeding him on soda-bread. Once in a while going back to Dublin and paying a smiling visit to Miss O'Toole who was housekeeper to the Parish Priest in Dundrum. Maybe articles about her in the Irish newspapers and about how the Pope was thriving on colcannon and coddle, macaroni quite given up. Nice pots of tea. Potato cakes. "Then, Miss O'Toole, he looked at me and 'Mrs. MacMahon' he said, 'This is a grand cup of tea,' and I said to him, 'Holy Father, the secret is to let it draw. Let it draw and warm the pot.' So he swallowed a cup of it with a nice hot slice of my soda-cake—I make it with raisins and the bit of butter and the egg—and he said, 'Mrs. MacMahon, let you give this to Us every morning at 11 and no more of that nasty old macaroni.'"

Miss O'Toole barely able to swallow with the bile churning inside her. "Well, 'tis a fine soft job you have landed for yourself."

And back I would say, gloated Mrs. MacMahon, "Faith then and it is not, for the devil ever so hard a man on socks you will meet. Sure I'm wore out with the mending of them, and then when himself sees me at them, sure he looks at me with a bit of a smile, the creature, and says the stone floors in the Vatican are very hard on them, and he wearing only the little biteens of red slippers, and the people kissing his foot. No, no," laughing lightly, "there's no formality in the family—'tis what he calls us himself, the family—'tis just like the man of the house, but holy. Miss O'Toole, the penances that man puts on himself! Amn't I always giving out to him?"

Or would it be more effective to shake her head and purse her lips at enquirers? "A vow, Miss O'Toole. We all have to make it. The Holy Father wouldn't like us to be blazoning it around what he had for breakfast." Miss O'Toole would feel the sharpness of that shaft, for she was forever complaining about Father Auger's enormous appetite, but in a proud sort of way like a mother would use in grumbling about a petted son.

The pain in her knees broke in on her daydreams, and when she consulted her watch she was surprised to see that it was only 11 o'clock. The Pope had still not appeared on the high altar to say Mass. There had not even been the flash of a Cardinal's scarlet or the peacock glint of a bishop. At home in Dundrum by this time, she would have taken in three Masses and had an enjoyable gossip with her cronies.

Churches seemed more interesting when there were neighbors to wonder at her sanctity.

"So tell me how you got on?" As she spoke Martha poured two glasses of dry vermouth and added a twist of lemon. It must have been a long day to half-past five for her mother; Martha had found her actually waiting at the colonnade and she had looked tired. "Where did you have lunch? At that little trattoria I showed you behind the pillars on the right?"

"No," shrugged Mrs. MacMahon, "I told you many's the time, I'd have nothing to do with that pasta stuff."

"Sure 'tisn't all pasta. Where did you go, then?"

It turned out that her mother had given the 4,000 lire to a poor priest.

"But there's no such thing," screamed Martha. "The fat of the land—a state salary—the Fondo del Culto—*my* money."

"It is our duty to give to those in need." A meek and holy look had made its appearance.

"But your own money, not mine."

"And was it not mine to buy my lunch? And all I could get with that amount was that pasta. A steak," she said pathetically, "or a nice bit of boiled ham, would cost double. The priest I gave the money to told me so. An Irishman he was," Mrs. MacMahon clarified. "A Maher from Tipperary."

"Have some more vermouth," said Martha hopelessly. "Cardinal Marconi says it's what every pilgrim needs after a day in St. Peter's." She swallowed her own hurriedly and poured herself more. She was going to need it.

"Ordained in Maynooth," reported her mother the following evening. "A very good family: they keep horses. His mother was a Nugent from Ballinasloe." She ate with a good appetite and remarked that she had had no lunch. Martha counted ten.

"Is he long in Rome?"

"I'll tell you tomorrow," said her mother through a fronded mouthful of spaghetti. (After she had dealt with a large plate of it and two goes of Parmesan cheese, she told Martha that she hated pasta.)

"Three months," reported her mother on Thursday evening. "Oh, the poor man. A priest of God. If I told you all I knew—!" She cried a little, then wiping the tears off her cheeks, went on, "But my lips are sealed. I've given my word and his confidence is safe with me. No! — raising her hand to still Martha's imagined question—"you needn't ask. I'll tell you nothing."

It turned out that he was in trouble with his bishop. "A Corkman," said Mrs. MacMahon venomously. "I've never heard good of one yet. But Father Maher will get to the Holy Father in the heel of the hunt, so he will. There's a certain crosier won't be raised high much longer. I'll say no more. I won't be quoted. But you can mark my words, my lady," a significant smile followed, and a grim shake of the head.

Later they went to a cocktail party given by an Irish diplomat whose sister, Eithne, worked with Martha in the United Nations. His flat was in a tall old building in Trastevere.

"And do you mean to tell me you want your mother—tired and old as she is—to climb those stairs? Oh, it's out of the question."

"But Cardinal Marconi will be here. He's expecting to meet you."

"Me?"

"He always meets the mothers."

"Oh 'always' indeed, is it," said Mrs. MacMahon tossing her nose in a dissatisfied way, but making fast for the stairs.

Martha had often met him before: a thin, sly, worldly looking prelate who frequented diplomatic cocktail-parties. He was always ready to meet the mothers of girls in the United Nations. It was a thing understood, but not mentioned, that he was kept supplied with duty-free goods from the staff commissary, for which he usually forgot to pay. It was only for her mother's sake (and to pass an evening) that Martha was attending the party. She had warned her lover, Giorgio, to stay away. She was missing him badly, but he was married and she would not feel easy under her mother's eye.

"Benedico te . . ." intoned the Cardinal over her mother's grizzled head. He helped her to her feet and asked her how she liked Rome, but before she could reply he turned towards the next arrival with real enthusiasm. This was a red-headed girl with a large creamy bust, generously displayed.

Martha urged her mother towards Eithne and the drinks.

"He wants to hear what I think of Rome."

"Sure can't you tell him later? He has to meet the guests."

"You mean meet the brazen straps," said Mrs. MacMahon with a venomous glance at her supplanter. Towards Eithne she behaved in a queenly manner. "And where are your people from? And where did you go to school?" Her eyes kept straying towards the redhead. "No brassiere on her," she whispered to Martha, "and the tops of her things sticking out like boils through her blouse. In front of the Cardinal, too."

"He needn't look at them, sure."

"Never forget that they are men too. If you were married you would know what I mean." She nodded her head portentously, but with something akin to sympathy for the affliction of a pair of testicles. Martha was surprised: Rome must be having a broadening effect. "And your friend, Eithne or whatever, is no example either. She certainly can put away the booze. Must spend a fortune on it. I know the price of it, remember—ah, who better? Your father. . . ."

"Not here you don't. We get it for half nothing at the commissary. Duty-free and non-profit-making."

"Ha!" said Mrs. MacMahon deeply. "And people starving. Starving. Bangladesh. Biafra. Here in Rome, even. The Cardinal is left on his own." She made for him with a surprising turn of speed and left Martha grinning into her drink as she saw her launch into what she presumed to be a condemnation of Rome. All the mothers did it. But the Cardinal's experienced face was growing wary, hunted. He looked furtively around for succor, smiled supplicatingly at Martha. When in leisurely pity she drew near she heard him saying, "But *cara signora,* it is not so easy. The only time we poor devils of Cardinals see him is when he wants his triple crown polished."

They watched him course across the room to the security of Eithne's brother. Mrs. MacMahon looked dissatisfied, but all she said was, "Ve-ry int-er-est-ed was the Cardinal. I'm telling you now, a certain miter is due for toppling." After a pause during which she swigged powerfully at her drink, she added, grievedly, "And I didn't even get a chance to speak to him about your father's soul."

Getting her out of bed the next morning was a task. After the cocktail party, Eithne had invited them to join her for dinner in a local trattoria. Her brother had come, too, and the red-headed girl with the bosom, and a meek Englishman with a long thin neck whom Eithne was trying to palm off on Martha. Mrs. MacMahon had held herself aloof from the food in a severe xenophobic attitude; however, she had allowed her glass to be filled and refilled with the straw-colored wine from the Castelli. Martha had had to undress her and put her to bed, while she talked of repentance and the sufferings of the Savior.

"I have to go now. The Conference will be under way." She looked uneasily at the old lady, whose face was leaden under two gay rosettes of rouge. "Would you not do better to rest at home today? The day after tomorrow is Sunday and we'll be going to St. Peter's to get the Pope's blessing. In the meantime—"

"For your father's soul. A vow is sacred." The old lips clamped together in a pleated mauve line of determination. "I've made a promise."

Yes, but what and to whom, Martha wondered. Her mother was carrying a bucket-bag which made a clinking sound of glass, and she had a presentiment that if she went to her drinks cupboard some of the Irish whiskey would be gone. Better to keep quiet about it. Her mother probably wanted an Elizabeth of Hungary situation, illicit alms turning into roses.

During the night a fine rain had fallen. It left a polish of damp on the stones of the square. The car-wheels skidded as Martha roared away, already late for the Conference. Half-way down the Via della Conciliazione however, she stopped the car, prompted by worry for an old woman in the grip of her first hangover. The small black figure was toiling across the immense space between the enfolding claws of the colonnade. One of her shoulders was dipping from the weight of the bucket-bag. "Christ! she must have taken the whole four," Martha said aloud.

It could have been worse. During the day the girls with visiting mothers compared notes. Freda Livingstone's sat all day in the entrance lobby, knitting a brown garment which was thought to be a Franciscan shroud. Letitia's had struck an Italian with a bottle in some obscure quarrel about cruelty to a cat.

"No one before has ever had a mother in Rebibbia prison. What shall I do? What shall I do?"

"The Lord save us, prison's nothing these days. Why should you be worrying about prison?" urged the Irish girls. But Letitia was English and respectable and would not be comforted.

"Mine has to have gruel in bed at night," contributed Catherine Kelly. "I had to buy oats from a stable at the race-track and grind them in my coffee-mill."

In the face of other people's trials Martha felt a little happier. That evening however, for the first time, her mother was not waiting for her. She appeared finally, after about half an hour, walking with tottering steps from the wrong direction. The bucket-bag swung lightly but her shoulders were bowed. Alarmed, Martha helped her into the car. Once inside, a strong smell of alcohol made itself felt. Grappa, and raw ignorant grappa at that. Hair of the dog. Oh dear.

They were in the thick of the Friday evening rush. Cars dashed vehemently across slippy intersections, trumpeting their anger at each other. As they turned up the green slope of the Aventine Hill the drizzle quickened in tempo; rain bounced back off the ground with a roaring noise. The film of oil on the cobbles made the car-wheels spin to the side, as horses' hooves might long ago have slipped and grabbed. It gave Martha an excuse to slow down to a crawl as she came near Giorgio's place, for she could see his pearl-gray outline, as he sat in his car. He stared with unconcealed interest at her mother, but made no sign, and she drove on. Giorgio was always cautious.

"Horrible staring oily people. Can't you be going on?" groaned Mrs. MacMahon. "The light is hurting your mother's eyes. I don't care for this place at all. Pagans in palaces, that's what they are." Lost on her was the gracious beauty of the villas set back amid lush gardens, where Horace and Lucullus would have felt at home; lost was the Byzantine splendor of the Aventine churches, and the paved square, with its perfection of carving around the gate to the garden of vines. All, all was alien: the stones, the strange historic hills, the olive staring faces, the ocher of the peeling buildings, even the quality of the light, for in the evening Rome was illumined from the West with a mirror reflection from the sea, which now glared slanting through the deluge. When she moaned "The light, light" she was mourning the dying of the sun against a moist Northern plain, and the gentleness of a city where sun and rain were benefactors, not tyrants. But she had fled to this place to escape the silence of her own house, and the cold bed whose springs were still dented by the shape of her husband.

Martha, making an effort to know all and to forgive all, could feel only an ache in her bone for Giorgio's touch and resentment that her mother's presence made meetings impossible. She wished she knew when her mother's air-ticket expired. A fortnight she could take — maybe three weeks. How long would Giorgio wait?

"I met Maura Cregg and I arriving* at the airport." An onslaught was preparing, for as she spoke Mrs. MacMahon was striking the palms of her hand together.

"Did you." Flat. Uninterrogative.

"A class behind you at school, wasn't she?"

"Before me."

"Just the year anyway. The one Year." From the corner of her eye Martha could see her mother's head nod meaningly. As no comment came back, she had to proceed unprompted. "Nine children she has, and a tenth on the way."

"Disgusting," said Martha. "Having them in litters like a rabbit or a guinea-pig."

"Ha, my lady, you wouldn't say that if they were your own," cried her mother in a triumphant tone. "That's what makes the difference — when they're your own."

"If they look anything like her, they must be a grim collection."

"She got her man, anyway, didn't she? Buck-teeth and all, she got her man." There was a respite while Mrs. MacMahon mused on the scalp tucked into Maura Cregg's belt, which conferred a superior status on her mother, old Mrs. Cregg. Martha would have been astonished had she heard her own mother's version of Martha's spinsterhood — the offers she had turned down, the Roman princes and bishops' nephews begging for her hand, and all turned down in favor of a career.

"And does the car and the flat really make up for everything?" she asked suddenly.

"I work for them," Martha replied obliquely. She knew that what appeared to be a question was really a statement: that she was being condemned for living an empty frivolous life in a foreign capital, instead of the penitential meritorious life of an Irish wife and mother.

"Horrible people," tittered her mother, peering through the misted window at two lorry-drivers abusing each other.

"Cardinal Marconi says anything south of Florence is mission territory, with cannibals."

"Not much I would think of him, to be abusing his own. Cardinal Macaroni *we* call him."

*This is idiomatic usage in Ireland.

Ha! We! thought Martha, disgusted. She changed the subject. "I don't have to work tomorrow so we can sleep on. I'll take you to the square on Sunday morning to see the Pope. 'Twas unlucky that the Conference was on."

"But you'll drive me to St. Peter's in the morning!" It was a frantic statement, not a request or a query.

When Martha said she needed to lie on and unwind, perhaps might bring her on a little stroll around the tombs of the Scipios in the afternoon and go to Nemi or Tivoli on Sunday afternoon, Mrs. MacMahon became incoherent with anxiety, which lasted through dinner. She passed from this into rage, and after a lengthy period of haranguing, into loud recriminations when Martha went into her own room and locked the door behind her. "I thought this was to be my holiday," came the voice through the keyhole. "What would I be wanting with your tombs?" A Conference, indeed! How well she knew that Martha could get away from it easily if she wanted. And then when her mother went back she would tell everyone how good she had been to her, the trouble she had gone to, the expense it had been.

It had been Mrs. MacMahon's secret intention to end her days in the Holy City. She had thought that her years of prayer and Mass-going had given her a lien on the Church of Rome, as if she would be coming to the house of her close kindred. Instead she found herself in a vast unfriendly museum, with paid attendants instead of the saintly clergy she had expected. The authority which she had expected to wield over Martha was become a weapon in Martha's hand, under Martha's roof and eating her food. And though Martha was being ostentatiously kind, she made it plain that it would last for a set term of weeks. The thought of returning to the silent house in Dublin made Mrs. MacMahon sick with terror, but Rome held no refuge. She was treated as an aged child with holiday whims to be gratified, and she knew (for she had overheard a phone-call) that her foibles were discussed and exchanged against the rival foibles of other visiting mothers. She was presented to a Cardinal as if he were something rare and diverting that would soothe a fractious toddler, and she was supposed not to notice but to be grateful to her daughter.

There was also the question of Martha's almost sinfully luxurious style of living, with a car as long and glittering as a railway train, and the way she was turning into an old maid, fussing about cigarette burns on the furniture, needing everything about her meticulous, so that the next thing would be a cat. She bent and shouted through the key-hole, "A dried-up old maid."

In the morning Martha lay in bed and listened to tinklings as her mother grappled with the phone-system. Later, they met coldly and inquired how each other had slept. Mrs. MacMahon had a fur-tive look on her face: checking her cupboard, Martha found a box of 500 cigarettes missing.

Saturday was a day of armed truce and scant words. Only on Sun-day as they drove towards St. Peter's did Mrs. MacMahon relax again into her accustomed tone of command, with admonitions to hurry. And then when they got to the square it was very little different from its weekday self. "You mean he appears for the blessing, and the Ro-mans know it and still don't come?" she cried, incredulous at the sparse huddled knots of foreigners. Her eyes were anxious, straining right and left obviously for some rendezvous.

Martha saw him first and recognized him out of the foreboding of her heart. He wore a black polo-neck sweater to hide the seediness of his Roman collar; his shoes were unpolished, which marked him out in that city of spruce princelings; about his clothes was that greasy look of the drinking civil-servant or the drinking priest. But his face was not bad, she conceded; no better than she had expected. A sort of ruined boyishness and vulnerability.

"Why, if it isn't Father Maher!" cried her mother. "If it isn't your-self!"

He acknowledged the greeting with a small anxious smile, and turned to Martha for the introduction. His blue eyes held apology and appeal. Martha might have softened if she had not known that it was her own whiskey which twitched in his hands and reached her in a powerful waft of alcohol and peppermint.

"And so few people," her mother went on busily. "I declare to God 'tis a scandal. If 'twas in Dublin he lived, the crowds would come, faith."

"The Italians aren't much," said Father Maher. He coughed and looked nervously at Martha.

"That's what I'm tired telling her, but she knows better than her mother. Oh they all do, these days. Nothing but Rome and the Ital-ians will do my lady here."

"Most of my friends are Irish or English," said Martha mildly.

"And Italian cardinals," laughed her mother with a wrinkling of her nose. "Oh yes, the Italian cardinals. Cardinal Macaroni, no less," she nodded to Father Maher.

At this point the Pope appeared on his balcony and the subject was dropped, but as they fell to their knees for his blessing, Martha saw a parcel and an envelope change hands. There go my brandy and my cigarettes, she thought, and my money too as sure as eggs. She stole a look at her mother who was sunk on the stones in an ecstasy of religion. She had joined her hands high and held them in front of her pointed at the balcony, while her eyes sighted along them as along the barrel of a rifle, at the mournful face with the large crooked nose and the black eyes and the obstinate complacent mouth, which embodied for her the living representative of Christ.

"He doesn't look as if he gets enough to eat, the poor Pope; that pasta couldn't be agreeing with him. Nasty greasy stuff it is too, that must incline his skin to pimples."

"Ah, sure if you're hungry you'll eat anything," said Father Maher.

"A life of penance," agreed Mrs. MacMahon. "And sure I suppose yourself, in the excitement, came out without any breakfast?"

They turned confident pre-arranged faces to Martha. As she weakly gestured them into the car she saw little conspiratorial smiles exchanged. It was blackmail, simply blackmail.

"Let Father Maher drive," Martha heard, and heard Father Maher magnanimously refuse. Oh, Ireland was the home of the priest, all right, where they could reign Turk-like over their seraglios. When she heard her mother pipe, "Not too fast, now; Father Maher doesn't like going too fast," she put her foot hard on the accelerator. At wicked speed they drove through the dusty outskirts of Rome, through the crowded country villages at the foot of the hills, along a road that nudged past lakes with antique names, towards the green mountain of Nemi where once the murderers had taken refuge in the Golden Grove.

Showing some fineness of spirit Father Maher kept up a jerky and one-sided conversation. Sunday customs in Italy. Officially Catholics. No true devotion. Admirable family spirit though too inclined (little cough) to the flesh. Italian driving. Opera. The food. And Mrs. Mac-Mahon, who had seen a magical sign indicating "Castel Gandolfo, Palace of Pope" abandoned her ritual cries of fear and lost herself in imaginings of how she, a poor Irish widow, would get to the Pope and reveal the injustices perpetrated by his underlings. "Mrs. Mac-Mahon. We knew nothing of this. Our subordinates have betrayed our trust." "Poor priests driven into a state of nerves and terror by these bishops. Corkmen, they are the worst." "Daughter, you have Our ear. Speak in confidence." All she needed to get to the Pope was someone with a little bit of influence who spoke Italian. Her daughter, now, would be the one to do it if she wanted to oblige her old mother. Had there been something odd in the way Cardinal Marconi had made himself scarce, and he so obviously well-known to Martha? Was it possible that she had turned the Cardinal against Father Maher out of jealousy? Huddled into a bundle she brooded on the brightness of the life she would have had, if only she had been blessed with a son like Father Maher. There would be first Masses and first blessings and anointed young male hands laid gently on the old grey head, not to speak of the admiration of all her butties who had to make do with being priests' housekeepers, having been left old maids on the shelf.

They had turned off the main road and looped up the mountain under a canopy of lime and pine. Martha caught sight of her mother's face in the rear mirror: it was tense, absorbed. Her hands were clenched and working. It is because she is at the end of her life, thought Martha, and has nothing to hope for. She must feel necessary to something, even if it is only to a leech. Once more she made the resolution that understanding all she would forgive all. Her mother would not have much longer in Rome. She would make this lunch a memorable one.

She had arranged to meet Olive and her mother, the jolly ex-cook Mrs. Whiteside, with whom Mrs. MacMahon had traveled. It was an unpropitious appointment but one which Martha had to keep, for she was under a few obligations to Olive in matters relating to her affair with Giorgio: messages had been passed on during difficult times. And after all, she reflected, in the exquisite surroundings of Nemi, who could feel anything but peace and goodwill? She parked the car beside the wall of the great towering castle, and they walked over the polished cobblestones of the square, dappled with small flying shadows as the swallows, crying in thin voices, dipped and wheeled against the sun, to where Baffone's restaurant clung to the edge of the cliff, a thousand dizzy feet above the lake.

The two Whitesides were sitting at a table under the trellis, in the young warmth of the Spring sun. As she approached, Martha saw them mutter to each other and gape. Their nods to Father Maher were barely perceptible, a minimum lowering of two sets of double chins, at which he seemed to shrink into himself and grow smaller.

Over the aperitifs the mothers eyed each other with the doubtful eye and bristling neck of dogs making up their minds to fight. Mrs. Whiteside had been in Rome a number of times before, and she took it on herself to patronize Mrs. MacMahon. "What! haven't seen the Trevi Fountain yet, dear, or the Spanish steps? Missing a lot, dear, aren't you?"

Mrs. MacMahon fought back creditably, her ground being that as a Catholic she was in the deepest sense a native of Rome.

"You wouldn't understand what we feel, Mrs. Whiteside. The sense of homecoming."

"Oh yes, and with the Father to show you around, no doubt." There was an unpleasant shade of meaning in her glance. Father Maher muttered something about not being very familiar with the place himself. "Oh, yes, the Vatican and St. Peter's." pursued Mrs. Whiteside. "*You* would know. Practically your own firm, I mean."

The waiter arrived with another round of drinks, which were paid for by Martha although they had been silently signaled for by Father Maher. Mrs. MacMahon, accepting hers, made the waiter a queenly gesture to keep Martha's change, and then, reversing roles, made democratic little remarks about Mrs. Whiteside's former life in service, and what a relief it must be now for her to sit back and let other people do the fetching and carrying. She urged her not to be a bit ashamed of her occupation. "No shame at all in any kind of honest work, so long as it is done for the love of God. Housework or kitchenwork or anything. I never treated my maids as anything less than the family, and I trained Martha the same way. It all depends after all on the position God has allotted us. NO SHAME AT ALL," in a loud slow voice, fixing Mrs. Whiteside's eyes with her own and slightly extending her hand as if she were raising her from the slime. "Remember that Christ called His apostles from the humblest fishermen."

"You do take things seriously. Laugh, that's my motto." Mrs. Whiteside wheezed out a jolly sound, but her eyes were cold and wicked
like pickled onions. She proceeded to tell far from Christ-like stories
about life below stairs.

Mrs. MacMahon bowed her head and puckered her lips as if she
were sucking a private slice of lemon. The hunch of her shoulders
showed her suffering in sympathy with Father Maher, whose mother
had been a Nugent of Ballinasloe. At a gap in the stream of narrative she interjected, "And do you mean to tell me, Mrs. Whiteside,
that you, a Christian, come to the Holy City without trying to set
eyes on our Holy Father? Fountains and restaurants, is that all it
means to you?"

"I saw him all right," said Mrs. Whiteside testily. "Looks as if he
suffered from his kidneys, doesn't he, with those yellow circles under
his eyes. Up all night running, I wouldn't doubt."

"A saint," said Mrs. MacMahon. "I saw him this morning. This
very morning."

"So did we see him this morning. Saw you, too, we did, and the
Father, di'n't we, Olive?" She laughed in a significant way and fished
a cherry out of her drink. Smiling down at it, she said, "Oh yes. Our
second time to meet the Father, i'n't it, Olive? Not that he remembers, I'll be bound."

"Cigarettes," said Father Maher. He looked around vaguely, and
then walked off across the piazza.

"Call the waiter for him, can't you, Martha," cried tender Mrs.
MacMahon.

"The widow's Curse," Olive contributed. She too laughed.

"The what? What do you mean?"

"That's what they call him. Came round trying to get money from
me in St. Peter's last week. Go away, I said, you'll get nothing from
me. My house is a house of prayer, I said, and I'll call those Swiss
in their uniforms and see what they have to say. Smelling of drink—
disgraceful *I* call it."

"Lucky we saw you to warn you," said Olive. "That's what Mum
said to me. Here, she said, we'll have to warn the MacMahons, didn't
you, Mum? But then you slipped away."

"Gave us quite a turn to see you walking over with him. Tries all
the women on their own, he does. Teaches you, doesn't it?"

"And one thing it doesn't seem to have taught you is charity," said Mrs. MacMahon in a trembling voice. "Judge not that ye may not be judged."

Mrs. Whiteside ate her cherry in a considering way. "Oh I don't know, I'm sure. Not that I'm judging. Think about these things differently in Ireland, don't you? Probably seems quite normal to you."

"And if a poor priest drinks too much occasionally, isn't it a disease? Who and what drives him to it?"

"Oliver Cromwell, I suppose. All you Irish are the same, anyway."

All pretense of a social neutrality had been abandoned. The two mothers, their faces congested, leaned across the table, only separated from blows by its fortunate width. Martha, cringing, looked furtively around at the other tables where three generations of happy Italian families guzzled. Loud voices at least would not be remarkable, but Giorgio sometimes brought his family to this restaurant.

"And after 700 years of tyranny by England is it any wonder? Plundered and oppressed. It's a wonder itself that you're not ashamed to look an Irish person in the face."

"Oh I don't know, I'm sure," said Mrs. Whiteside, dealing with another cherry. Through the masticated pieces she added, "Seems to me anything Oliver Cromwell did, you've done worse in England. Drinking all day long on Social Welfare. Going home at night to have more children at our expense. Fights all the time, drink, and the priests as bad as any, I ask you."

"And what about that English clergyman, so-called, at Castle Sant' Angelo last week? Over all the papers in Rome. With young boys. A sin that I didn't even know existed until here. Martha read it all out to me. Faugh!" — tossing her head about and stretching her neck as if she were about to be sick — "*We* keep ourselves clean. Natural."

"Ho, natural indeed," shrilled Mrs. Whiteside. "Nice natural daughter you have too." Martha felt an intense pain in her ankle as Olive's foot, lashing towards Mrs. Whiteside, missed its target. "Ask her how she got her promotion. Ask her how she runs her big car and gets all the time off."

"How dare you? Liars, all the English."

"Liars? Made off quick enough, your priest did. Drunken Irish. You ask your daughter —"

"And you ask yours what she said to the whole office about her mother the ex-cook. The way she is ashamed to have you here with your dirty stories."

"Liar," panted Mrs. Whiteside. "My Olive is a fine girl."

"No maid-servant is going to say anything in front of me about Martha that was reared in a decent Irish home, far from the likes of ye."

Neither Martha nor Olive looked at each other as they led away the aged gladiators in opposite directions. It was the kind of thing that always happened in the mothers' season.

"Sinful slanderous lies."

Martha agreed.

"First on to the poor priest that she thought had no-one to defend him. Then as if that was not enough, on to you."

"Appalling."

"As if," said Mrs. MacMahon, "I would believe what she said about you, and she after taking the character of Father Maher. We're better off without her and her snib of a daughter. Supposing Cardinal Marconi had seen us with the likes of them, what would he think? A cook, by your good leave. We'll have lunch instead in that nice town of the Pope's we passed on the way up."

"Castel Gandolfo," said Martha hopelessly. Father Maher's seedy black figure was leaning against the bonnet of her white car, like something symbolic. Even at that distance she could detect the timid ingratiating smile.

"Father Maher knew how to deal with them. Just up, and quietly left them to it. I feel ashamed of myself for exposing him to people like that. His mother was a Nugent of Ballinasloe, too, you know."

By this [time] they were close enough for him to see the victory flush and the conquering tilt of the black-winged Viking hat. His own outline seemed to swell in sympathetic relief.

"We've had enough of that lot," explained Mrs. MacMahon. She climbed grunting into the rear seat.

"My mother fancies lunch in Castel Gandolfo."

"If that's all right with you, Father," cried the anxious voice from behind.

Father Maher nodded his agreement.

"We might meet someone useful—Cardinal Macaroni, maybe. Or the Pope might be spending the afternoon there."

Another nod from the clerical incubus.

"You must be tired," solicitously. "That little tiny airless room of yours you told me about — sure you could never get a decent night's sleep."

They had just turned downhill from the town, into an alley of budding limes which cut off the sunlight, and Martha felt a simultaneous access of cold to her heart. She knew what her mother was planning. And all her life her mother had won. Not one but two Old Men of the Sea were planning to mount on her back. Where would Giorgio fit in? Except in the office they had had no contact since her mother arrived, and already he was becoming impatient. It was not the passionate impatience of a Romeo, but the tetchy impatience of someone kept waiting in a supermarket.

"Do you know," said her mother, thrusting her great black hat between the priest and Martha, "I had been dreading the journey home in the plane, back to the empty house, and sure I think Martha, the poor creature, wasn't looking forward either to being left on her own, for all that we've had our little differences. Martha sees now that her mother was right, for all that I've never been out of Ireland before. Faith, Martha walked off on them quick enough, that vulgar pair, when they started in on Ireland and the clergy. And on her mother, on her mother. For all she's been living in Rome, Martha's Irish."

The hat was withdrawn. Two thuds indicated shoes kicked off. After a long musing pause Mrs. MacMahon added in a cozy tone, "Sure it just goes to show you, that the Irish never appreciate each other, until we encounter the foreigners, the Italians and the English."

Aimez-vous Colette?

ITA DALY

As I walk to school in the morning, or go for my groceries at the weekend, or perhaps pay a visit to the local public library, I often wonder—
do I present a figure of fun? I should I suppose: provincial schoolmistress; spinster; wrong side of forty. Certainly I must seem odd to
those pathetic rustic minds to whom any woman of my age should
be safely wed, or in a nunnery, or decently subdued by her continu-
ing celibacy. I teach in a convent. No ordinary convent, mind you,
for the nuns are French, and as you might expect this gives the school
a certain cachet among our local bourgeoisie. Most of the girls are
boarders—day girls are tolerated with an ill grace—and many of them
spring from quite illustrious lines. The leading merchant has two
daughters here; the doctor and the dentist three apiece. Even the
surgeon in the County Hospital has sent his Melissa to us.

The town in which I work and live is one of those awful provincial
Irish towns which destroys without exception anyone of any sensitivity who must live there. It is every bit as narrow, snobbish and anti-
thought today as it was twenty years ago. It is the sort of town which
depraved Northerners—Swedes, Dutch and the like—are captivated
by. They always assure us, on departing, that our unique attitude
towards life and our marvelous traditions must be preserved, at all
costs, against encroaching materialism.

ITA DALY (b. 1955) has received two Hennessy Literary Awards for her fiction. Her story collection, *The Lady with the Red Shoes,* was issued by Poolbeg
in 1980; and her novel *Ellen* by Jonathan Cape in 1986. A second novel, *A
Singular Attraction,* was published by Blackstaff in 1987. Ms. Daly, who comes
from Drumshanbo, County Leitrim, has lived in Dublin for many years.
She was educated at University College, Dublin.

As you may have guessed, I do not like this town: neither, however, does it make me unhappy. Unhappiness, I am beginning to realize, is a condition of the young. I realize it more as I spend a whole day—sometimes as much as a week—without being actively unhappy myself. Even those mediocrities who surround me do not upset me excessively any more. At most I occasionally feel something a little sharper than irritation at their absurd attempts at liberalism. Such as collections and fasts outside church doors for the Biafrans, when every mother within twenty miles would lock up her daughter if a black man came to town. And would be encouraged by their priests to do so.

But on the whole, as I said, I live life with a modicum of enjoyment. I have a small house, and a cat. I grow vegetables and flowers and I buy beautiful and expensive clothes in Dublin and London. I cook well, and I enjoy a glass of wine with my meals. I have no friends, but I do not feel the need of them. When I leave the victim daughters of the bourgeoisie behind, having duly carried out my daily efforts at subversion with the help of Keats and Thomas, I return to my little house and close my door on the outside world. Then I read. As Miss Slattery in the Public Library says, I am a terrible reader. I prefer the French to the English novel, and with the best, the most sophisticated and subtle minds for company, why should I care about an Ireland that continues to rot in obscurantism and neurosis?

I particularly like the novels of Colette. I have always been drawn to her work. She creates an ambience which I have never found elsewhere, except in poetry. Indeed I often think that if it were not for Colette, I should have left this wretched place years ago. But her books are so peopled with village school-mistresses, leading romantic and smouldering lives in some distant town, I may foolishly have thought that something similar might happen to me, here in *my* distant Irish town. But Irish towns are not French towns. Or perhaps the whole point is that they are: if I were living deep in the Midi, teaching the daughters of the local bourgeoisie at the local Lycée, I would perhaps find myself surrounded by just such nonsense and stupidity as I do here. It is, after all, the romantic vision of Madame Colette which transforms and enhances.

I have often thought of writing myself. I am sure I could, for I consider myself to be intelligent and perceptive enough and my retired life is ideally suited to such an occupation. I have hours of un-disturbed solitude, all the bodily comforts that I need, and a job which if dull is not overtaxing — and yet I have never written. Not a line, not even an elegy for Sitwell, my dear cat, when he died last Spring aged twelve years.

Of course, really, I know perfectly well why I do not write; why I will never write. I have nothing to write about. Now I appreciate that this may seem a lame excuse to many; a writer, they will say, a real writer, can write about anything. Look at Jane Austen. Jane Austen, I notice, is always cited in this context, why I don't know, as she has always seemed to me an excessively sociable person with a myriad human relationships. While, by comparison, I am a hermit. It is true that I work and live among people but my relationships with them are invariably tangential. I never exchange a word with my head-mistress, my girls, my butcher, except in the course of business. And I have lived like this for twenty years. Before that, it is true, there was the odd relationship which may appear to have had slightly more sub-stance: a shadowy involvement with my parents, the occasional girl-ish exchange during my years at a gloomy and indifferent boarding school. On the whole, however, my life could be said to be arid. But, be assured, I do not use the word pejoratively. I am pleased with this aridity. Just as I like the dryness of my skin. I cannot abide clammy skin — it makes me quite ill to come into contact with. But when my hand brushes my cheek and I feel and hear the dry rasp, I experience something akin to pleasure.

In my entire life there is only one incident about which I could write. No, it was not an incident, it was an interlude — a period of joy. I could write about it with ease, for I recall it often and I remember it still with clarity though its pain is no longer as sharp.

Can you imagine me at twenty? I have always been a plain woman, but whereas nowadays I seldom think of this, even when I look in my mirror, at twenty it was the over-riding factor in my life. At school I had never thought about my looks — I don't think any of us did. Cleverness was what counted, and anyway, nobody who spent nine months of the year in the same greasy gym-frock and washed her hair every two months could have any pretensions to prettiness. And when I left my boarding school and went, clutching my County Council scholarship, to pursue my studies at University in Dublin, my terror was so overwhelming that it blotted out every other sensation from my consciousness. As I stood for the first time in the Great Hall of the College, I literally trembled from head to foot.

Today my most outstanding character trait is probably my independence, but in those days I was like a puppy. I became a slave to anybody who threw me a kind word. Perhaps this is why I dislike dogs so much. I prefer my cats — elegant independent beasts, who stalk off, indifferent to all shows of affection. Every time I see a silly pup, wagging his tail furiously, even when he is being kicked out of the way, I am reminded of myself at twenty.

I was staying at Dominican Hall, where I lived for my four years at University. Initially I was even too shy to have tea with the others in the dining-room and I would buy a bun and an apple and eat them by myself in my bedroom. Then, after about a month, I began to venture downstairs and eventually I became accepted. People came to know my name and they'd nod to me as I crossed the Green. I was even included in the tea-time conversations. I was a good listener, and quite a subtle flatterer (though to be fair to myself, I think it was often genuine admiration on my part). I did not make a close friend, but this new-found camaraderie was quite enough. Then, as I gained confidence, and was known even to timidly initiate a conversation myself, I began to realize that I was finding much of my companions' conversation unintelligible. It was all about boys, love affairs and dating; unknown territory to me. Just as I had never thought about my looks, so I had never thought about boys. But now I did. I even began to notice them as I sat in the lecture halls, and it was easy to see what interested the other girls so greatly. Suddenly I was caught up in the excitement of potential romance, just like all the rest. I stopped thinking of myself as an outsider. I felt I was becoming normal.

I began to pay visits to Woolworths, to buy lipsticks and powder and even a home permanent. I could discuss such purchases with the other girls, even sometimes offer them advice on bargain hunting. I woke up every morning with a feeling of anticipation, and instead of going straight to the library, increasingly I found myself going for coffee and a gossip.

At this stage, the question of boy-friends was largely academic as few of the girls actually had one, but we all talked about them constantly. I believed I was attractive to boys. I think I trusted in the magic properties of the make-up I used and I felt that each time I clumsily applied my morning mask I was being liberated from myself and my inadequacies. Of course I was still too shy to actually look directly at boys, but whenever I had to pass a group of them I felt sure that they were all looking at me.

Eventually it was decided (by whom I cannot now recall) that I should join some of the other girls at the Friday evening student dance. I was overwhelmed. I felt far more nervous than I had ever felt sitting for an examination. But I was determined to go, so I took myself in hand and was ready, painted and coiffured, at the appointed time on the Friday.

I went to three dances before I would allow myself to admit that something was wrong. The first night, I was genuinely puzzled. As the evening wore on I couldn't understand why nobody was asking me to dance. Maybe because I didn't know the place and looked awkward as I blundered around searching for the Ladies. Maybe because these boys only danced with the regulars, the girls who came here every week, and they would have to get used to my face before they asked me. At the end of the night I had convinced myself that there was no need to worry and indeed I was looking forward to the next Friday when I would avoid so many mistakes and would surely emanate a new confidence.

But the following week it was the same story, and the week afterwards. That night when I came home I locked myself in the bathroom and stood in front of the mirror. A heavy, rather stupid-looking face stared back at me. The skin was muddy, the hair dull and limp. Even to my novice eyes the inexpertly applied make-up appeared garish and pathetic. The dress which I had chosen with such care hung in sad folds over my flat bosom. I felt myself blush—a deep blush of shame. What a spectacle I must have made of myself. What a fool I must have looked, standing there with a hopeful, grateful expression on my lumpy face, waiting to be asked to dance.

I think most people, when they look back on their youth, find, or pretend to find, these intense emotions rather amusing. It seems to me that this is just another aspect of the sentimentalization of youth which is so commonly indulged in in middle age. I know that the misery I experienced that night was far greater than anything I have experienced, or could experience, since.

I left the bathroom and I took my lipstick, my powder and my cheap perfume, made a bundle of them, and threw them over the railings into the bushes in Stephen's Green. I resumed my earlier habits, and returned to my reading in the library, where I kept my eyes firmly downcast in case by chance I should meet the pitying gaze of some of those boys whom I had so beseeched at those dances. I took my tea earlier to make sure of avoiding contact with my friends. They never appeared to miss me, and I suppose they were relieved to be rid of someone whom they had tolerated only out of kindness. How had I ever imagined that I could fit in amidst their gay and careless chatter—I, who carried around with me a smell of deprivation and humility which singled me out from these confident grocers' daughters?

I became a most serious student, and it was in this period of my life that I developed my taste for vicarious living. I did not have to totally relinquish my world of romance, for now I found it in the pages of Flaubert, and Hardy and Stendhal.

After a time I became less actively unhappy, and once I could close my door on the world at night I knew peace. I was no longer tormented by my ugliness and ineptitude—there was nobody there to sneer at my clumsy attempts at man-catching—and my antidote against loneliness continued to give me solace as I read late into the night. But with the coming of Spring and the longer evenings, I began to feel restless. An animal stirring perhaps? I found myself gazing around the library, day-dreaming, instead of reading the books lying in front of me. It was in this manner, one day, that I first noticed Humphrey. I was toying with a pencil, idly thinking of nothing, when it rolled away from me across the table. As I retrieved it, again idly, I happened to glance at the man sitting opposite. He had been staring at me, but quickly looked away. It must have been the embarrassment with which he looked away that first aroused my interest, for after that I noticed him practically every day, and he always seemed to find a seat near mine. Sometimes I would catch him gazing at me; at other times he would be totally involved in his work.

At this period there were quite a number of African students at the University, but I think Humphrey was the blackest man I had ever seen. He was quite small, with a rather large head covered in fuzzy down, and long, curiously flat arms. He seemed very ugly to me, but I was flattered by his obvious interest in me and I had all

sorts of fiercely-held liberal attitudes which must have affected my reaction towards him. I pitied him too, for I thought that anyone who
could find me an object of interest must be desperate indeed.

Soon, when I found him looking at me I would look back, not
quite smiling, but in a reasonably friendly manner. I took to saying
"Excuse me," vaguely in his direction when I left the table. Then one
day we literally bumped into each other outside the library door and
both of us involuntarily said hello. After this we always exchanged
greetings and then about a month later as we sat working I found
a note pushed across the table towards me. It read (and I still remember the wording clearly): "Dear Miss, would you care to break into
your morning studies and refresh yourself with a cup of coffee?"

We were soon meeting regularly. As if by agreement, though neither
of us ever mentioned it, we never met outside, and we never went anywhere. But every Saturday afternoon at about four o'clock, I would
catch the bus to Rathmines, to Humphrey's bed-sittingroom. He lived
in a large run-down house, at the top of a hill, just off the Rathmines
Road. The house seemed to be let out entirely to African and Indian
students, and I can still recall vividly the strong, individual aroma
that filled it. It was made up of exotic cooking smells and perspiration
and stale perfume. All the other students seemed to entertain their
girl-friends on Saturday afternoons too, and I got to know some of
them (though we never spoke) as we traveled on the bus or stood on
the door-step together. Their approach was either furtive or brazen
and I was sure that I was the only undergraduate among them. It
made me very angry that these girls should feel that they had to act
like this, and also, that these boys should have to have such girlfriends;
but when I thought of myself and remembered my own ugliness I
was often reminded of a favorite saying of one of the students in Dominican Hall as she prepared for the Friday night dance — "Any port
in a storm."

Perhaps this was true for me initially, but as I got to know Humphrey I began to realize that he was a person of unusual qualities.
He was very gentle — he didn't seem to have any aggression in his
make-up at all. He laughed often and easily. He was a cultivated person, and whereas I was a crammer — with my peasant equation: learning equals getting on — he was a scholar.

Each Saturday when I arrived he would very formally shake hands and take my coat and make me comfortable. Then we would sit and talk, I with ease for the first time in my life, discovering too that I could be witty and interesting and that Humphrey obviously thought so. We always listened to music, and I was taught to understand something of its magic. We would sit for hours, listening to string quartets and looking out over the darkening roof-tops. During these periods I grew genuinely to like Humphrey. He seemed so lonely and yet so calm sitting there in the shadowy room. I admired his calm, and my natural kindness and crude radicalism made me suffer what I imagined he was suffering.

Later, when it was quite dark and the light was put on and the spell broken, he would make me a chicken stew. It was of a most spicy, succulent oiliness which I have never tasted since and have never been able to capture in my own cooking. Afterwards he would kiss me and fondle me for half an hour, maybe an hour, and then I'd get up, put on my coat and catch my bus home.

Oh, they were marvelous evenings — oases of brightness in my gray, dull weeks. His kisses healed me, and if they excited him, I never knew. I was too young, too unconscious, for the relationship to have been a sexual one, even in texture. And I am so glad now that I was unschooled in the sex-manuals with their crude theories of the potency of the black man. Our relationship was a relationship of love.

I had never in my life been given a present, not even by my parents who were too busy struggling to keep me at school to have been able to pay for presents. Now Humphrey gave them to me. He would suddenly present me with a flower, or a hairband, or a book. He taught me to open myself, he told me I was pretty, and while I was with him I believed it, for I knew by the way he looked at me that *he* believed it. Most of the time in that bed-sitting room, I was happy. I learned to forget myself and my tortured inadequacies.

I don't know how I thought it would end. I knew at the back of my mind that I would not marry Humphrey, but I never really admitted it to myself — I kept it well out of sight and continued to enjoy the present.

Then one Saturday, about three weeks after he had duly carried off a double first in History and Politics, Humphrey handed me a large white envelope as I came in the door. It was an invitation to any of

Mr. Ozookwe's friends to the forthcoming conferring ceremonies, and afterwards, to a cup of tea with the President of the College.

"Well," said Humphrey, "we'll buy you a new hat. I know exactly the kind you should wear . . ."

This was a shock—I had never thought of it. Not once. I began to feel sick. I thought of all those girls in Dominican Hall, and all the boys who had ignored me at those Friday night dances. I thought of me in my finery, and their comments and their sneers. So this was all I could produce. This was where I ended up. Humphrey was no longer my kind, gentle friend—he was a black man.

"Humphrey, no," I said, "you know how I hate social occasions. I won't even go to my own conferring—if I ever get that far." The little joke could not disguise the panic in my voice. "I'll tell you what— afterwards, we could . . ." but the expression on his face stopped me. He looked as if he was in physical pain. But his voice was gentle when he spoke.

"Yes, I see," he said. "I should have seen all along—it was stupid of me. I am sorry for embarrassing you. I think you'd better go now, please."

Well, of course, I changed my mind the next day. Humphrey would be going away, it was the least I could do for him, give him this. I would miss him. I would sorrow after him.

I wrote to him but he did not reply. I called at his house, and the second time an Indian answered the door and told me that he had moved, left no address. I never saw him again. He may have been killed in the Biafran War (he was an Ibo), or he may be rich and prosperous, living somewhere in Nigeria, with several wives perhaps. I hope, do you think, that he has forgotten me?

Saints and Scholars

MARY BECKETT

The two women sat on either side of the fire, the one old, the other young—both gray. The sour heart-burn of resentment had aged them both. The older woman said: "You've been a great disappointment to me, Lena. I don't mind telling you I thought a lot of you once. The first day you stepped out of your father's car in the yard I thought what a fine capable girl you were and how safe Malachy would be in your keeping. 'If I die, I'll know that he's cared for,' I said to myself. But I should have known, for you laughed when you met him."

"How could I guess then, the deadly sin that was. But it wasn't at him that I laughed; it was the way that you introduced him. 'Here's my dairy,' you said, 'and here's my byre, and here's my tractor, and riding on it, here's my son.' And his big dark eyes behind thick glass widened and blinked and widened again and he shook hands and mumbled 'Pleased to meet you' and went into the house to change in my honor. I could just as easily have cried for surely he disappointed me after the warmth in the eyes of his mother."

"The only way to please me was through him. But the neighbors all warned me no good would come of a match arranged between parents now, when the custom's died out. But he and his father left all

Mary Beckett (b. 1926) is the quintessential Belfast writer. Though she married and left the North for Dublin more than thirty years ago, her fiction still recreates troubled life in the Ardoyne with a wrenching realism. Ms. Beckett has published in *Threshold*, the *Bell*, *New Irish Writing*, and other "little mags." *A Belfast Woman*, a 1980 collection from Poolbeg Press, brings together eleven of her finest pieces.

to me and what could I do? You weren't being forced into it either unless by your own hard, grasping nature."

"Is it hard or grasping to want a husband and home and a family? What other way would I get them except by making much of the boys in the dance-hall who were afraid of my education."

"Malachy had more education than you."

"Why has it always been used as a millstone to tie around my neck — my half dozen years at the convent? Because of it I was urged neither to marry nor to stay at home with my father and brother. Instead I was to go to the city and sit at a desk and write out accounts, and add numbers. I told my father I'd just as soon sit on a stone in the heart of the desert till the sun would soften my head. Then it held up my marriage until Malachy took himself off to the town to learn music and French because I knew a little of both."

"Many a one would be glad of a husband taking such trouble."

"It showed he resented my having merits at all that he thought competed with his. He wanted to know what marks I had got in exams years before. Even after my hasty subtraction, the jealous light in his eye didn't aid the growth of respect between us."

"You insulted his books the first day you met him."

"So, even then he complained to you! I said what a pity it was he had no books I could read since he had acquired no others beyond those he needed in school and in the Training College. That was all."

"Why would he need any more after his uncle had left him the farm?"

"Why then did he send to the town for a copy of every book that was in our bookcase at home? Even *Little Women* and *What Katy Did* because I had read them. He could have borrowed them or even kept them, God knows. But no, he had to do it in secret. Aren't they standing inside there behind glass doors and green curtains, tempting me to mock him every time I dust them. Does he not see how ludicrous it is — this pillar of his scholastic reputation? Do you know what came into my head that first day when I saw his pitiful collection of grammars and algebras and expurgated Shakespeare? I made a great joke to myself for I thought in the face of his puffed up pride in his learning 'It went to his head, but it never got in.' I was ashamed of my lack of loyalty then, but now you can think what you like!"

"Oh, there never was decency in you."

"There was till he outraged it!"

"You're no fit wife for any man, let alone for my son. Did you never think to make any return for the home and the name that he gave you? Do you never remember you're the mother of his son?"

"His son! There's no drop's blood's resemblance between them, thank God. Peter's like my people, like my mother, God rest her."

"Have you no respect then for your husband?"

"I can feel no respect for my husband. Don't you see that it grieves me! Don't you see that in despising him I'm despising myself for being his wife? I have built him up and bolstered him up and he keeps the edifice for the neighbors to see and crawls out to me for pity. Did you never think why I've read nothing but these magazines you complain of, since Peter was born? Did you never think I was sick looking at faces in them empty of all but their lipstick? Just because I discovered that Malachy tortured himself with scrambling after my reading, I confined myself to these so that he could feel his lofty supremacy. I have gone to all lengths to encourage his self-respect. And now you fear he might get wild notions from reading these stories. All right, I'll burn them and buy no more. Let him do what he likes; I'll help him no more. His wish is for me to treat him as I would a toddler seeking comfort after falling. You began it. You deserve to know how your rearing has prospered, and the half-grown boy of forty I have for a husband."

"I brought him up well. If he's changed for the worse it's your doing."

"Do you notice how we both deny him a will of his own? Your kind of love and my hate both annihilate."

"You can't say you hate him. You mustn't say that. It's a terrible sin."

"It is, and what's worse, a wife unloving, unloved, loses caste. He made me pity him and my pity grew rancid and turned into hate."

"You had no call to pity him."

"He asked for it from the day and hour of my marriage. He began to show off the gay dog he had been in the town. He told me my clothes were not smart; I should dress in dark grays and light browns like a girl he had met. I laughed and said I wasn't the type; I was too short and my hair was just brown. Then he agreed that this girl had been slender and tall and fair-haired and that indeed I might be too dull. I was cross and said it wasn't the usual thing to tell a wife she's plain until after the honeymoon's over. Now would you not think it a pitiful thing to boast to a new wife of past conquests?"

"You must have made him think that you didn't admire the way he looked after you."

"Nor did I. The room he had booked was poor with paper-thin walls so that he whispered whenever he wanted to talk and the food was rough and badly-cooked and served by a girl with a sty on her eye who said 'Now' when she put down each dish as if the meal was a triumph. But would he complain to them or let me point out that the milk was sour and sauce had stained the cloth some time before we came!"

"It was little enough to put up with."

"That I know now. But then I had hopes that marriage with Malachy might prove to be good and I dreaded to see the beginning spoilt. After the second day I cared no more."

"It does you no credit to remember and complain so long afterwards."

"There never was anything good to blot out the memory of Malachy debasing himself to me by bemoaning the fact that this girl had laughed at him — this elegant girl whom I was to copy. And I had to reassure him every day that no girl could laugh in the face of his grand education, his hundred acres and his thousands of pounds. I wanted to smother him, to strangle him, but instead I praised him when he gloated aloud over the way he had answered the girl when she refused to go to the pictures with him 'just in the way of friendship.' 'I have a girl of my own at home you know,' he said. That was me and still he appealed to me with glee in his voice, 'Wasn't I right? Lena, wasn't I right to show her I could get somebody else?' Till the day I die I'll remember the loathing I felt."

"Why do you make me listen to this? After all I am his mother."

"I couldn't tell anyone else, but you must hear my side to balance with his. He runs to you when I am more mocking than meek. But he doesn't even make any pretense of affection for me. He wasn't long back beside you and his barns and his beasts before the story had changed. 'If a man falls out with a girl, that's bad enough but it can always be mended,' he said one night when John Lavery and Eddie O'Rourke were in. 'But supposing to spite her he marries another.

What then? His life is ruined: so's hers.' Then he leaned back and stuck out his stomach and sighed his melancholy for them both to condone. You should have seen the way their eyes darted from him to me. I airily said that I wouldn't imagine the wife would have a great time either but it didn't put them off. You needn't pretend you didn't hear the story. But I can see it's now out-of-date. There's a better one now. First for money, then for spite. But the new one you and he have concocted makes my skin crawl. He married me for the sake of religion, for such was the will of God!"

"There's no need to sneer. And I don't know what disturbs you so much about that. I've always thought you were fairly devout. What are you so angry about?"

"I don't know but it sickens me, disgusts and repels me. Malachy mouthing to God about me."

"You'll be sorry if you say any more."

"You're right, I suppose."

"I'm warning you, Lena, don't try him too far. These magazines have stories in them tempting men to leave their wives. They'd put ideas into his head when he's hankering after this girl in the town. As he hinted to me, it's only his religion keeps him from going."

"Oh, I wish he would go and be done with it!"

"You said that before and I shouldn't be listening even. If he wishes for her it's your fault and the sin's on your soul."

"How nice for him. Let us say then that it is for the good of *my* soul that I wish he would go and find out this girl, if she even existed. But he won't. Think what would happen! It's eight years you must remember. She's hardly plucking roses in the garden all these years waiting for him to return. Do you not imagine she'd laugh again at our poor Don Juan arriving to carry her off to Omeath, we'll say, or Blackrock; Dublin's too dear. She might even be more unkind than I am. He would have to face up to the fact that it's a clown he is and not a hero. It's much more comforting to be a martyr at home and respected as such, no matter what his mind is like. His thoughts don't let him down before the priest and parishioners."

"Lena, you're talking foolishness, he told me he wanted to marry the girl but he was swayed by me and came home to you since you were trusted already. The girl hadn't a halfpenny."

"So the will of God was for him to marry money. All right. That offends me the least. But that isn't the whole, just the same. I was the easy way out. He needn't blame God when all he did was to take the line of least resistance."

"The Church says be advised by your parents."

"The Church says drunkenness is forbidden, still he gets drunk when he knows no one will see him. The Church says give to every man his own; still he boasts when he drives a hard bargain when he catches a man in a corner. But when it says love your parents he thinks he should hug himself into the shadow of your shawl till his bones are jelly and his blood flows anaemic and thin."

"I needn't talk any more. Your mind is made up that you won't accustom yourself to his ways. I'll go home. If it wasn't for my son and my grandson I would trouble you little again."

"I have no quarrel with you. I would value your company."

"There's Peter now, swinging on the gate and stubbing his boots on the screenings. The roofs are wet. There must be a mist of rain."

"Peter, come in at once. You'll get wet. Let me see what your jersey is like. Dear goodness, it's soaking. Go and change. And your shoes. You'll have to change every stitch you have on and then I'll give you hot milk to keep you from catching a cold."

"You're fussing a lot, Lena, over a bit of a mizzle of rain."

"I dare not take any risk. I have no parents, no husband worth talking about. But no one on earth can deprive me of Peter. Remember; I too have a son." And her fingers dug in through wet wool and took hold of his bone and muscle.

The Empty Ceiling

F. D. SHERIDAN

ONE

I have to choose with care my place at the window. A few inches and the hills and sheep are blotted out. The ridge where the lambs learn to play is missing. There is a danger, too, of not seeing the gulls as they rest, silver, in the sunlight beside the sheep.

So I move my chair carefully, if a little arthritically. But only a little, for I can still hold the exquisite, luminous needle, so light and fine, unlike the needles I used unwillingly in my role of materfamilias. Silk married to steel and buried by steel into more silk. This is what I love, what makes my world go round in the center of the evergrowing jungle. And no one can quite believe me. So, every now and then, to temper the chiding voices, I put on my disguise of well-cut hair, lipstick and scent and seem somehow to say and do the right things. And after the smart lunches, still in disguise, I invent reasons for incurious shop assistants and buy more colored wisps. My daughters and friends appear mollified and I can continue again to put my chair each week an inch or two away from its previous position and bury the precious, undauntable steel into the deceptive silk.

It is growing, my feather bed, my curtain, my casket, my everflowing delight. Its gently graded colors surround me. In memory I look at the drawers of butterflies at Muckross House. My eyes play

F. D. SHERIDAN (b. 1929) was born in Dublin and resides now near Lucan. Since graduation from University College, Dublin, she has lived abroad in England, Italy, and Spain. Her first volume of stories, *Captives*, was published by Co-op Books in 1980.

across the spectrum of color as if they were hands on a harpsichord. A bittern stands close to these countless drawers. A man's delicate passion.

The chair is now a problem, for the jungle grows as if in a tropical heat. Its noise reaches me more closely each day, but I will stay my ground, for at least I know what is happening and understand. And isn't to understand to forgive? I think of the proud king, absolute father, protector to seven hundred people, in his different, more acceptable jungle. And they took him to Rio for a few days just to show him what civilization was really like. Their monarch (and I am no respector of the royal condition), their needed one, returned to his people, broken, that the world was so large, so peopled, so noisy. No illusion his. No hanging on like pathetic European puppets. He broke, so that the road could be built. Is, after all, to understand to forgive? The road continued. Just as soon I shall have to shutter my windows and sit dark in the daylight like an aging Spanish widow.

TWO

Well, it has happened now. I am surrounded, not by gray brick upon brick, but by desolate concrete, empty faces, grim and too old for their age, with cares about three day weeks and will their children stay out of mischief and only a car at the door and a colored telly as props. They won't last, They can't. The people who carried stones from around Chartres to help build their cathedral must have had better props. I wonder how many of them really believed, for we live as we all know so well, in danger of believing too much of our legends.

Today, I thought I heard Tom. I don't mean come to the house as a ghost, but it was his walk, his ring when he forgot his key. It was a new postman. I must remember in future to bury my head somewhere when he passes. I don't believe in ghosts. But we've all had those curious time lapses, those peeps to the future that scientists now tend to want to explore. What if time were to go the other way? My prop, my reason, my sense of the absurd, my Finnish trees, my Swedish lakes, my being able to see through the evening light into more light, would they—Tom's gifts to me—like my respect for Erasmus, leaving town each time a plague broke out (in spite of his final passion "liberame deus"), would they return?

For it is grotesque that at fifty eight I have not learned to wed my twin identities. Other people do. But then I had no name either and it didn't help. Christened Prudence, I called myself Bobby. It solved nothing, pretending to be a tomboy, when all I did was sit in the apple tree. I staked my claim and it was respected. No, I don't think tomboys pinch their tiny breasts to make them bigger or nearly weep with excitement at their first period. And when matured they don't go through pregnancies with no idea of what morning sickness is like with no "picas," begging for dates, old rope or dried ginger. And they certainly don't have to remind themselves sternly, constantly that the world would be empty if they were, in fact, the first creatures with a moving creature inside them. No, Bobby didn't really help, though it was better than Prudence and by eight or nine, irreversible.

The silk, with its tiny stitches, now fills the large room. Fold over fold the spectrum grows, recedes. It is useless. I am a hardworking parasite and all the bile comes up and there is no Tom to strike the balance, to call the right tune.

There is a spider on the ceiling. Recently, I read, that apart from humans, spiders are the only known species to react to L.S.D. They build a more intricate web. But I don't want drugs, drinks or even cigarettes. After all the years of working, family life, pleasures now lost forever, I want only to pause with my silken threads — to simplify. I look at the ceiling and see the empty center-piece. We would have crystal, or like the great collector of Bantry, Spanish iron graced by little Dresden snowdrops. Perfection, madness or nothing. But an idea has come to mind.

I've given the idea some thought and have decided it is not crazy. I am a practical woman; good with my slightly arthritic hands and I'm not afraid of heights. There is plenty of wire and cord in the house. I have decided to turn the silk into a tent, hanging from the empty ceiling.

THREE

It is finished now and stands a tent no king ever lay in before battle. And it can turn. In the mornings I can read through ivory to cinnamon and later I can lie with green grass reflected through the windows, or lilac. It may even be useful. Perhaps one child of all the hundreds may look in from the terrible jungle and see, really see, the translucent colors as they gently move.

I lie here on silk and cushions, encased in more silk. Neither Prudence nor Bobby, Mary by inclination, Martha by necessity, am I now beginning, at last to look outside myself? Have I been too propped up all these busy years? Jobs, home, children and Tom, the assuager of all my woes.

I don't spend all the day in my lair, my cocoon and soon, I think, I'll fold it up. I won't emerge a golden drinking moth. The use of silk has, I suspect, acted as a filter and golden moths are susceptible to passing birds as I have been susceptible to guilt these past years of relative inactivity, coinciding with the horror of my island. Partly assuaged only because I see no solution and how can I work for something I do not even see?

Arthritic, perhaps symbolically, could a bomb ever affect me again as one did two years ago when a policeman sat on a dark, wet pavement holding a boy's severed head, his tears pouring into the rain? I had admonished that head only a few days earlier. His hair cut, no longer was his Italian face framed as in a sixteenth century portrait. He stood that September morning in the sun, the shining sea reflected in his face, our favorite bus conductor. He stood laughing and waving to me. "Never mind," I shouted to the wind, "I'll tell you again." Not of his Italian beauty of which he had no idea.

You can die of remaining doubled up in agony, so a certain setting aside becomes part of the routine. I shall have to start to read the newspapers again, at a distance this time to look at them and past them.

But steel and silk have taught me a little strength, though I shall need more to face the layers and layers of jungle around us all, showing itself clearly in the honest ugliness around us and then more and more insidiously in parklands of extraordinary calm: at conference tables, in bookless rooms, in shouting, mindless voices.

Bird swoops on moth to kill. Steel wounds silk to enhance. Moth or silk.

Perhaps, after all, I'll leave the swirling colours moving quietly in an empty room — a minor confrontation; a reminder to some untouched memory. If even one child.

Housekeeper's Cut

CLARE BOYLAN

Edward kept looking into the refrigerator. It gave him a sense of faith.
This peculiar sensation billowed inside his chest in the manner com-
petently wrought by carol singers and card senders at Christmas. It
was not the same as religious faith. Edward was too modest for that.
He was experiencing another sensation never before aspired to in his
life, a faith in ordinary things.

There was butter and bacon, eggs, milk, ice-cream; a clutter of
untidy vegetables — carrots, cabbage, onions, mushrooms. He had pur-
chased them recklessly from a stall in a food market, cramming his
string bag with scabby-looking roots with the air of a man who knows
exactly what he is doing. He had no notion of any practical applica-
tion for such primitive nutrients. They might have been employed by
men who lived in caves to club their enemies. He was familiar with
food that came in plastic bags and could be persuaded, with boiling
water, to imitate a meal.

He knew, all the same, in the way a blind man knows that the
world over his head is blue and grey and the world under his feet is
green and grey and the top part is safer, that these items belonged
at the very heart of things and that this was where he was going.

The thing that pleased him most was his roast. It held the cen-

CLARE BOYLAN (b. 1948) has worked as an editor and a journalist. Her first
novel, *Holy Pictures,* won her international critical recognition in 1983; *Last
Resorts* followed in 1984, and *Black Babies* in 1989, all from Hamish Hamilton. She has one story collection to date, *A Nail on the Head,* also published
by Hamish Hamilton in 1983. Ms. Boylan was born and educated in Dublin, but lives now in Wicklow.

ter of the refrigerator, lightly covered in butcher's paper. He had
watched it in the meaty window for several minutes before striding
in and claiming it. He did this by pointing because he had no idea
what it was. He was appalled at the price. It cost over four pounds.
He was neither poor nor mean, merely accustomed to buying a slice
or two of roast beef from the delicatessen or a couple of spiced sau-
sages, and there was always plenty of change left over from a pound.
Now that it was his he could see that it was worth the money, swirling fat and flesh tied with a string in the middle; already he could
hear the clash of knives being sharpened, the rattle and scrape of plates,
like sounds of battle imagined by a child in a history class.

He used to meet Susan between meals. She was worn out from
making excuses and he had to give her glasses of wine to make her
look the way he imagined her when she was not there. She grumbled
about the needs of her children, the demands of her husband, his capacity for chops and potatoes and apple tarts. It appeared that her
whole life was dragged down by the weight of her husband's appetite;
she was up at dawn wringing the vitamins from oranges, out ham-
pered by enormous sacks of groceries during the day. Afternoons were
taken up with peeling and grating, marinating, sieving. After a time
her abused features would soften and she would say: "It would be
different if it was for you. I always think of that when I'm cooking.
I always pretend it's for you." She would come to him then, dipping
her face to his lips. She sat across his legs as if he was a see-saw. "If
you were with me," he would say, "I would give you six months of
tremendous spoiling. Then I'd put you to work."

Sometimes he did, just to watch her, just for fun. He put her beside the cooker with mushrooms and cream, small morsels of fish,
tasty things.

She was too tired. The food got burnt, the mushrooms went rub-
bery. Or they became distracted. He would come up behind her and
put his arms around her and she would swivel round and burrow to
him. When they were in bed smells of burning food and sounds of
music drifted up from rooms below.

Inside her, he found a love that wanted to be taken advantage
of and although he did not wish to hurt her, he found himself complaining about the comfortlessness of his life; the meals taken in restaurants with people who meant nothing, just to fill an evening. He

dined out most evenings because he was lonely in the house without her. She never asked about his companions, but about the interior features of the restaurants, the designs on menus and then in detail, the meal. "It's a waste," he said, "to be anywhere without you."

When he went back to the city he forgot about her. There were moments when he felt a hollowness which he recognized as the place in him where she had been, but he had always known it would come to an end. He looked on love as a seasonal pleasure, like sunshine. Only a savage expected the sun to shine all year round.

She telephoned from public call boxes. Her voice was the ocean in a seashell. He remembered that they had made together a splash of happiness on a pale canvas but he knew that she did not carry this glow alone, without him. When they said goodbye for the last time, he had watched her running away, a drooping figure, disarrayed, a spirit fleeing an exorcism. He listened to the cascade of coins following the operator's instructions and then after a pause, her weary voice. "I miss you." He saw her in a headscarf with a bag of groceries at her side and small children clawing on the outside of the glass, trying to get at her.

He was at home now, busy, surrounded by people who were skilled in the pleasures of living—conversation and lovemaking—as people in the country had never been.

Even she, to whom he had leapt as determinedly as a salmon, held within her a soft hopelessness which begged, come in to me, fill me up, I have nothing else.

One day on the phone her voice sounded different: "I'm coming up," she said. He frowned into the machine receiving the bubbles of her tone. This possibility had not occurred to him. She was too firmly anchored with groceries. "Two whole days," she was telling him through her laughter, gasping about excuses and arrangements so complicated that he knew she would tunnel under the earth with her hands to reach him if necessary. "That will be very nice," he said inadequately. "I'll look forward to that." It was when he had replaced the receiver and was still washed by echoes of her foolish joy that he understood properly what she was saying. She had disposed, for a time, of all the open mouths that gaped at her for sustenance. She had put them aside. She was coming to do her proper task. He was tenderly agitated by the thought of her frail figure scurrying from one area of usefulness to another. This was blotted out by the shouts of his own areas of deprivation, crying out to be seen to. He wanted her to look after him.

When he met her at the station she was tremulously dressed up, a country woman on an outing. She threw him a reckless smile from under a hat. Alarming blue carnations sprang up around her skull. She dropped her cases and raced into his arms. Her feet flailed heedlessly and the flowers on her hat dipped like the neck of a heron. She thudded into him and he felt the needy probing of her tongue. He held her patiently, employing his training as a man to grind down the stone in his chest, of disappointment, that she had not kept a part of herself solid and available to his needs.

"Look at that!" She kept stabbing at the window of the car with her gloved finger, demonstrating pigeons and churches and department stores. "Look!" "You sound like a tourist," he said. She kept quiet after that. She hadn't ever been to the city before.

Inside his flat she walked around all the rooms, inspecting his clothes on their hangers, patting the bed, trying out chairs. He was surprised when she sat down without giving a glance to the refrigerator. "What shall we do?" she said.

She was slouched in a red leather armchair, her white skirt bunched under her thighs. He imagined that she ought to be in the kitchen doing something with the roast. He could picture it bulging in a tin, strung about with peeled potatoes and onions. He wanted to watch her bending at the oven, her frowning face pink, her straight hair shriveling into tiny curls around her face. He had bought an apron for her. It was white with a black and red frill at the bottom. It hung on a nail by the sink. He had no clear idea of what they would do with all the time they now had to spend together. She was the one who was married, who was skilled in the sectioning of time. He had vaguely imagined that women liked to be busy in a house, arranging flowers, punching pastry, stirring at saucepans on the stove, and that it was a man's role to encircle this ritual with refinement, music and drinks and occasional kisses, creating a territory for their contentment, a privacy for their love.

He had not set his heart on this course of events. He did not mind if she preferred to take a nap or read a book or sit on his knee.

The thing that was foremost in his mind was that their pursuits of the afternoon would be overlaid by ovenly aromas, snaps and splutterings and the delicious sting on their senses of roasting meat.

He asked if she was hungry and she said that she was, standing up instantly, brushing down her skirt. She took a mirror from her bag and gazed at her face, pressing her lips together, peering into her eyes for flaws. He took her hand and led her through to the kitchen. He pulled open the door of the refrigerator as if he was drawing back a stage curtain and she peered, awed, at the overcrowding of nourishment. "What are you going to do with all this?" she said, and he laughed. "There's cold meat and cheese," he said. "We could have that for lunch." She stood gazing into the fridge with a melancholy expression while he removed the slices of ham and the tubs of potato salad and the oozing triangle of Brie.

When he had set the table and opened a bottle of wine he came back to find her still transfixed in front of the open cabinet with that expression housewives have, and he thought she was sizing up the contents, planning menus. "That," he said, pointing in at his slab of meat on the shelf as if it was a lovely trinket in a jeweler's window, "is for dinner." She sat down at the table without a word. He sensed, as she ate her ham and potatoes and swirled her wine around in the glass, that she was disappointed. This feeling communicated to himself and he poured wine into his leaden chest, blaming himself. He had probably pre-empted her plans for lunch. She might have been planning to surprise him with a homemade soup. She raised bleak eyes to him over her glass. She was not her normal self, full of cheerful complaint and breathless love. She was ill at ease and sad. "Aren't we going out?" she said. The thought to him was preposterous. Now that they finally had a stretch of privacy, she wanted to race out into the cold where they would be divided by elements and the curious looks of strangers.

He drove her to a park and they huddled under some trees against the cold, watching cricket players and a family of deer in the distance like an arrangement of dead branches. He had brought a box of sweets that she had sent him. It had seemed a sentimental gesture, saving them to share with her. Now that he was pulling off the wrapper he could see it was tactless, taking them out so much later. She would think he had not wanted them. He laid the open box in the grass. After a moment or two, the arrangement of confectionery was swarming with ants.

He was tired when he got home and beginning to get hungry. Susan wanted a bath. He took the meat from the fridge and laid it on a plate on the counter. He hazarded the skinning of several potatoes. He carried a clutch of jaundiced-looking parsnips and placed them in a bowl, close to the liquidizer. This tableau was completed with a blue tin of curry powder. Once, in a restaurant, he had been given a curried parsnip soup and it was delicious.

When she joined him in the kitchen she was wearing a black dress down to her feet. Her mouth was obscured in magenta. He put his arms around her and kissed her laundered neck but she struggled from his grasp and pointed to the ranked ingredients. "What are you doing?" she said. "Just hamming." He smiled guiltily.

She looked from him to the food, back again. Her hands, he noticed, wrestled with the string of a tiny evening bag. "I thought," she said, "that we'd be going out." "Going where?" he said, exasperated. "I don't know." Her shoulders drooped. "The theater, a restaurant." He could not keep her still, draw her back to the things that mattered. "Do you really want to go out?" She nodded her head. He sighed and went to telephone a theater. When he came back the counter had been cleared of his work and offered instead a meager plate of toast and a pot of tea.

In the city she was happy. She sipped cocktails and laughed, showing all her teeth, raising her eyebrows larkily. Although her clothes were not suited to the theater, not suited to anything really, she carried her happiness with dignity. Men looked at her, old ones, young ones, brown, gray. She was aware of this but her eyes were for him. He thought he understood now. She was sure of herself on this neutral territory. She did not wish to be plucked by him from their complicated past. Here, she was a woman alone. She wanted him to court her. He took her hand and kissed her cheek, catching scents of gin and perfume. He felt desire. This seizure of lust was new. It had not touched him when they were in the park or shut up in his living quarters. He had felt love and compassion but no selfish stirrings.

During the play he watched her, writing his own theme, making her free and carefree as his needs required, as her loud laughter would lead anyone to believe.

Afterwards he turned the car quickly homeward. She kept looking out the window, like a child. When they were home she said fretfully: "We haven't had anything to eat, not really." He was no longer concerned about food. There was plenty, in any case, in the fridge. She cooked some eggs and a packet of little onions, frozen in sauce. It was a strange combination but he drove the food into his mouth and pronounced it delicious.

They went to bed. Their sex was full of need and passion. They came with angry shouts. They could not find their love. "I love you," she said. "Yes," he said. "Yes." And then they were silent, each saying to themselves: "Tomorrow will be different."

In the morning she was up early to make his breakfast, her toes crackling with joy as she reached up to shelves for coffee and marmalade. She felt wrapped around him as a cardigan. As she waited for the coffee to boil she sensed a warm splash on her feet and it was his seed, languorously detaching itself from her. She felt a minute sense of loss, wanting to let nothing go, wanting to be pregnant.

Edward had to work after breakfast. He did not mind leaving her on her own. She seemed happy as she punished pillows and washed out the breakfast things. He found himself whistling as he bent over his set square. After a time she came and sat beside him. She had been washing her hair. She combed it over her face in long strokes that emanated a faint creak. Inky streamers swam through the air and clung to his clothing. He could not work. He gave her an irritated glance and she went away. She came back dressed in high shoes and a blue suit—a costume, rather, he thought—her face matt and piqued with make-up. She was carrying cups of coffee. When she put his coffee down she quickly sought his hand with hers, and although their grasp was warm and steady there was some central part of them that was trembling and they could feel it through their palms. "Now," he thought, "we could go to bed. We could love each other." It made sense. They had always done their loving in the day. Her bright armor kept him distant.

"I'd like," she said, "to see the sights."

He took his hand away and wrapped it around the cup of coffee, needing warmth. He did not look at her. "There's nothing to see out there," he said. "Believe me. We could have a quiet lunch and listen to some music. We could read to each other." "But it's London!" she protested.

He said, thinking to stop her: "You go if you want. I must work for a little while. I couldn't bear to see the sights." He did look up then and saw her soft round face boxing up a huge hurt in an even larger resolve. She kissed the side of his face and he wanted the salt of her mouth but she was so different, so devoid of humor and generosity, that he believed even her taste might have changed. She clopped off on her high heels and he heard the sorrowful bang of the door.

He could not work. He was exasperated to distraction. There crept in on him thoughts, malice-filled whispers. He shook them off as if they were wasps at his ears.

He had established in his mind, long months before, that she was the one in his life who truly loved him, wanting nothing, knowing that nothing was possible. When they parted he had savored the sorrow of it, knowing that this was real. They had been severed by fate, an outsider, a true professional. There would be no festering, only a clean grief gleaming like stainless steel around the core of a perfect happiness, safely invested in his center. He had been content to leave it at that. He would have loved her, at the back of his head, until his death.

It was she who had come back like a vengeful spirit to incorporate him in her discontent, to mock his faith, to demonstrate to him, in her ghostly unreachableness, the great stretch of his own isolation.

He went to look for some lunch. There was nothing in the refrigerator that he could understand. He was exploring parcels of foil, hoping for some forgotten cheese, when he heard a commotion coming from the garden.

Susan was in a restaurant. She had a chocolate éclair that she was breaking with the side of her fork. She had taken a taxi to Madame Tussaud's and the Planetarium. Outside each was a long queue of foreigners and a man selling balloons on a stick for fifty pence. There was no glamour, no sense of discovery. They were like people queueing for food in the war. She had wanted him to take her to a gallery of famous paintings and show her the pictures he liked. No point in going on her own; she could never understand pictures, always wanted to see the scene as it really was.

She left the stoic queue and went back to the taxi rank. She could not think where to go. "Bond Street," she said to the driver, liking its sound. She did not know where it was but it seemed to her, as the streets unraveled like red and gray bandages, she was being taken further and further away from Edward. When they got to Bond Street, she was ordered out of the dark enclosure. She tried to thrust a fan of notes at the back of the driver's neck, through the sliding glass door, but he was suspicious and made her go out on the street and put them through a side window.

She stumbled along in front of the smart shops. She ached to be with Edward, to feel his hand or even the cloth of his jacket; and then, perversely, she felt lonely for home, wanting to butter toast for the children or to fluff the top of a shepherd's pie for her husband. She understood their needs. She knew how to respond. When she had exhausted several streets she found a café and she went in and ordered herself a cake. A tear dropped into it and she did not want to eat it. She would go back, she promised herself. She would talk to him.

He was standing at the window, shoulders bent, head at a quizzical angle and sunlight teasing his hair into infantile transparency. She had let herself in with the key he had given her and he did not notice her. Watching his back, she felt as if all the ordinary things had been vacuumed out of her body and replaced by love, lead-heavy, a burden. "I want to talk to you," she said. "Shhh," he said, not turning around. "Edward?" she begged. He turned to her. His face was white, filled with horror. "It's a bird," he said.

"What are you talking about?" She went to the window and looked out. She could see a ragged tomcat standing at a tree, his back arched. She ran to the back door and out into the garden, down the length of the path.

The tree was root deep in rattling leaves and when she got to it she could see that the leaves were in permanent motion as if agitated by a slow motor under the earth. She saw then that it was a dowdy gray bird, lopsided, helplessly urging an injured wing to flight. The cat held its victim with a gooseberry gaze. She picked up the cat and put it on the wall, slapping its behind to make it jump into the next garden. "Bring me a box," she shouted out to Edward's white face at the window. He advanced with a shoe box. She snatched it from him, piling it with leaves, roughly cramming in the damaged bird. She slammed the lid on the bird's head and carried it indoors. She looked, Edward thought, like a housewife who has just come upon some unpleasant item of refuse and means to deal with it; but when she got indoors she sat in a chair and emptied bird and leaves into her blue linen lap. She held the bird in cupped hands and crooned gently into its dank feathers.

He brought her tea and fed it to her, holding the cup to her mouth. She minded the bird like a baby, making noises with her lips, rocking back and forth as once she had minded him. He was unnerved by a pang of jealousy. "Did you have a nice morning?" he said. "Oh, yes," she said, distantly, rocking. He could see that she was in her element. He was excluded. He crumbled bread into a bowl of milk and pushed little spoons of it at the dry nib of the bird's beak. The bird seemed to be asleep. She pushed his hand aside and swept the bird, leaves and all, back into the box. "Open the bedroom window," she said. She followed him upstairs and put the box on the ledge without its lid. "If his wing isn't broken he'll fly away," she said. "But if it is broken?" he said helplessly. "He'll die," she said.

In the course of the morning he had taken the meat and vegetables from the fridge once more. There had been nothing readily edible and he was hungry. When they came downstairs again she saw them and said: "I have to phone my husband," as if they had reminded her of him, which they had.

He heard her on the phone. She sounded as if she was defending herself. She said then: "I miss you." It was an echo from his distant past. He went in and found her sitting on the sofa, her fist to her mouth, crying. He touched her hair lightly with his fingers, afraid to do more. "I'll just put the meat in the oven," he said hopefully. "What?" She glared at him. Her tearful face was full of scorn. "Have you still got your heart set on that?" "I bought it for you," he said. "You bought it for me? I have tasted prawns and sole in my life, you know. I have had fried steak." She was attacking him. He didn't know what was the matter. He assumed her husband had said something to upset her. "It's all right," he soothed. He tiptoed out as if she were sleeping.

The potatoes, peeled from yesterday, had blackened. He flung them hopefully into the tin. He peeled four onions and tucked them into the corners, in the center, as he had imagined it, the round of juicy meat.

It looked perfectly fine. He put a pat of butter on the top and a sprinkling of salt and pepper. He cut up a clove of garlic and scattered it over the food. He thought he had seen other women doing something like this. He turned the oven up to a rousing temperature and pushed the tin inside. It was done. There was nothing to it.

He blamed himself for Susan's outburst. He should not have left her to wander around the city on her own. She was used to a more protected way of life. He must make it up to her.

He took champagne from a cool cupboard and dug it into a bowl with ice. He found music on the radio. He brought the wine with glasses to the bedroom. Music drifted up from downstairs. He drew the curtains and switched on a little lamp. "Susan," he called.

He heard her dragging steps on the stairs. A face loomed round the door, self-piteous. Her sharp eyes flashed about suspiciously, took in the details—and were radiant. She was a child; all troubles erased in a momentary delight. She ran to him and was caught in his arms. They stroked hair, pulled buttons, tasted flesh. She laughed greedily. At last they had met.

They made love boastfully, tenderly, certain of their territory. He held her feet in his hands. She took his fingers in her mouth. They embroidered one another's limbs with their attentions. He felt with his lips for the edges of her smile and could find no end. They were separated only by the selfishness of their happiness. Afterwards, she gave a deep unlikely chortle from her satisfied depths and he laughed at her.

They drank the champagne crouching at opposite ends of the bed in the intimate gloom, striking up flinty tales of childhood for sympathy.

When they crawled towards each other, he with bottle and she with empty glass, only their mouths met and he took the breakable things and put them on the floor because they had to make love again.

They emptied the bottle of champagne. They lay beside each other, gazing. "I must look awful," she said. He surveyed her snarled black hair and the matching dark scribble under a carelessly disposed arm; the smear of make-up under her eyes, her sated face scrubbed pink.

"You look fine to me," he said. He felt exuberant, relieved, re-born, at ease. "You look," he teased, but truthfully, "like my mistress."

She swung away from him, rolled over and clung to her pillow, a mollusc on a rock. He could not tell what was in her head. He patted her back but she shook him off and murmured sadly through the pillow: "I smell something." She looked up at him, one moist eye rising above its ruined decor. He had offended her. But when the rest of her face rose above the sheets he could see that her eyes were watering with laughter.

"What is it?" he smiled tenderly. "It's perfect," she said. "It's exactly as it used to be—us, together, the music and the smell of burning food." She laughed.

He jumped out of bed and ran to the kitchen. Smoke gusted out around the oven door. The air was cruel with the taint of burning beast. He pulled open the oven door and his naked body was assaulted by the heat of hell. He dragged the roasting tin clear of the smoke with a cloth. The cloves of garlic rattled like blackened nails on the tarry ruin.

He was worn out. He felt betrayed. He could not believe that it had happened so quickly, so catastrophically. He felt his faith sliding away. "Edward?" Susan called out from the bedroom. "It's all right!" he shouted; and after he had said it he felt that it had to be. He opened the window to let out the smoke and went to the bathroom for a dressing-gown.

Bolstered by champagne and the satisfactoriness of the afternoon's loving he made himself believe that the meat could be repaired. He whistled loudly as if it was the dark and he was afraid. He forked the meat on to a scalloped plate and began to hack away with a sharp knife at the charred edges of the tormented flesh.

He was agreeably surprised to find that the meat was still quite rare on the inside—almost raw, in fact. He found it hard to make an impression with the knife but he put this down to lack of practice and the fact that the carving implements were not much in use. He sawed, glad of the little box of cress in the fridge which would decorate its wounds and the rest of the vegetables which Susan would cook and toss in butter while he put on his clothes.

Susan came up behind him. She had been standing in the doorway in a night-dress like a flourbag, frilled on cuff and sleeve. She tiptoed on bare feet, so that he sensed her at the last moment, tangled wraith blanched and billowing.

"It's no use," she whispered. "It's fine," he said. "It's not bad at all." "It's no use," she cried brokenly. "There's no Bisto, no stock cubes. There's nothing in your cupboards, nothing ordinary—no flour or custard, there isn't a packet of salt. It's all a pretense."

She put out a hand, and he reached for it, needing something to hold. Her hand shot past him. She struck at the meat. It sailed off the plate and landed on the floor, blood gathering at its edges. "That's all you think of me," she said violently, through trembling jaws. "You think that's good enough for me! Housekeeper's Cut! I wouldn't have that on my own table at home. I wouldn't give that to my children if they were hungry. That's all I'm worth."

They ate in an Italian restaurant close to where he lived. It was not a place he had been before. The tables were bright red and the menu leaned heavily to starch but there was no time to book a proper restaurant. He had to have something to eat.

"Have some veal," he said. "That should be good." He poured wine from a carafe into their glasses. She ordered a pizza. Her hair fell over her face. He could see her knuckles sawing over the fizzing red disc but none of it seemed to go to her mouth. The waiter said that the lady should have an ice-cream. She shook her head. "Cassata!" he proclaimed. "It means," he wheedled, "married."

Edward laughed encouragement but she did not see. Her head was turned to the waiter, nodding, he could not tell whether in request or resignation.

In the morning she was gone. The sheets still burned with the heat of her body. She had been up at six, packing, making coffee, telephoning for a taxi. Her feet, on the floor made a rousing slap like the sound of clapping hands. At one point he heard her whistling. He knew that he should drive her to the station but he would not hasten her back to the disposal of her lawful dependents. He would not.

"Edward!" Her hands clung to the end of his bed and she cried out in distress, her face and her night-dress trailing white in the gray morning light. "Yes, love," he said inside, but he only opened a cautious eye and uttered a sleepy "Mmm?" "I bought nothing for the children," she said. "They'll be expecting presents. I always buy them something."

She stood at the window, dressed in hat and coat, in the last moments, waiting for her taxi. "Edward!" she cried. He sat up this time, ready to take her in his arms. "The bird!" she said. "He flew away."

When she was gone he traced with his fingers her body in the warm sheets, bones and hair and pillows of maternal flesh. He kept his eyes closed, kept her clenched in his heart. The day bore in on him, sunshine and telephone bells and the cold knowledge that she did not love him. All the time she pretended to care for him, she had been jealous of his wealth, greedy for glamour. She was a pilgrim, stealing relics of the saints.

It was not him she desired. She wanted to snatch for herself some part of a glittering life she imagined he was hoarding. He tried to bring her face to mind but all he could see was a glass box, clawed by children, and inside, a housewife in a headscarf, bags of groceries at her side.

Susan did not cry until she was on the train. The tears fell, then, big as melted ice cubes. There was a man sitting opposite with a little boy. The child had been given a magic drawing pad to occupy his hands and he made sketches of her melting face, squinting for perspective.

As the tears dashed from her eyes she felt that she was flying to pieces. Soon there would be nothing left of her; at any rate, nothing solid enough to contain the knowledge that he did not love her.

She had expected so little. She only wanted to fill up the gaps in their past. Often, when they were together, he had spoken of the hurt of being anywhere without her; the wasted nights with strangers; the meals in restaurants, not tasted. It was terrible to her that she had only given him her leftover time. She had to make it up to him. She wanted him to know that she would risk anything for him. She would shine beside him in the harsh glare of public envy. For a very little time she would be his for all the world to see, whatever the world might say.

Now she did not know what she would do except, in time, face up to her foolishness. He had not been proud of her. He wanted to hide her away. Established in his own smart and secret life, he had been ashamed of her.

The man on the seat opposite was embarrassed. It was her huge tears, her lack of discretion, the critical attention of his little boy. He felt threatened by their indifference to proper codes of behavior. He snatched the magic pad and threw it roughly to the far end of the seat. The boy gazed idly out the window.

Accustomed to inspecting the creative efforts of the children, Susan reached for the sketch pad. The boy was not as clever as her own. His portrait was a clown's mask, upside down. She rubbed out his imprint and sat with the pad on her knee, acquainting herself with the raw, hurting feeling of her mind and her skin, settling into the pain. She had to stop crying. The children would notice. Tomorrow she would buy them presents. Tonight, they would have to content themselves with ice-cream. "Ice-cream" she scratched absently on the magic pad. Her tired mind grizzled over the necessities of tea and she wrote, without thinking, "eggs, bacon, cheese"; and then, since days did not exist on their own but merely as transport to other days, and since she on this vehicle of time was a stoker, she continued writing: "carrots, cabbage, onions, mushrooms."

Five Notes After a Visit

ANNE DEVLIN

Monday 9th February 1984

I begin to write.

The first note:

"You were born in Belfast?" the security man at the airport said.

"Yes."

"What is the purpose of your visit there?"

To be with my lover. Well, I didn't say that. I had written "re-search" on the card he was holding in his hand. I remind him of this.

"I would like *you* to answer the questions," he says.

"I am doing research."

"Who is your employer?"

"Self." I stick to my answers on the card.

"Oh! The idle rich," he says.

"I live on a grant."

I might have expected this. It happens every time I cross the water. But I will never get used to it.

"Who is paying for your ticket?"

"I am."

"What a pity." He smiles. "And what have you been doing in England all this time?"

ANNE DEVLIN (b. 1951) has won numerous literary awards—the Hennessy in 1982 for "Passages," and the Samuel Beckett Award for Television Drama in 1984 for *The Long March*. Ms. Devlin, born in Belfast, sets her work in her native city. Her recent filmscript, *Naming the Names,* has been cited for veritism and sensitivity. Ms. Devlin has lived in Birmingham, England, for the past several years.

"Living." Trying.

"There was a bomb in Oxford Street yesterday. Some of your countrymen."

Two feet away some passengers with English accents are saying goodbye to their relatives. A small boy holding his mother's hand is smiling. Two feet between the British and the Irish in the airport lounge: I return the child's smile. Two feet and seven hundred years.

"He's a small man doing a small job!" Stewart says, when he meets me at the other side. "Forget about him." I won't. "Now don't be cross with me. But you could save yourself a lot of trouble if you'd only write British under nationality."

"I think—" I start to say, but don't finish. Next time I'll write "don't know."

I come back like a visitor. I always do. And I'm treated like one. On the Black Mountain road from the airport it is getting dark, when the taxi driver says, "Do you see that orange glow down there? Just beyond the motorway?"

"Yes."

"Those are the lights of the Kesh."

Like a football stadium to the uninitiated.

"And just up there ahead of us," he points to a crown of white lights on Divis ridge, "that's the police observatory station. That's where they keep the computer."

"Is it?"

"I had to do a run up there once. But I never got past the gates."

We plunge down Hannastown Hill in the dark towards the lights of a large housing estate. If I don't speak in this taxi, perhaps he'll think I'm English.

"What road is this?" Stewart asks, as we pass my parents' house. His father is a shipyard worker.

SINN FEIN IS THE POLITICAL WING OF THE PROVISIONAL IRA is painted on the gable. WESTMINSTER IS THE POLITICAL WING OF THE BRITISH ARMY.

"This is Andersonstown," the taxi driver says.

There is barbed wire on the flowerbeds in my father's garden. A foot patrol trampled his crocuses last spring. Tomorrow I'll go and tell them I've come home. But not yet. Stewart isn't keen.

"They won't approve of me," he says, "I've been married once before. They'll persuade you to go back to England."

"They won't!" I insist. But I have the same old fear. His first wife lives in East Belfast.

Tuesday 10th January 1984

The second note:

I am looking at the bus that will take me to my mother. Through the gates I can see the others waiting too. I hear myself say: "Mother, I've come back!"; and I hear her ask me, "Why?"

I have let him lure me from my undug basement garden in an English town; one egg in the fridge and the dregs of milk; my solitude wrapped around me like a blanket for those six years until he came — and presented me with the only kind of miracle I ever really believed in.

I hear her ask me, "Why?"

I remember the summer months, our breakfasts at lunchtime in my garden, our evening meals on the raft, my bed. When term began again, he said: "I've got a job in Belfast. Will you come and live with me?"

"Oh, I can't go back," I said. "I can't — live without you," I tell him at the airport when I arrive.

I hear her ask me why?

My house is empty and the blinds are down. The letters slip into the hall unseen. The tanks will still turn onto the Whiteladies Road out of the Territorial Army Barracks and pass the BBC. And the black cab driver will drive someone else from the station. "Where to?" Blackboy Hill.

A For Sale notice stands in the uncut grass. .

I hear her ask me why? I turn away from the stop.

Wednesday 1st February 1984

I have not kept an account of the days in between because I am too tired after work to write. And anyway I go to bed with him at night.

The third note:

It is the third day of the third week of my visit. I am working in the library.

"On the 1st of January 1957 the Bishop of Down and Connor's Relief Fund for Hungarian Refugees amounted to £19,375 0s 6d. Further contributions in a daily newspaper for that morning include: Sleamish Dancing Club, £5; Bon Secours Convent, Falls Road, £10; The John Bosco Society for the Prevention of Communism, £25; A sinner, Anonymous—"

"Love?"

"£5. Three months later, in April of the same year, the Lord Mayor of Belfast welcomed the first 500 refugees. It was the only issue on which the people of Belfast East and West agreed."

"Love."

He is standing at my table.

"Oh, I'm sorry, I didn't see you."

"Love. My wife's just rung. I'll have to go and see her. She was crying on the phone. She wants to discuss us getting back together. If only you knew how angry this makes me!"

"Will you tell her about me?"

Below the library window voices reach me from the street. The students are assembling for a march. They shoulder a black coffin: RIP EDUCATION is chalked in on the side.

Maggie. Maggie. Maggie. Out! Out! Out!

Police in bulletproof jackets flank the thin demonstration through the square. The wind tosses the voice back and forth; I only catch an odd phrase here and there: "Our comrades in England . . . The trade union movement in this country . . ."

"We have to keep a low profile for a while," he said. "And don't answer the phone in case it's her."

When I was young I think, watching the demonstration pass. I must have been without fear. I make a resolution: I will go there after dark.

Thursday 2nd February 1984

The Feast of the Purification. And James Joyce's birthday. I always remember it.

This is the fourth note:

He is scraping barnacles off the mussels when I come back after midnight. "Where were you?" he asks.

"I went to see my mother."

"How was it?"

"She asked the usual questions. Did I still go to Mass? She said she'd pray for me."

"Did you tell her about me?"

"I talked about my research: The Flight of Hungarian Refugees to Belfast in '57. Can't think why. She said when I was leaving: 'Keep your business to yourself.' She was talking about you."

"My wife cried when I told her. She thinks it's a phase I'm going through—and I'll get over it."

There are pink and red carnations in a jug on the table, the man-next-door's music is coming through the walls. A trumpet. Beethoven. I'm getting good at that.

"He's obsessive," Stewart says. "He's played that piece since ten o'clock."

At the table, I make a mistake: I push my soup away, I'm not as hungry as I thought.

"Go back! Go back to England then! You said you *could* live with me."

"I am trying."

When I wake the smell of garlic reaches me from the bottom of the stairs. It was the mussel soup he lifted off the table. "Go back! Go back to England! You're not anybody's prisoner!"

"I am trying!"

Mussel shells, garlic, onion, tomato paste, tomatoes and some wine, he threw into the kitchen. But the garlic hangs over everything this morning; and the phone is ringing in a room downstairs.

In some places, he said last night, amid the broken crockery, before a marriage they smash the dishes, they break the plates to frighten off the ghosts. Perhaps this is necessary after all.

When he wakes, I whisper: "Love, I'll stay."

"I've found you again," he says.

The phone is still ringing in a room downstairs. It is 2:30 in the afternoon.

"Send your Fenian girlfriend back where she belongs, or we'll give her the works and then you."

He is staring at the clock.

"I wonder how they knew?" he says.

"The estate agent has been writing to me from England. It was too much trouble to explain the difficulty of it. The postman would notice a Catholic name in this street. The sorters in the Post Office too. Or maybe it was the man collecting for the football pools—"

"Football pools?"

"The other night a man came to the door, he asked me to pick four teams or eight, I can't remember now. Then he asked me to sign it."

"You should have given my name."

"I did. But I don't know anything about football. And I think I gave myself away when—"

"What?"

"I picked Liverpool. Or it could have happened at the launderette when I left the washing in. They asked: 'What name?' And I forgot. Or it could have been the taxi I got last night from here to—"

"I suppose they would have found out some time." He is sitting on the bed.

"Could it have been—your wife?"

He looks hurt: "I never told her that!" he says. "I suppose they would have found out some time. I think I'd better call the police."

I get up quickly: "Do you mind if I get dressed and bathe and make the bed before you do?"

"Why?"

"Because they'll come round and look at everything."

I am packing a large suitcase in the attic where we sleep when he comes upstairs.

"The police say that anyone who really meant a threat wouldn't ring you up beforehand. They're not coming round."

"Listen. I want you to take me to the airport. And I want you to pack a bag as well."

"I'm teaching tomorrow," he says. "Please leave something behind, love. That black dress of yours. The one I like you in."

It is still hanging in the wardrobe. I leave my scent in the bathroom and on his pillow.

"It's just so that I know you'll come back."

At 3:40 we are ready to leave the house. The street is empty when we open the door. The curtains are drawn.

"We're a bit late," he tells the driver. "Can you get us to the airport in half an hour?"

In the car he kisses me and says: "No one has ever held my hand so tightly before."

"What will you do?" I ask, as I'm getting on the plane.

"I'll have to give three months notice."

"Do it."

"Teaching jobs are hard to come by," he says, looking around. "Whatever this place is — it's my home."

5:45. Heathrow. Without him I walk from the plane. Who are they watching now? Him or me? Suddenly a man steps out in front of me. Oh Jesus!

"Have you any means of identification? What is the purpose of your visit . . . ?"

Friday 3rd February 1984

The fifth note.

A bell is ringing. I go cautiously to the door. I have slept with all the lights on. I see a man through the glass. He is wearing a combat jacket. This is England, I remind myself. The milkman is smiling at me.

"I saw your lights," he says.

I tell him I've come back and will he please leave one pint every other day.

He tells me his son's in Northern Ireland in the Army. "No jobs," he shouts, walking down the path. "Were you on holiday?"

"No, I was working."

The bottles clink in the crate.

"It's well for some."

He is angry, I begin to think, because I do not drive a milkfloat.

I am shopping again for one. At closing time I go out to the supermarket. It is just getting dark. There are two hundred people gathered in the road outside the shopping precinct. A busker is playing a love song. The police are turning away at the entrance the ones who haven't noticed.

"What is it?" I ask a woman who is waiting at a stop.
"A bomb scare. It's the third one this week."
I should think before I speak.
"There were 14 people killed in London, in a bomb in a store."
I am hoping that she hasn't noticed. Some of your countrymen?
Then she says, "Doesn't matter what nationality you are, dear. We all suffer the same."

The busker is playing a love song. I am shopping again for one.

Noday. Nodate 1984
I keep myself awake all night so I am ready when they come.

Lilacs

MARY LAVIN

"That dunghill isn't doing anyone any harm, and it's not going out of where it is as long as I'm in this house," Phelim Mulloy said to his wife Ros, but he threw an angry look at his elder daughter Kate who was standing by the kitchen window with her back turned to them both.

"Oh Phelim," Ros said softly, "if only it could be put somewhere else besides under the window of the room where we eat our bit of food."

"Didn't you just say a minute ago people can smell it from the other end of the town? If that's the case I don't see what would be the good in shifting it from one side of the yard to the other."

Kate could stand no more. "What I don't see is the need for us dealing in dung at all."

"There you are, what did I tell you?" Phelim said. "I knew all along what was in the back of your minds, both of you. And the one inside there too," he added, nodding his head at the closed door of one of the rooms off the kitchen. "All you want, the three of you, is to get rid of the dung altogether. Why on earth can't women speak

MARY LAVIN (b. 1912) came to Ireland from East Walpole, Massachusetts, with her parents as a child of ten. She is one of the most prolific and prestigious writers of fiction in Ireland, winner of every major literary award. Ms. Lavin's stories have been published in the *New Yorker* over many years. She has produced seventeen volumes of short fiction and two novels since 1942. She served from 1972 to 1974 as president of the Irish Academy of Letters and received the D. Litt. from University College, Dublin, in recognition of her considerable artistic achievements.

out, and say what they mean. That's a thing always puzzled me."

"Leave Stacy out of this, Phelim," said Ros, but she spoke quietly. "Stacy has one of her headaches."

"I know she has," said Phelim, "and I know something else. I know I'm supposed to think it's the smell of the dung gave it to her. Isn't that so?"

"Ah Phelim, that's not what I meant at all. I only thought you might wake her with your shouting. She could be asleep."

"Asleep is it? It's a real miracle any of you can get a wink of sleep, day or night, with the smell of that harmless heap of dung out there, that's bringing good money to this house week after week." He had lowered his voice, but when he turned and looked at Kate it rose again without his noticing. "It paid for your education at a fancy boarding school, and for your sister's too. It paid for your notions of learning to play the piano, *and* the violin, both of which instruments is rotting away inside in the parlor and not a squeak of a tune ever I heard out of the one or the other of them since the day they came into the house."

"We may as well spare our breath, Mother," Kate said. "He won't give in, now or ever. That's my belief."

"That's the truest word that's ever come out of your mouth," Phelim said to her, and stomping across the kitchen he opened the door that led into the yard and went out, leaving the door open. Immediately the faint odor of stale manure that hung in the air was enriched by the smell of a fresh load, hot and steaming that had just been tipped into the huge dunghill from a farm cart that was the first of a line of carts waiting their turn to unload. Ros sighed and went to close the door, but Kate got ahead of her and banged it shut, before going back to the window and taking up her stand there. After a nervous glance at the door of the bedroom that her daughters shared, Ros, too, went over the window and both women stared out.

An empty cart was clattering out of the yard and Phelim was leading in another from which, as it went over the spud-stone of the gate, a clod or two of dung fell out on the cobbles. The dunghill was nearly filled, and liquid from it was running down the sides of the trough to form pools through which Phelim waded unconcernedly as he forked back the stuff on top to make room for more.

"That's the last load," Ros said.

"For this week," Kate said. "Your trouble is you're too soft with him, Mother. You'll have to be harder on him. You'll have to keep at him night and day. That is to say if you care anything at all about me and Stacy."

"Ah Kate. Can't you see there's no use? Can't you see he's set in his ways?"

"All I can see is the way we're being disgraced." Kate said angrily. "Last night, at the concert in the Parish Hall, just before the curtain went up I heard the wife of that man who bought the bakehouse telling the person beside her that they couldn't open a window since they came here with a queer smell that was coming from somewhere, and asking the other person if she knew what it could be. I nearly died of shame, Mother, I really did. I couldn't catch what answer she got, but after the first item was over, and I glanced back, I saw it was Mamie Murtagh she was sitting beside, and you can guess what that one would be likely to have said. My whole pleasure in the evening was spoiled."

"You take things too much to heart, Kate," Ros said sadly. "There's Stacy inside there, and it's my belief she wouldn't mind us dealing in dung at all if it wasn't for the smell of it. Only the other day she was remarking that if he'd even clear a small space under the windows we might plant something there that would smell nice. 'Just think, Mother,' she said, 'just think if it was a smell of lilac that was coming in to us every time we opened a door or a window."

"Oh Stacy has lilac on the brain if you ask me," Kate said crossly. "She never stops talking about it. What did she ever do to try and improve our situation?"

"Ah now Kate, you know Stacy is very timid."

"All the more reason Father would listen to her, if she'd speak to him. He may not let on to it, but he'd do anything for her."

Ros nodded. She'd never speak to him, all the same, Stacy would never have the heart to cross anyone."

"She wouldn't need to say much. Didn't you hear him, today, saying he supposed it was the smell of the dung was giving her her headaches? You let that pass, but I wouldn't not that he'd have taken much more from me, although it's me has to listen to her moaning and groaning the minute the first cart rattles into the yard. How is it that it's always on a Wednesday she has a headache? And it's been the same since the first Wednesday we came home from the convent." With that last thrust Kate ran into the bedroom and came out with a raincoat. "I'm going out for a walk," she said, "and I won't come back until the smell of that stuff has died down a bit. You can tell my father that, too, if he's looking for me."

"Wait a minute, Kate. Was Stacy asleep?" Ros asked.

"I don't know and I don't care. She was lying with her face to the wall, like always."

When Kate went out, Ros took down the tea-caddy from the dresser and put a few pinches of tea from it into an earthenware pot on the hob of the big open fire. Then, tilting the kettle that hung from a crane over the flames, she wet the tea, and pouring out a cup she carried it over to the window and set it to cool on the sill while she went on watching Phelim.

He was a hard man when you went against him. A man who'd never let himself be thwarted. He was always the same. That being so, there wasn't much sense in nagging him but Kate would never be made see that. Kate was stubborn too.

The last of the carts had gone, and after shutting the gate Phelim had taken a yard-brush and was sweeping up the dung that had been spilled. When he'd made a heap of it, he got a shovel and gathered it up and flung it up on the dunghill. But whether he did it to tidy the yard or in order not to waste the dung, Ros didn't know. The loose bits of dung he'd flung up on the top of the trough had dried out, and the bits of straw that were stuck to it had dried out too. They gleamed bright and yellow in a ray of watery sunlight that had suddenly shone forth.

Now that Kate was gone, Ros began to feel less bitter against Phelim. Like herself, he was getting old. She was sorry they had upset him. And while she was looking at him, he laid the yard-brush against the wall of one of the sheds and put his hand to his back. He'd been doing that a lot lately. She didn't like to see him doing it. She went across to the door and opened it.

"There's hot tea in the pot on the hob, Phelim," she called out. "Come in and have a cup." Then seeing he was coming, she went over and gently opened the bedroom door. "Stacy, would you be able for a cup of tea?" she asked bending over the big feather-bed.

Stacy sat up at once.

"What did he say? Is it going to be moved?" she asked eagerly.

"Ssh, Stacy," Ros whispered, and then as Stacy heard her father's steps in the kitchen she looked startled.

"Did he hear me?" she asked anxiously.

"No," said Ros, and she went over and drew the curtains to let in the daylight. "How is your poor head, Stacy?"

Stacy leaned toward Ros so she could be heard when she whispered. "Did you have a word with him, Mother?"

"Yes," said Ros.

"Did he agree?" Stacy whispered.

"No."

Stacy closed her eyes.

"I hope he wasn't upset," she said.

Ros stroked her daughter's limp hair. "Don't you worry anyway, Stacy," she said. "He'll get over it. He's been outside sweeping the yard and I think maybe he has forgotten we raised the matter at all. Anyway, Kate has gone for a walk and I called him in for a cup of tea. Are you sure you won't let me bring you in a nice hot cup to sip here in the bed?"

"I think I'd prefer to get up and have it outside, as long as you're sure father is not upset."

Ros drew a strand of Stacy's hair back from her damp forehead. "You're a good girl, Stacy, a good, kind creature," she said. "You may feel better when you're on your feet. I can promise you there will be no arguing for the time being anyway. I'm sorry I crossed him at all."

It was to Stacy Ros turned a week later, when Phelim was taken bad in the middle of the night with a sharp pain in his chest that the women weren't able to ease, and after the doctor came and stayed with him until the early hours of the morning, the doctor didn't seem able to do much either. Before Phelim could be got to hospital he died.

"Oh Stacy, Stacy," Ros cried, throwing herself into her younger daughter's arms. "Why did I cross him over that old dunghill?"

"Don't fret, Mother," Stacy begged. "I never heard you cross him over anything else as long as I can remember. You were always good and kind to him, calling him in out of the yard every other minute for a cup of tea. Morning, noon and night I'd hear your voice, and the mornings the carts came with the dung you'd call him in oftener than ever. I used to hear you when I'd be lying inside with one of my headaches."

Ros was not to be easily consoled.

"What thanks is due to a woman for giving her man a cup of hot tea on a bitter cold day? He was the best man ever lived. Oh why did I cross him?"

"Ah Mother, it wasn't only on cold days you were good to him but on summer days too. Isn't that so, Kate?" Stacy appealed to Kate.

"You did everything you could to please him, Mother," Kate said, but seeing this made no impression on her mother she turned to Stacy. "That's more than could be said about him," she muttered.

But Ros heard her.

"Say no more, you," she cried. "You were the one was always at me to torment him. Oh why did I listen to you? Why did I cross him?"

"Because you were in the right. That's why," Kate said.

"Was I?" Ros said.

Phelim was laid out in the parlor, and all through the night Ros and her daughters sat up in the room with the corpse. The neighbors that came to the house stayed up all night too, but they sat in the kitchen, and kept the fire going and made tea from time to time. Kate and Stacy stared sadly at their dead father stretched out in his shroud, and they mourned him as the man they had known all their lives, a heavy man with a red face whom they had seldom seen out of his big rubber boots caked with muck.

Ros mourned that Phelim too. But she mourned many another Phelim besides. She mourned the Phelim who, up to a little while before, never put a coat on him going out in the raw, cold air, nor covered his head even in the rain. Of course his hair was as thick as a thatch. But most of all, she mourned the Phelim whose hair had not yet grown coarse but was soft and smooth as silk, like it was the time he led her in off the road and up a little lane near the chapel one Sunday when he was walking her home from Mass. That was the time when he used to call her by the old name. When, she wondered, when did he stop calling her Rose? Or was it she, herself, gave herself the new name? Or perhaps it was someone else altogether, someone outside the family. A neighbor maybe? No matter, Ros was a good name anyway, wherever it came from. It was a good name and a suitable name for an old woman. It would have been only foolishness to go on calling her Rose after she faded and dried up like an old twig. Ros looked down at her bony hands, and her tears on them. But they were tears for Phelim. "Rose," he'd said that day in the lane, "Rose, I've been thinking about ways to make money. And do you know what I found out? There's a pile of money to be made out of dung." Rose thought he was joking. "It's true," he said. "The people in the town, especially women, would give any amount of money for a bagful of it for their gardens. And only a few miles out from the town there are farmers going mad to get rid of it, with it piling up day after day and cluttering up their farmyards until they can hardly get in or out their sheds. Now, I was thinking, if I got hold of a horse and cart and went out and brought back a few loads of that dung, and if my father would let me store it for a while in our yard, I could maybe sell it to the people in the town. I could sell it by the sack to women for their gardens."

"Women like the doctor's wife," Rose said, knowing the doctor's wife was mad about roses. The doctor's wife had been seen going out into the street with a shovel to bring back a shovelful of horse manure.

"That's right; women like that. After a while the farmers might deliver the loads to me. I might offer to pay for it myself. Then if I made as much money as I think I might, maybe soon I'd be able to get a place of my own where I'd have room to store enough to make it a worthwhile business." To Rose it seemed an odd sort of way to make money, but Phelim was only eighteen then, and probably he wanted to have a few pounds in his pocket while he was waiting for something better. "I'm going to ask my father about the storage today," he said, "and in the afternoon I'm going to get hold of a cart and go out the country and see how I get on."

"Is that so?" Rose said, for want of knowing what else to say.

"It is," said Phelim, "and do you know the place I have in mind to buy if I make enough money? I'd buy that place we often looked at, you and me when we were out walking, that place on the outskirts of the town, with a big yard and two big sheds that only need a bit of fixing, to be ideal for my purposes."

"I think so," Rose said. "Isn't there an old cottage there all smothered with ivy?"

"That's the very place. Do you remember we peeped in the windows one day last Summer. There's no one living there."

"No wonder," Rose said.

"Listen to me, Rose. After I'd done up the sheds," Phelim said. "I could fix up the cottage too, and make a nice job of it. That's another thing I wanted to ask you, Rose. How would you like to live in that cottage, after I'd done it up of course, live in it with me?" he added when he saw he'd startled her. "Well Rose, what have you to say to that?"

She'd bent her head to hide her blushes, and looked down at her small thin-soled shoes that she only wore on a Sunday. She didn't know what to say.

"Well?" said Phelim.

"There's a very dirty smell of dung," she said at last in a whisper.

"It only smells strong when it's fresh," Phelim said, "and maybe you could plant flowers to take away the smell."

She kept looking down at her shoes.

"They'd have to be flowers with a strong scent," she said, but already she was thinking of how strongly sweet rocket and mignonette perfumed the air of an evening after rain.

"You could plant all the flowers you liked, you'd have nothing else to do the day long," he said. How innocent he was, for all that he was thinking of making big money and taking a wife. She looked up at him. His skin was as fair and smooth as her own. He was the best looking fellow for miles around. Girls far prettier than her would have been glad to be led up a lane by him, just for a bit of a lark, let alone a proposal of marriage. "Well, Rose?" he said, and now there were blushes coming and going in his cheeks too, blotching his face. She could see that he was bent on carrying out his plan. "You ought to know, Rose Magarry, that there's a lot in the way people look at a thing. When I was a young lad, driving along the country roads in my father's trap, I used to love looking down at the gold rings of dung dried out by the sun, as they flashed past underneath the horses' hooves."

Rose felt like laughing, but she knew he was deadly serious. He wasn't like anybody else in the world she'd ever known. Who else would say a thing like that? It was like poetry. The sun was spilling down on them and in the hedges little pink dog roses were swaying in a soft breeze.

"Alright, so," she said. "I will."

"You will? Oh, Rose. Kiss me so," he said.

"Not here Phelim," she whispered. People were still coming out of the chapel yard and some of them were looking up the lane.

"Rose Magarry, if you're going to marry me, you must face up to people and never be ashamed of anything I do," he said, and when she still hung back he put out his hand and tilted up her chin. "If you don't kiss me right here and now, Rose, I'll have no more to do with you."

She kissed him then.

And now, at his wake, the candle flames were wavering around his coffin the way the dog roses wavered that day in the Summer breeze.

Ros shed tears for those little dog roses. She shed tears for the roses that were in her own cheeks in those days. And she shed tears for the soft kissing lips of young Phelim. Her tears fell quietly, but it seemed to Kate and Stacy that, like rain in windless weather, they would never cease.

When the white light of morning came at last, the neighbors got up and went home to do a few chores of their own and be ready for the funeral. Kate and Stacy got ready too, and made Ros ready. Ros didn't look much different in black from what she always looked. Neither did Stacy. But Kate looked well in black. It toned down her high color.

After the funeral Kate led her mother home. Stacy had already been taken home by neighbors, because she fainted when the coffin was being lowered into the ground. She was lying down when they came home. The women who brought Stacy home and one or two other women who had stayed behind after the coffin was carried out, to put the furniture back in place, gave a meal to the family, but these women made sure to leave as soon as possible to let the Mulloys get used to their loss. When the women had gone Stacy got up and came out to join Ros and Kate. A strong smell of guttered-out candles hung in the air and also a faint smell of the lilies that had been on the coffin.

"Oh Kate! Smell!" Stacy cried, drawing in as deep a breath as her thin chest allowed.

"For Heaven's sake, don't talk about smells or you'll have our mother wailing again and going on about having crossed him over the dung-hill," Kate said in a sharp whisper.

But Ros didn't need any reminders to make her wail.

"Oh Phelim, Phelim, why did I cross you? Wasn't I the bad old woman to go against you over a heap of dung that, if I looked at things rightly, wasn't bad at all after it dried out a bit. It was mostly yellow straw."

"Take no heed of her," Kate counseled Stacy. "Go inside you with our new hats and coats, and hang them up in our room with a sheet draped over them. Black nap is a caution for collecting dust." To Ros she spoke kindly, but firmly. "You've got to give over this moaning, Mother," she said. "You're only tormenting yourself. What harm was it for you to let him see how we felt about the dung?"

Ros stopped moaning long enough to look sadly out the window.

"It was out of the dung he made his first few shillings," she said.

"That may be. But how long ago was that? He made plenty of money other ways as time went on. There was no need in keeping on the dung and humiliating us. He only did it out of obstinacy." As Stacy came back after hanging up their black clothes, Kate appealed to her, "Isn't that so, Stacy?"

Stacy drew another thin breath.

"It doesn't smell too bad today, does it?" she said. "I suppose the scent of the flowers drove it out."

"Well, the house won't always be filled with lilies," Kate said irritably. "In any case, Stacy, it's not the smell concerns me. What concerns me is the way people look at us when they hear how our money is made."

Ros stopped moaning again for another minute. "It's no cause for shame. It's honest dealing, and that's more than can be said for the dealings of others in this town. You shouldn't heed people's talk, Kate."

"Well, I like that!" Kate cried. "May I ask what do you know, Mother, about how people talk? Certain kinds of people I mean; good class people. It's easily seen you were never away at boarding school like Stacy and me, or else you'd know what it feels like to have to admit our money was made out of horse manure and cow dung."

"I don't see what great call there was on you to tell them," Ros said.

"Stacy, Stacy, did you hear that?" Kate cried.

Stacy put her hand to her head. She was getting confused. There was some truth in what Kate had said, and she felt obliged to side with her, but first she ran over and threw herself down at her mother's knees.

"We didn't tell them at first, Mother," she said, hoping to make Ros feel better. "We told them our father dealt in fertilizer, but one of the girls looked up the word in the dictionary and found out it was only a fancy name for manure."

It was astonishing to Kate and Stacy how Ros took that. She not only stopped wailing but she began to laugh. "Your father would have been amused to hear that," she said.

"Well, it wasn't funny for us," Kate said.

Ros stopped laughing, but the trace of a small bleak smile remained on her face.

"It wasn't everyone had your father's sense of humor," she said.

"It wasn't everyone had his obstinacy either," Kate said.

"You're right there, Kate," Ros said simply. "Isn't that why I feel so bad? When we knew how stubborn he was, weren't we the stupid women to be always trying to best him? We only succeeded in making him miserable."

Kate and Stacy looked at each other.

"How about another cup of tea, Mother? I'll bring it over here to you beside the fire," Stacy said, and although her mother made no reply Stacy made the tea and brought over a cup. Ros took the cup but handed back the saucer.

"Leave that back on the table," she said, and holding the cup in her two hands she went over to the window, although the light was fading fast.

"It only smells bad on hot muggy days," she said.

Kate gave a loud sniff. "Don't forget Summer is coming."

For a moment it seemed Ros had not heard, then she gave a sigh.

"It is and it isn't," she said. "I often think that in January it's as true to say we have put the Summer behind us as it is to say it's ahead." Then she glanced at a calendar on the wall. "Is tomorrow Wednesday?" she said, and an anxious expression overcame the sorrowful look on her face. Wednesday was the day the farmers delivered the dung.

"Mother! You don't think the farmers will be unmannerly enough to come banging on the gate tomorrow, and us after having a death in the family?" Kate said in a shocked voice.

"Death never interfered with business yet, as far as I know," Ros said coldly. "And the farmers are kind folk. I saw a lot of them at the funeral. They might think it all the more reason to come, knowing my man was taken from me."

"Mother!" This time Kate was more than shocked, she was outraged. "You're not thinking, by any chance of keeping on dealing with them; dealing in dung?"

Ros looked her daughter straight in the face.

"I'm thinking of your father and him young one day, and the next day, you might say, him stretched on the bed inside with the neighbors washing him for his burial." She began to moan again.

"If you keep this up you'll be laid alongside him one of these days," Kate said.

"Leave me be," Ros said. "I'm not doing any harm to myself by thinking about him. I like thinking about him."

"He lived to a good age, Mother. Don't forget that," Kate said.

"I suppose that's what you'll be saying about me one of these days," Ros said, but she didn't seem as upset as she had been. She turned to Stacy. "It seems only like yesterday, Stacy, that I was sitting up beside him on the cart, right behind the horse's tail, with my white blouse on me and the gold chain he gave me bouncing about on my front, and us both watching the road flashing past under the horse's hooves, bright with gold rings of dung."

Kate raised her eyebrows. But Stacy gave a sob. And that night, when she and Kate were in bed, she gave another sob. "Kate, it's not a good sign when people begin to go back over the past, is it?"

"Are you speaking about Mother?"

"I am. Did you see how bad she looked when you brought her home from the grave?"

"I did," said Kate. "It may be true what I said to her. If she isn't careful we may be laying her alongside poor father before long."

"Oh Kate. How could you say such a thing?" Stacy burst into tears. "Oh Kate. Oh Kate, why did we make her go against father over the dunghill? I know how she feels. I keep reproaching myself for all the hard things I used to think about him when I'd be lying here in bed with one of my headaches."

"Well, you certainly never came out with them," Kate said. "You left it to me to say them for you. Not that I'm going to reproach my-self about anything. There was no need in him keeping that dung-hill. He only did it out of pig-headedness. And now, if you'll only let me, I'm going to sleep."

Kate was just dropping off when Stacy leant up on her elbow.

"You don't really think they will come in the morning, do you, Kate, the carts I mean, like our mother said?"

"Of course not," Kate said.

"But if they do?"

"Oh go to sleep Stacy, for Heaven's sake. There's no need facing things until they happen. And stop fidgeting. You're twitching the blankets off me. Move over."

Stacy faced back to the wall and lay still. She didn't think she'd be able to sleep, but when she did, it seemed as if she'd only been asleep one minute when she woke to find the night had ended. The hard, white light of day was pressing on her eyelids. It's a new day for us, she thought, but not for their poor father laid in the cold clay. Stacy shivered and drew up her feet that were touching the icy iron rail at the foot of the bed. It must have been the cold wakened her. Opening her eyes she saw, through a chink between the curtains, that the crinkled edges of the big corrugated sheds glittered with frost. If only, she thought, if only it was Summer. She longed for the time when warm winds go daffing through the trees, and when in the gardens to which they delivered fertilizer, the tight hard beads of lilac buds would soon loop out into soft pear-shaped bosoms of blossom. And then, gentle as those thoughts, another thought came into Stacy's mind, and she wondered whether their father, sleeping under the close, green sods, might mind now if they got rid of the dunghill. Indeed it seemed the dunghill was as good as gone, now that father himself was gone. Curling up in the warm blankets, Stacy was preparing to sleep again, when there was a loud knocking on the yard-gates and the sound of a horse shaking its harness. She raised her head off the pillow, and as she did, she heard the gate in the yard slap back against the wall and there was a rattle of iron-shod wheels traveling in across the cobbles.

"Kate! Kate!" she screamed, shaking her. "I thought I heard Fa-ther leading in a load of manure."

"Oh shut up, Stacy. You're dreaming, or else raving," Kate muttered from the depths of the blankets that she had pulled closer around her. But suddenly she sat up. And then, to Stacy's astonishment, she threw back the bedclothes altogether, right across the footrail of the bed, and ran across the floor and pressed her face to the windowpane. "I might have known this would happen," she cried. "For all her lamenting and wailing, our mother knows what she's doing. Come and look."

Out in the yard Ros was leading in the first of the carts, and calling out to the drivers of the other carts waiting their turn to come in. She was not wearing her black clothes, but her ordinary everyday coat, the color of the earth and the earth's decaying refuse. In the raw cold air, the manure in the cart she was leading was still giving off, unevenly, the fog of its hot breath.

"Get dressed, Stacy. We'll go down together." Kate ordered and grabbed her clothes and dressed.

When they were both dressed, with Kate leading, the sisters went into the kitchen. The yard door was open and a powerful stench was making its way inside. The last cart was by then unloaded, and Ros had come back into the kitchen and began to warm her hands by the big fire already roaring up the chimney. She had left the door open but Kate went over and banged it shut.

"Well?" said Ros.

"Well?" Kate said only louder.

Stacy sat down at once and began to cry. The other two women took no notice of her as they faced each other across the kitchen.

"Say whatever it is you have to say, Kate," Ros said.

"You know what I have to say," said Kate.

"Don't say it so. Save your breath." Ros said, and she went as if to go out into the yard again, but Stacy got up and ran and put her arms around her.

"Mother, you always agreed with us. You always said it would be nice if . . ."

Ros put up a hand and silenced her.

"Listen to me, both of you," she said. "I had no right agreeing with anyone but your father. It was to him I pledged my word. It was him I had a right to stand behind. He always said there was no shame in making money anyway it could be made, as long as it was made honestly. And another thing he said was that money was money, whether it was in gold coins or in dung. And that was true for him. Did you, either of you, hear what the priest said yesterday in the cemetery? 'God help all poor widows.'" That's what he said. And he set me thinking. Did it never occur to you that it might not be easy for us, three women with no man about the place, to keep going, to put food on the table and keep a fire on the hearth, to say nothing at all about finery and fal-lals."

"That last remark is meant for me I suppose," Kate said, but the frown that came on her face seemed to come more from worry than anger. "By the way, Mother," she said, "You never told us whether you had a word with the solicitor when he came with his condolences? Did you by any chance find out how father's affairs stood?"

"I did," Ros said. But that was all she said as she went out into the yard again and took up the yard-brush. She had left the door open but Stacy went over and closed it gently.

"She's twice as stubborn as ever father was," Kate said. "There's going to be no change around here as long as she's alive."

Stacy's face clouded. "All the same, Kate, she's sure to let us clear a small corner and put in a few shrubs and things," she said timidly.

"Lilacs, I suppose," Kate said, with an unmistakable sneer, which however Stacy did not see.

"Think of the scent of them coming in the window, Kate."

"You are a fool, Stacy," Kate replied. "At least I can see that our mother has more important things on her mind than lilac bushes. I wonder what information she got from Jasper Kane? I thought her very secretive. I would have thought he'd have had a word with me, as the eldest daughter."

"Oh Kate." Stacy's eyes filled with tears again. "I never thought about it before, but when poor mother . . ." she hesitated, then after a gulp she went on "when poor mother goes to join father, you and I will be all alone in the world with no one to look after us."

"Stop whimpering, Stacy," Kate said sharply. "We've got to start living our own lives, sooner or later." Going over to a small ornamental mirror on the wall over the fireplace, she looked into it and patted her hair. Stacy stared at her in surprise, because unless you stood well back from it you could only see the tip of your nose in that little mirror. But Kate was not looking at herself. She was looking out into the yard, which was reflected in the mirror, in which she could see their mother going around sweeping up stray bits of straw and dirt to bring them over and throw them on top of the dunghill. Then Kate turned around. "We don't need to worry too much about that woman. She'll hardly follow father for many a long day. That woman is as strong as a tree."

But Ros was not cut out to be a widow. If Phelim had been taken from her before the dog roses had faded in the hedges that first summer of their lives together, she could hardly have mourned him more bitterly than she did when an old woman, tossing and turning sleeplessly in their big brass bed.

Kate and Stacy did their best to ease her work in the house. But there was one thing Kate was determined they would not do, and that was give any help on the Wednesday mornings when the farm carts arrived with their load. Nor would they help her to bag it for the townspeople although as Phelim had long ago foreseen, the townspeople were often glad to bag it for themselves, or wheel it away in barrowfuls. On Wednesday morning when the rapping came at the gates at dawn, Kate and Stacy stayed in bed and did not get up, but Stacy was wide awake and lay listening to the noises outside. And sometimes she scrambled out of bed across Kate and went to the window.

"Kate?" Stacy would say almost every day.

"What?"

"Perhaps I ought to step out to the kitchen and see the fire is kept up. She'll be very cold when she comes in."

"You'll do nothing of the kind I hope. We must stick to our agreement. Get back into bed."

"She has only her old coat on her and it's very thin, Kate."

Before answering her, Kate might raise herself up on one elbow and hump the blankets up with her so that when she sank back they were well pegged down around her. "By all the noise she's making out there I'd say her circulation would be kept up no matter if she was in nothing but her shift."

"That work is too heavy for her, Kate. She shouldn't be doing it at all."

"And who is to blame for that? Get back to bed, like I told you, and don't let her see you're looking out. She'd like nothing better than that."

"But she's not looking this way, Kate. She couldn't see me."

"That's what you think. Let me tell you, that woman has eyes in the back of her head."

Stacy giggled nervously at that. It was what their mother herself used to tell them when they were small. Then suddenly she stopped giggling and ran back and threw herself across the foot of the bed and began to sob.

After moving her feet to one side, Kate listened for a few seconds to the sobbing. Then she humped up her other shoulder and pegged the blankets under her on the other side.

"What ails you now?" she asked then.

"Oh Kate, you made me think of when we were children, and she used to stand up so tall and straight and with her gold chain and locket bobbing about on her chest." Stacy gave another sob. "Now she's so thin and bent the chain is dangling down to her waist."

Kate sat up with a start. "She's not wearing that chain and locket now, out in the yard, is she? Gold is worth a lot more now than it was when father bought her that."

Stacy went over to the window and looked out again. "No, she's not wearing it."

"I should hope not," Kate said. "I saw it on her at the funeral but I forgot about it afterwards in the commotion."

"She took it off when we came back," Stacy said. "She put it away in father's black box and locked the box."

"Well, that's one good thing she did anyway," Kate said. "She oughtn't to wear it at all."

"Oh Kate!" Stacy looked startled.

"What?" Kate asked, staring back at her.

Stacy didn't know what she wanted to say. She couldn't put it into words. She had always thought Kate and herself were alike, that they had the same way of looking at things, but lately she was not so sure of this. They were both getting older of course, and some people were not as even-tempered as others. Not that she thought herself a paragon, but being so prone to headaches she had to let a lot of things pass that she didn't agree with, like something Kate said recently about the time when they were away at school. Their mother had asked how many years ago it was, and while Stacy was trying to count up the years, Kate answered at once.

"Only a few years ago," she said. That wasn't true but perhaps it only seemed like that to Kate.

Gradually, as time passed, Stacy too, like Kate, used to put the blankets over her head so as not to hear the knocking at the gate, and the rattle of the cart wheels, or at least to deaden the noise of it. She just lay thinking. Kate had once asked her what went through her head when she'd be lying saying nothing.

"This and that," she'd said. She really didn't think about anything in particular. Sometimes she'd imagine what it would be like if they did clear a small space in the yard and planted things. She knew of course that if they put in a lilac bush it would be small for a long time and would not bear flowers for ages. It would be mostly leaves, and leaves only for years, or so she'd read somewhere. Yet she always imagined it would be a fully grown lilac they'd have outside the window. Once she imagined something absolutely ridiculous. She was lying half awake and half asleep, and she thought they had transplanted a large full grown lilac, a lilac that had more flowers than leaves, something you never see. And then, as she was half-dozing, the tree got so big and strong its roots pushed under the wall and pushed up through the floorboards, bending the nails and sending splinters of wood flying in all directions. And its branches were so laden with blossom, so weighted down with them, that one big pointed bosom of bloom almost touched her face. But suddenly the branch broke with a crack and Stacy was wide awake again. Then the sound that woke her came again, only now she knew what it was, a knocking on the gate outside, only louder than usual, and after it came a voice calling out. She gave Kate a shake.

"Do you hear that, Kate? Mother must have slept it out."

"Let's hope she did," Kate said. "It might teach her a lesson, it might make her see she's not as fit and able as she thinks."

"But what about the farmers?"

"Who cares about them," Kate said. "I don't. Do you?"

When the knocking came again a third time, and a fourth time, Stacy shook Kate again.

"Kate. I wouldn't mind going down and opening the gate," she said.

"You? In your nightdress?" Kate needed to say no more. Stacy cowered down under the blankets in her shame, then suddenly she sat up again.

"There wouldn't be anything wrong with mother, would there?" she cried. This time, without heeding Kate, Stacy climbed out over her to get to the floor. "I won't go out to the yard, I promise, I'll just go and wake mother," she said and ran out of the room.

"Come back and shut this door," Kate called after her. Stacy mustn't have heard. "Stacy. Did you hear me?" Kate shouted.

Stacy didn't come back.

"Stacy." Kate yelled. "Stacy?" At last she sat up.

"Is there something wrong?" she asked. Getting no answer now either, she got up herself.

Stacy was in their mother's room, lying in a heap on the floor. As Kate said afterwards, she hardly needed to look to know their mother was dead, because Stacy always flopped down in a faint the moment she came up against something unpleasant. And the next day, in the cemetery when the prayers were over and the gravediggers took up their shovels, Stacy passed out again and had to be brought home by two of the neighbors, leaving Kate to stand and listen to the stones and the clay rumbling down on the coffin.

"You're a nice one, Stacy. Leaving me to stand listening to that awful sound."

"But I heard it, Kate," Stacy protested. "I did. Then my head began to reel, and I got confused. The next thing I knew I was on the ground looking up at the blue sky and thinking the noise was the sound of the horses going clip-clap along the road."

Kate stared at her.

"Are you mad? What horses?"

"Oh Kate, don't you remember? The horses mother was always talking about. She was always telling us how when she and father were young, she used to sit beside him on a plank across the cart and watch the road flashing by under the horse's hooves, glittering with bright gold rings of dung?"

Kate, however, wasn't listening.

"That reminds me. Isn't tomorrow Wednesday?" she said. "Which of us is going to get up and let in the farm carts?" When Stacy stared vacantly, Kate stamped her foot. "Don't look so stupid, Stacy. They came the day after father was buried, why wouldn't they come to-morrow? Mother herself said it was their way of showing that as far as they were concerned the death wouldn't make any difference."

"Oh Kate. How do you think they'll take it when you tell them . . ."

"Tell them what? Really Stacy, you *are* a fool. Tomorrow is no day to tell them anything. We'll have to take it easy, wait and see how we stand, before we talk about making changes."

Kate was so capable. Stacy was filled with admiration for her. She would not have minded in the least getting up to open the gate, but she never would be able to face a discussion of the future. Kate was able for everything, and realizing this, Stacy permitted herself a small feeling of excitement at the thought of them making their own plans and standing on their own two feet.

"I'll get up and light the fire and bring you a cup of tea in bed before you have to get up, Kate," she said.

Kate shrugged her shoulders. "If I know you, Stacy, you'll have one of your headaches," she said.

Stacy said nothing. She was resolved to get up, headache or no headache. On the quiet she set an old alarm clock she found in the kitchen. But the alarm bell was broken, and the first thing Stacy heard next morning was the rapping on the gate. When she went to scramble out, to her surprise Kate was already gone from the room. And when Stacy threw her clothes on and ran out to the kitchen, the fire was roaring up the chimney, and a cup with a trace of sugar and tea leaves in the bottom of it was on the windowsill. The teapot was on the hob but it had been made a long time and it was cold. She made herself another pot and took it over to sip it by the window, looking out.

Kate was in the yard, directing the carts and laughing and talking with the men. Kate certainly had a way with her and no mistake. When it would come to telling the farmers that they needn't deliver any more dung, she'd do it tactfully and they wouldn't be offended.

One big tall farmer, with red hair and whiskers, was the last to leave, and he and Kate stood talking at the gate so long Stacy wondered if, after all, Kate mightn't be discussing their future dealings with him. She hoped she wouldn't catch cold. She had put a few more sods of turf on the fire.

"Do you want to set the chimney on fire?" Kate asked when she came in. Stacy didn't let herself get upset though. Kate was carrying all the responsibility now, and it was bound to make her edgy.

"I saw you talking to one of the men," said she. "I was wondering if perhaps you were giving him a hint of our plans and sounding him out?"

"I was sounding him out alright," Kate said, and she smiled. "You see, Stacy. I've been thinking that we might come up with a new plan. You mightn't like it at first, but you may come round when I make you see it in the right light. Sit down and I'll tell you." Stacy sat down. Kate stayed standing. "I've been looking into the ledgers, and I would never have believed there was so much money coming in from the dung. So, I've been thinking that, instead of getting rid of it, we ought to try and take in more, twice or three times more, and make twice or three times as much money. No. No. Sit down again, Stacy. Hear me out. My plan would be that we'd move into a more suitable house, larger and with a garden maybe."

When Stacy said nothing Kate looked sharply at her. It wouldn't have surprised her if Stacy had flopped off in another faint, but she was only sitting dumbly looking into the fire. "It's only a suggestion," Kate said, feeling her way more carefully. "You never heed anything, Stacy, but when I go out for my walks I take note of things I see, and there's a plot of ground for sale out a bit the road, but not too far from here all the same, and it's for sale. I've made enquiries about the cost of that too."

But Stacy had found her tongue. "I don't want to move out of here, Kate," she cried. "This is where we were born, where we were so happy together, where my mother and father . . ." She began to cry. "Oh Kate. I never want to leave here. Never. Never."

Kate could hardly speak with fury.

"Stay here so," she said. "But don't expect me to stay with you. I'm getting out of here at the first opportunity that comes my way. And let me tell you something else. That dunghill isn't stirring out of where it is until I've a decent dowry out of it. Cry away now to your heart's content for all I care." Going over to their bedroom Kate went in and banged the door behind her.

Stacy stopped crying and stared at the closed door. Her head had begun to throb and she would have liked to lie down, but after the early hour Kate had risen she had probably gone back to bed. No.

Kate was up and moving about the room. There was great activity going on. Stacy felt better. She knew Kate. Kate had never been one to say she was sorry for anything she said or did, but that did not always mean she didn't feel sorry. She must be giving their room a good turn-out. Perhaps this was her way of working off her annoyance and at the same time show she was sorry for losing her temper. Stacy sat back, thinking her thoughts, and waited for Kate to come out. She didn't have long to wait. In about five minutes the knob of the bedroom door rattled. "Open this door for me, Stacy. My arms are full. I can't turn the handle," Kate called and Stacy was glad to see she sounded in excellent form, and as if all was forgotten. For the second time in twenty-four hours Stacy felt a small surge of excitement, as Kate came out, her arms piled skyhigh with dresses and hats and a couple of cardboard boxes, covered with wallpaper, in which they kept their gloves and handkerchiefs. She'd done a real spring cleaning. They hadn't done one in years. She hadn't noticed it before but the wallpaper on the boxes was yellowed with age and the flowery pattern faded. They might paste on new wallpaper? And seeing that Kate, naturally, was carrying only her own things she ran to get hers, but first she ran back to clear a space on the table so Kate could put her things down.

But Kate was heading across the kitchen to their mother's room.

"There's no sense in having a room idle, is there?" she said, disappearing into it. "I'm moving in here."

There was no further mention of the dunghill that day, nor indeed that week. Stacy felt a bit lonely at first in the room they had shared since childhood. But it had its advantages. It had been a bit stuffy sleeping next to the wall. And she didn't have so many headaches, but that could possibly be attributed to Kate's recent suggestion that she ought to ignore them, and not give in to them.

Every Wednesday Kate was up at the crack of dawn to let in the carts and supervise the unloading. As their father had also foreseen, they were now paying the farmers for the manure, but only a small sum, because the farmers were still glad to get rid of it. The townspeople on the other hand were paying five times more than before for it. Kate had made no bones about raising her prices. The only time there was a reference to the future was when Kate announced that she didn't like keeping cash in the house, and that she was going to start banking some of their takings. The rest could be put as usual in the black box, which was almost the only thing that had never been taken out of their mother's room. A lot of other things had been thrown out.

Kate and Stacy got on as well as ever, it seemed to Stacy but there were often long stretches of silence in the house because Kate was never as talkative as their mother. After nightfall they often sat by a dying fire, only waiting for it to go out, before getting up and going to bed. All things considered, Kate was right to have moved into the other room, and Stacy began to enjoy having a room of her own. She had salvaged a few of her mother's things that Kate had thrown out and she liked looking at them. If Kate knew, she never said anything. Kate never came into the old room anymore.

Then when Con O'Toole, the whiskery farmer with whom Kate had been talking the first day she took over the running of things, started dropping in to see how they were getting on, Stacy was particularly glad to have a room of her own. She liked Con. She really did. But the smell of his pipe brought on her headaches again. The smell of his tobacco never quite left the house, and it pursued her through the keyhole after she had left him and Kate together, because of course it was Kate that Con came to see.

"How can you stand the smell of his pipe?" she asked Kate one morning. "It's worse than the smell of the dung." She only said it by way of a joke, but Kate, who had taken out the black box and was going through the papers in it, a thing she did regularly now, shut the lid of the box and frowned.

"I thought we agreed on saying fertilizer instead of that word you used."

"Oh but that was long ago, when we were in boarding school," Stacy stammered.

"I beg your pardon. It was agreed we'd be more particular about how we referred to our business when we were in the company of other people, or at least that was my understanding. Take Con O'Toole for instance. He may deliver dung here but he never gives it that name, at least not in front of me. The house he lives in may be thatched and have a mud wall, but that's because his old mother is alive and he can't get her to agree to knocking it down and building a new house, which of course they can well afford. I was astonished at the amount of land he owns. Of course, you understand, Stacy, that I am not urging him to make any changes. So please don't mention this conversation to him. I'll tell him myself when I judge the time to be right. I'll make him see the need for building a new house. He needn't knock down the old one either. He can leave the old woman in it for what time is left her. But as I say, I'll bide my time. I might even wait until after we are married."

That was the first Stacy heard of Kate's intended marriage, but after that first reference there was talk of nothing else, right up to the fine blowy morning when Kate was hoisted up into Con O'Toole's new motor-car, in a peacock blue outfit, with their mother's gold chain bumping up and down on her bosom.

Stacy was almost squeezed to death in the doorway as the guests all stood there to wave goodbye to the happy couple. There had been far more guests than either she or Kate had bargained on because the O'Tooles had so many relations, and they all brought their children, and, to boot, Kate's old mother-in-law brought along a few of her own cronies as well. But there was enough food, and plenty of port wine.

It was a fine wedding. And Stacy didn't mind the mess that was made of the house. Such a mess: Crumbs scattered over the carpet in the parlor and driven into it by people's feet. Bottle tops all over the kitchen floor. Port wine and lemonade stains soaked into the tablecloth. It was going to take time to get the place to rights again. Stacy was almost looking forward to getting it to rights again because she had decided to make a few changes in the arrangement of the furniture, small changes, only involving chairs and ornaments and she intended attacking the job that evening after the guests left. However, when the bridal couple drove off with a hiss of steam rising out of the radiator of the car, the guests flocked back into the house and didn't go until there wasn't a morsel left to eat, or single drop left to refill the decanters. One thing did upset Stacy and that was when she saw the way the beautiful wedding cake on which the icing had been as hard and white as plaster had been laid waste by someone who didn't know how to cut a cake. And the children that hadn't already fallen asleep on the sofas were stuffing themselves with the last crumbs. Stacy herself hadn't as much as a taste of that cake, and she'd intended keeping at least one tier aside for some future time. Ah well. It was nice to think everyone had had a good time, she thought, as she closed the door on the last of the O'Tooles, who had greatly outnumbered their own friends. Jasper Kane, their father's solicitor, had been the principal guest. He had not in fact left yet, but he was getting ready to leave.

"It will be very lonely for you now, Miss Stacy," he said. "You ought to get some person in to keep you company, at least for the nights."

It was very kind of him to be so concerned. Stacy expressed her gratitude freely, and reassured him that she was quite looking forward to being, as it were, her own mistress. She felt obliged to add, hastily, that she'd miss Kate, although to be strictly truthful, she didn't think she'd miss her as much as she would have thought before Con O'Toole had put in his appearance.

"Well, well. I'm glad to hear you say that, Miss Stacy," Jasper Kane said, as he prepared to leave. "I expect you'll drop in to my office at your convenience. I understand your sister took care of the business, but I'm sure you'll be just as competent when you get the hang of things." Then for a staid man like him, he got almost playful. "I'll be very curious to see what changes you'll make," he said, and she saw his eye fall on a red plush sofa that Kate had bought after Con started calling, and which Stacy thought was hideous. She gave him a conspiratorial smile. But she didn't want him to think she wasn't serious.

"I intend to make changes outside as well, Mr. Kane," she said, gravely. "And the very first thing I'm going to do is plant a few lilac trees."

Jasper Kane looked surprised.

"Oh? Where?" he asked and although it was dark outside, he went to the window and tried to see out.

"Where else but where the dunghill has always been. You see I am going to get rid of it," Stacy said, and just to hear herself speaking with such authority made her almost light-headed.

Jasper Kane remained staring out into the darkness. Then he turned around and asked a simple question.

"But what will you live on, Miss Stacy?"

A Minor Incident

MAURA TREACY

The Army truck had passed them earlier on the road. The driver had kept close to the edge, forcing them to pull the prams onto the grass verge, to press back against the hedge until the briars pricked their shoulders. The covered truck passed so close to them, looming above them, that the children cried with fright. Then it was gone. Shaken, they stepped out into the road again. From the back of the truck the soldiers grinned.

Captain barked as he raced along on the other side of the hedge. He had broken away from them earlier and now he rushed back to the sound of the motor, scrambling through a gap to shake himself and bark at the truck. But it was too far off by then and when Sara shouted to him, he gave up and came back to her. He squatted in front of her, still panting, his pink tongue rippling between the white rows of spiky teeth, his bushy tail swishing clouds of dust off the road. He blocked her way until she patted him and talked to him, and then he fell in behind and followed tamely for another while.

They had walked too far in the heat and now on the way home Sara lagged behind the others. Her mother and Mrs. Martin walked on in front, pushing their prams. Mrs. Flynn stooped to lift up her child. He had stumbled again and dropped his bottle of milky tea and she would have to carry him the rest of the way. She was going to have another baby soon. Her leg was bandaged. Her hair kept on

MAURA TREACY (b. 1946) was born in Kilkenny. Poolbeg published her popular story collection, *Sixpence in Her Shoe,* in 1977; and her novel *Scenes from a Country Wedding* five years later. Ms. Treacy won the Listowel Writers Award for short fiction in 1974.

falling in around her face and when she was out of earshot Mrs. Martin would whisper about her until she caught up with them again. When their own baby awoke, Sara's mother sat him up and lifted Mrs. Flynn's child onto the end of the pram.

As they walked on, back over the bridge and around the turn, they hurried towards the shade of the tall trees that grew on either side of the road, the branches meeting overhead. Here they lingered, feeling kinder towards each other. The river slurped against the arch of the bridge and when they moved on they could hear inside the walls of the estate the sharp rap back and forth of a tennis ball. They followed the staccato rhythm of the game and heard the voices of the Corbetts and their friends who were spending the summer there. As they passed the green door in the wall through which they might see the lawns, the tennis court, the shrubbery and the glasshouses, Mrs. Flynn winked at Sara to come and peep too, but her mother had turned around and was beckoning her to come on. They were out on the open road again, with low banks on either side topped by barbed wire fences, when they heard the distant sound of an engine on the road behind them. Sara's mother and Mrs. Martin looked at each other.

"They're coming back," Mrs. Flynn said. "Come on, quick, we'll be as far as your house."

"Oh, it might not be them at all," Sara's mother said. But she reached back and grabbed Jamie's hand and he trotted along beside her, looking back, and stumbling. "Sara!" She turned to her and smiled. "That dog, is he gone again? Oh well, he's probably home by now."

They were hurrying towards Martin's house when the truck came roaring down the road behind them and Captain reappeared, darting out under the wire. They had just reached the front of the house from the road and were walking in single file on the grassy margin.

The truck drove up beside them, the wheels spewing clouds of dust, and Captain came running after it, barking at the rolling wheels and at the men in the back of the truck who were yelling at him. Mrs. Flynn called Captain to come back. The truck braked suddenly and Captain too skidded to a halt behind it. He crouched there, yapping at the jeering men as they pelted him with small stones and pellets of hardened mud they picked off the floor of the truck. He whim-pered when they hit him and would cower for a moment. But he would not stay away. Mrs. Flynn and Sara caught him between them and tried to coax him and lead him away. And all the time the engine churned the stillness of the day to shreds. Mrs. Flynn held him back, her arms binding him against her legs while he struggled, quivering and panting with excitement, to escape. Mrs. Martin whispered to Sara's mother that they should all go into the house. "Maybe they won't mind us," she said. But her mother shook her head and stayed there. She was trying to soothe Jamie and Mrs. Flynn's child who had begun to cry.

"Come on, let him out, Missus," one of the men shouted to Mrs. Flynn. He was sitting nearest to the opening, facing them. He held his rifle across his knees. Mrs. Flynn tightened her arms around the dog and looked to the other women. "Come on, Missus, let him off." He swiveled around, resting on one knee, the rifle against his shoulder. The other soldiers looked on, and the driver rested his elbow on the ledge of the window and adjusted the mirror.

Then another soldier poised his rifle, grinned and said, "Leave him to me, I can take him where he is." But the first soldier pushed him aside with his elbow. He shrugged his shoulders and sat back. Sara searched all their faces. There was one soldier, a thin pale man with a dark moustache, who sat there with his hands clasped between his knees. He looked on with none of the anticipation of the others, but neither with impatience, as if all this had been bound to occur and he must bide while it lasted.

"Ah, what do you want with the poor dog," Mrs. Flynn said. She smirked as she glanced at the other women to see what they thought, and to blame their presence if her tactics were not the most effective she might have used. "He belongs to the little one here. Sure you wouldn't harm him."

The soldier with the moustache stretched his leg, turned away and looked across the flat countryside. It was to him Sara felt they should have appealed to stop it. Now she too turned away. She stood there waiting, her head bowed, her fingers twisting the fringe of the baby's sunshade. She heard the soldier saying, in his alien accent, "Maybe you'd rather I'd shoot him where he is . . . take two birds. . . ." She heard them whispering and someone laughed, "Three birds, aye. What do you say, Missus?"

Mrs. Flynn's arms went limp. The truck began to trundle away from them. Captain slipped from her arms. He stood still for a moment, unsure of his freedom. But as the truck picked up speed, he streaked away after it again, barking excitedly, flurries of dust in his wake. The soldier aimed and fired, and fired and fired again until the barking stopped. And when Sara looked up, the truck was near the top of the hill, clouded in dust as it gathered speed. The soldier was still shooting, into the air now, every shot puncturing the fragile blue shell of the day. Frightened birds flew squawking out of the hedges and trees, and in Martin's paddock a mare and her foal left their grazing and ran to the far side and the stamping of their hooves vibrated along the hard ground. And when the noise had stopped and the dust cleared she saw Captain lying on the road at the foot of the hill, unbelievably still as they approached him. Blood oozed through his brown and white coat in darkening patches and trickled onto the road and was absorbed in the dust.

The Cobweb Curtain

RITA KELLY

"It can't be . . . Julie?"

"Yes it is. How are you?"

The coolness of it, clipped, London. Still pretty, so casual, straight cords, always could wear anything.

"Must be years, let me see . . ."

"About twelve I should say."

"And you haven't"

"Changed a bit! Kate, let's not go through the clichés. Care for a drink?"

"Yes, that's an idea. I've been moping about the old town. I suppose you have noticed the changes too, even the shops."

"All plate-glass, impractical and understocked. One pharmacy after the other, I merely wanted a packet of cotton wool, and when they didn't have it they tried selling me 500 meters of the stuff, one could insulate an attic."

Still the same Julie, sprightly, yet not the same, alien almost.

"And I see they've swept the old post office away."

"And poor Larry Molloy's house beside it, car-for-hire, you remember?"

"Died, didn't he?"

RITA KELLY (b. 1953) writes in Irish and English. Her first collection, *The Whispering Arch and Other Stories,* was published by Arlen House in 1986. Her short fiction has appeared, over the years, in the *Irish Press,* the *Literary Review,* and other journals. She has won the *Irish Times*/Merriman Poetry Award and the Maxwell House Prize for short fiction. Ms. Kelly, a native of Ballinasloe, County Galway, lives now in Enniscorthy, County Wexford.

"Only three months ago, and all the journeys he made to Clondelara, visitors, Christmas . . ."

"And late Saturday nights when my father had drunk himself out of memory and whatever miserable money he had."

"Julie, you must miss him, I didn't know how to bring it up . . ."

"Shall we try the hotel?"

"It's so awkward, impossible almost . . ."

"The hotel?"

"Sympathizing."

Along the footpath, Julie's fashionable heels pricking the stone. Not a walk, an elegant glide. Her hair is dark against the sunlit street, soft style, flowing with her footsteps. Her hair was always dark even when cut to the bone, to deal with nits, her industrious mother rubbing in pomade and paraffin oil, Kate got the whiff of it over the years, the ghost of a barelegged little girl, now this suave young woman.

"Please Kate, I invited you therefore I insist on buying the drinks."

"Very well then, gin and lime."

"Ice?"

"No thanks."

To reach across the years. Perhaps it is impossible. What will she drink, something rather exotic no doubt. Nice handbag too, wonder what she does. Married? Must be, and a family? Strange she bothers to come home, and the mother, god love her, well . . . hopelessly ineffectual. The jacket is becoming, she can wear it, but it's just a trifle common, superstore stuff, mustn't be a bitch, things at Scotts were never easy.

That day by the well, overgrown now no doubt, it was a place of mossed stones, hazels and wild strawberries. They had come to get spring-water for the butter, the elastic gave in Julie's knickers and they fell about her ankles. Kate had laughed, Julie threw a whole can of water in her face and walked off leaving the pink knickers on the grass.

"Sorry for being so long, this takes time."

"A pint, I, I didn't think—"

"Good for the blood, why not, besides I enjoy it."

"Of course, I just thought—"

"You know Kate, I too must avoid the clichés, I was about to ask where you were now, and what you are doing. So silly, isn't it."

"Cheers."

"Cheers. However, let me ask how your parents are, I know that it's a relatively safe question."

"I imagine, Julie, that you know all there is to know about them. They sold the old place about eight years ago, and they're now quite comfortable—at least mother is—on the Elm Drive side of town. Quite up to date, though Dad still hankers after Clondelara, insists on pottering about, can't fully accept it you know."

"I'd say that being in town quite suits your mother. She was always, shall we say, lost in the country."

"Thanks for the understatement. You never did particularly care to, but would you like to come up and see her now?"

"Sorry, I told Mark to expect me about six."

"Mark?"

"My son. Gone five, the youngest."

"You have more then?"

"Yes Kate, two more. They didn't come, they've slightly outgrown my mother as you might understand."

She did. Julie's mother in Clondelara, that easy way with things, excruciating really, but so likable, and the homely kitchen face having nothing in common with the fresh-air face across the lounge table.

"And your husband?"

"No Kate, Clondelara is not his idea of happiness, and he is made to feel, well . . ."

"Out of it? It can happen, particularly if . . ."

"If he's English, no Church, abstemious, and rather vocal."

"Yet you still come back, Julie?"

"Don't we all. But don't misunderstand me, it would be less bother to write or telephone, nothing about the place draws me, I come annually for a week, it keeps my mother in touch, and as she'll neither write nor come to us, it seemed the most practical solution."

"Yes, and . . ."

"And it can't go on much longer, a few years perhaps, and then I shan't ever come. No reason."

"But Julie, how can you be so definite. And the children?"

"Quite simple really, when one nurtures no sentimental attachments. As for the children, they'll always be strangers in Clondelara, it means nothing to them, except a point on the planet where Mummy was born. It could be anywhere, and they'll find nothing of me there."

"But Julie, all your past is there, locked within the landscape, the turns and bends of the road, the furzy hills, the . . ." She stopped. She had almost said the well in the hazelwood.

"Don't be daft. The road has been flattened and steamrolled, the corners and bends bulldozed away. Trees have been cut, lanes choked with briars and nettles. Hazel hedges ripped asunder giving on to new bungalows."

"I haven't been out there in years."

"Even your own house Kate, I wouldn't recognize it, all shuttered up. And this morning I saw some cows in the front lawn."

"Would you like another drink?"

"No thank you, one is sufficient, and I must do something about a taxi."

"Listen Julie, let me drive you out, I can spare the time and it will save you the bother."

"All right then. I hitched in, a Wakefield chap from way up, you know, the Attykill side, gave me a lift, I hadn't an idea who he was, and he kept insisting that I ought to know. What these people take one for."

"You don't mean that you hitched in."

"Well I'd defy you to manage mother's battered old bicycle, and the bus passes only two days a week, marvelous system. I did think of tackling the pony, but found the collar in shreds, and a draught-chain pulled off to tie a starved mongrel to the spokes."

"Your father always kept the harness, very particular about them I remember."

"Much good it has done."

"He loved dogs about the yard too."

"Dogs yes, not curs, and he did manage to feed them."

"I know. Now that he's gone . . ."

"He too began to feel the futility of keeping the weeds from the gate."

"You're quite sure that you won't have another drink?"

"Yes, quite."

"Mind if I go to the ladies' room, and then we can start. I left the car on the Square."

"And Kate, thanks for the lift."

"Not at all. My turn anyway, think of all the times you put me

on the carrier of your bike and left me at the haggard-gate because
I was too afraid to pass the well on my own."

"Wonder if you still are?"

There was a full-length mirror in the lavatory. "Good," she thought,
the suit is still sitting properly, if I wasn't so long and skinny. The
hair, I'm not sure now of the ash-blonde, Julie's looks far more natural. Strange meeting her after all these years, not the same person
really, I can't see her knickerless among the hazels. My mother never
liked her. "Bad company Kate," she said, "living wild with horses and
dogs in that ramshackle house." Attractive house, attractive girl, beautiful skin, even today no need of make-up, I liked that house, I loved
those days with Julie. So changed, elegant aloofness, hitched into town
and drank a pint of Guinness. Unpredictable. I can still feel the ice-
cold water full on my face. Indeterminate face, a little old half-and-
half, a bit of a changeling, that is Mrs. Scott's voice, here now as in
that antique kitchen, but why indeterminate? A little more eye-shadow,
perhaps. Why do my fingers fumble, nervous of Clondelara? Glad of
the excuse to go down there again with Julie, too late for the wild
strawberries, that was in June, we lay in the long grass after. God,
I am afraid to go back.

She found herself reading, "Insert soiled sanitary towel and re-
close the drawer firmly." Damn, she said, and banged the door going
out.

"Ready Kate?"

"Yes. How long have you got?"

"Until Wednesday."

"I was thinking," what was she thinking anyway? "I was thinking we might go to a film, perhaps. Dinner together. There's a new
place on the Woodpark Road, quite good, they do an excellent Beef
Wellington."

"Thanks a lot Kate, but I didn't come back for that kind of thing.
Besides, we should very definitely run out of things to talk about."

"I see. It was just an idea. Maybe I don't agree with you, fully."

"Exhausting our topics of conversation? Well, just try it. There
can't be any real contact, and you know it. Whatever we may have
been to each other is long since past. And digging up all the details
could do neither of us any good."

"It can help, sometimes."

"Sorry, but I'm not necromantic."

Untouchable, thought Kate, she is probably right too. Might be interesting to see more of her, but one mustn't grasp. Her tones are so final and well-formed, such a change from the Clondelara cadence. We all adapt, more or less, to the new, but something drags, something to make one uneasy.

"I say Kate, what a car. Doing all right for yourself, eh. Mother will be stupefied when she sees this thing stop at the gate. What you bet, she'll kick a few chickens from the kitchen, God between us and all harm, posh visitors and the place in a mess."

"It's nothing really, well as cars go, Brendan ordered it for me, Easter."

"Stereo, sun-roof and sheep-skin covers, the lot. A bit of all right. Did I hear you say Brendan? Some fellow this Brendan of yours."

"I didn't mean to show off. Or did I?"

"Forget it Kate. Are you up in town for long? Or are you a lady of leisure?"

"The weekend. I come from time to time, and Brendan likes the golf-course here, it's relaxing for him."

"Play yourself?"

"A little, but it doesn't mean the same to me. And the ladies' end of it can be a bore, you know, comparing nappy-rash, exam results and adulteries."

"I can imagine. What's he do?"

"Brendan?"

"Yes."

"He's attached to the county hospital, pathology."

"I remember now, mother did have a big story for me, a doctor, a few years back."

"Six years."

"Kids?"

"None, well . . ."

"Better off maybe, sorry Kate, that's the cliché response, forgive my asking."

"Not at all. At least you spared me the marked pause, you know that silence while the other person wonders which of us is sterile."

"Does that still give nowadays?"

"You'd be surprised Julie, what still gives. I haven't been on this road for so long, I had almost forgotten how narrow it is."

"Or how big your car is."

"Perhaps you're right, things go out of perspective."

"Yes Kate, and rather quickly too. There's the letter-box, remember the mail-van at six p.m. and the cows had to be back in the paddock across the road before it came, speeding as always."

Mail-van. Pathetic really. What creates a rhythm and a routine, anything at all to mark time. This impossible road of bushes, might be a stone round the next bend, pushed off by a full-grown lamb. Briars scrape the side of the car, how dazzling the red paint-work must seem in this tunnel of tired green. Stubble, blotched and burned, might be a harvester coming along, slowly. Cubes of straw. And Kate, there's Flynns's. Who's there now? Haven't an idea, never see them. Flynns's thresher would come into the haggard, such excitement, tumbling in the chaff, and field-mice scurrying from the stack, Julie's father came to throw sheaves. Blackberries and fresh cream, the sweet tang of it, wash off all those maggots, the fear of getting a crawly thing on the tongue. Yes, and Duffys's, they have cut the apple trees. Too old I suppose. Marking time. How small the fields are, cattle under trees swishing flies, swarms of midges in the quiet of the evening, brushing by each other against the setting sun. The long drawn out decline of the sun. And Walshes's. What ever became of Helen?

"Kate, there's your old house."

Thought we could slip past it, keep talking, God, nothing, why won't she keep talking, anything.

"There it is Kate, see what I mean? Pity too, such a fine house, I'm sure someone would have been glad of it. Look."

Christ, the bleak blue light, the shuttered windows. Sure someone would have been glad of it, such a fine house, oh yes, nettles growing half-way up the door, the gate choked, fine house, as if nothing else mattered, what's she know about it. The front wall plundered.

"That's life Kate. Move on."

"That's not life, that's . . ."

"Ah well, no point in moaning."

"Who's moaning?"

"You are."

"No, I'm not."

"Yes, you. Don't let's argue, it's childish."

"And if you had a can of water you'd throw it."

"You know I had quite forgotten that. Funny wasn't it."

"Oh yes, very funny."

"Kate, you don't mean."

"No, I don't mean anything."

There all the time, shuttered, sealing something from the light. Undisturbed for years, but spiders tenuously tying things together. A tentative opening of a door might rend the webs, making an unpleasant mess of dust, fluff, and fly-bodies. A constant killing in the quiet. Damp moldering rooms, doors would creak, and a foot-step ring hollow on the floor, where Red Riding Hood was read by the fire before mother's brisk—"Time for bed." Empty echoing rooms, brittle paint and plasterwork, a trapped air smelling of decay. An empty shell.

"Kate, we're not being pursued, are we?"

Eyes fixed suddenly on the road ahead, Kate jabbed the gearlever back, and came out of the bend with a lurch.

"Julie, did you fly?"

"No, the boat still works out less expensive."

"Of course, but it can be such a bother, especially with children."

"Mark's no trouble, and he enjoys the adventure of being at sea." Letting the wind blow through his hair, and gripping the handrail, and "Mummy are there whales down there, is it really very deep?" Peering across the blue distance, there just might be a gull. The salt tang and the slap of the water, the furtive child's considering look back along the wake where Dad and Jenny and Alison remain. Then that tug at a sleeve, "Mummy look, there are gulls."

"But Julie, the plane is so fast and convenient."

"One might as well be in the Tube."

The blue light in her eyes. Kate suddenly glimpsed her, scarved, on deck, the wind billowing her skirts out from her long legs, her voice through it lively and vibrant, Mark, Mummy. Kate felt bleak, out of it. A new realization of Julie. Living on the cheap, but liking it, somehow alive. A quiet self-reliance, hitching a lift, going her own way, grown-up. Kate felt small, flushed, frustrated . . .

"Slow up Kate, we're here. At least there's smoke."

The same smoke rising up through the beech trees. Cobweb lace on the windows, gate needs paint, the old piers are mossed and one of the caps is askew. And a huddle of out-houses tucked into the sand-hill, and still the grass path and the dandelions.

"Would you like to come in, say hello to my mother, and have a cup of tea?"

"She'd be upset if I didn't. Also, I might like to meet Mark."

"He won't mind, probably up to his neck in Clondelara mud by now. It tends to attach itself to one you know."

"Julie, you're being ironic."

"Not really, just factual."

The old dog barked, she feared that he was about to jump up at her with his friendly filthy paws. A wrinkled face had appeared at the window, the curtain slips back. Then Mrs. Scott was at the door wiping her hands in her apron, the grey hair untidily pinned back, no bottom teeth.

"Musha, I thought 'twas someone. I couldn't know who on earth was coming in with Julia. And you're heartily welcome, Lord save us but 'tis years."

"How are you, Mrs. Scott?"

"Pulling the devil by the tail, and there's no loss on yourself by the look of it."

"Mother, Kate drove me out from town."

Dazed coming in from the bright light, smell of sour milk and soap-powder, and that tireless voice flowing in warmish waves over her.

"Wasn't that awful good of her, always a good-natured young one, seems no length since you were running into me here in the kitchen, day you turned the pram upside-down, and the child in it, I'm sure 'twas a pure accident, and your mother in the hospital, how is she?"

A wipe of her apron on the table, she bangs a couple of buckets together and fusses a few chairs out of the way.

"She was having your little sister at the time, what's this her name was, a grown woman now, married and all I suppose. Miriam. It had always been Miriam. And you did marvelous yourself, a doctor I'm told, sure you won't have far to go for the bit of medical attention. I never heard, but did you have a family?" She was standing, brush in hand.

"No mother, Kate has no children. I'll put the kettle on."

"Ah well, God is good, and there's plenty of time."

The can of spring water on a table. The same old dresser with the milk jugs, and cups on hooks, can't keep the ashes off. She comes with an armful of turf and piles it on the fire. Kate's hand goes to take the tongs, so many times, the half-heard voice, the flapping flame.

"Sure they can't do enough for me, God love them. There's Julia comes home every year without fail, sends the few bob from time to time. And the little lad, what's this his name is, a cure to have child round the house again, sticks his nose in everything, I'm sure he's up to something. Run down Julia, he was with the hens before you came, you wouldn't know what he might drink out there in the shed."

"Mother what's the oven doing? Are you baking?"

"I was just going to make a cake when I heard the car."

"But you know that there's plenty of bread in the house."

"And you kept the open-fire, Mrs. Scott?"

"Ah I did Katie, sure the kitchen wouldn't be the same without it."

"Yes mother, you'd miss the smoke and the ashes in everything."

"Run out will you and see to the child."

The bake-oven and lid warming against the fire, just like it used to be, and she'll put the coals on the hob under it, getting the tongs again and being let put the coals on the lid. All those days, and Julie too used to make a little cake from the remainder of the dough and put it on the coals. On the hearth, watching the flames peep out through the turf, the warmth, the rippling glint on the saucepan lids and on the delph. Harsh March days, the fire reflected in the windowpane as if it was out in the hedge. In the primroses. And sitting on the hob itself, watching the smoke whirl up into the blue.

"Now that she's gone, will you tell me what in the name of God do you think of her."

"Well, Mrs. Scott, Julie knows her own mind."

She has sat down too, in the armchair scratching the ashes with the tongs. Hushed intimate tones.

"How right you are, Katie, did she say anything about her man? A bit odd he is, between ourselves, not one of our kind you know what I mean, has ideas and notions about everything, doesn't come much, oh I'd say he's very good to her and all that. Just the way she talked about things long ago, and she would take a Woodbine from behind the tea-caddy, and a bag of bull's eyes, sweet and sticky. Hush now, I hear her coming."

"Here he is. Say hello to Kate, then you may wash your hands."

"Hello. Please Mummy who is Kate? May I go now?"

"Well isn't he the little stranger." Cool English consonants, inquiring eyes, goes his own way. Gone.

"Well, isn't he the distant little creature, I don't know, but at his age, honest to God but it's not natural."

"Children should not be petted, mother."

Was Julie smiling slightly, smiling at her as she looked across the firelit kitchen? The old woman was murmuring about tea. She stood up, decided.

"No thanks, Mrs. Scott."

Go. She had a sudden sense of a salt breeze on a boat-deck. Her own voice, get out of this suffocating cave of a room.

"Don't fuss mother. We mustn't detain Kate."

Clipped and final, we mustn't detain. Dragging slattern heels across the concrete floor, murmuring of eggs, might have the half-score, to bring back with you, God blast the same hens, wait now till I see.

"Thank you Mrs. Scott, but I wouldn't like to leave you short."

"Plenty of eggs when we're all dead and gone. Wait now till I give them a rub of a cloth."

Rub of a cloth, dab of breadsoda and a spit. Good-natured, hobbling. Hen dung trodden into the pitted concrete floor, stupid to have come, a ragged chicken drinking off the floor, some blue-gray mixture, milk and slop. Fussing about newspaper to wrap the eggs. And, "Julia if you had a nice bit of a box." She had. It had held Mark's new shoes.

"Where's Mark, Julie?"

"Reading. His refuge."

Yes, his own way, his own world, shutting out the interminable voice.

"You'd want to mind his eyes, Julia, too much of that reading altogether, now if I had a bit of straw for the bottom of the box."

"Mother, for goodness sake, Kate isn't on a bicycle."

"I'll say goodbye to you so. Mind the eggs. Julia will see you out to the gate. Lord, but I've ruined your glove with flour, wait till I get the old cloth."

"It's all right, they're an old pair anyway. Goodbye Mrs. Scott, and . . . thank you."

"If only I'd known you were coming—"

Out into the fresh air, cool against flushed cheeks. Getting dark. There was hay down, a smell of meadowsweet. First touch of fog.

"Well Kate, that's it."

"Yes. Mark is nicely behaved. Congratulations."

"Thanks."

"I suppose Julie, I shan't see you before you go?"

"No. And I don't think you'll really want to."

"You don't?"

"No."

"Goodbye then. And Julie . . . I'm glad we met."

"Me too. Kate, have you forgotten?"

A pause. In the twilight Kate caught the ghost of a smile. A clasp across the void, quick and eager, a cool impression on the lips. Go, or the moment will have spent itself. Break.

She stopped the car at the mouth of a laneway. Taking the box with her she strode along between the hazels, wisps of fog hung in the leaves, there were the beginnings of nuts in their pale green frills. She found the well in a thicket of briar and blackthorn, a cow-track torn through it to a glint of black water.

I'll keep the box, she thought. Nice child. One by one she dropped in the whole half-score, light in her hand they went down like stones.

A Pot of Soothing Herbs

JULIA O'FAOLAIN

I'd like to make this brief, but I doubt if I shall. Like my friends, I talk a great deal. *Why* is probably going to become clear from this letter. (Is it a letter? That too may become clear.) The depressing thing about our talk is that it is not about activity. It is about talk. I'm told the Irish were always that way — given to word-games since the sixth century. It is typical of us too to say "the Irish" instead of "I": a way of running for tribal camouflage. I am trying to be honest here, but I can't discard our usual rituals. In a way, that would be more dishonest. It would mean trying to talk like someone else: like some of my friends, sheep in monkeys' clothing, who chatter cynically all day in pubs, imitating the tuneful recusancy of a Brendan Behan while knowing damn' well all the while that they'd tar and feather anyone who seriously threatened the comfortable values of the Irish Republican Middle Classes. Not that anyone is likely to. We're a modest, solid little oligarchy. The bloodshot eyes of our drunks are the pinkest things about us. So we can be smug. And in a way we are. And in a way we aren't. The collective memory ripples in our sky like a damp, nostalgic flag. A red flag. Our parents didn't work their way up selling underwear or sweat out their fantasy for scholarships. They fought — they meant to fight — a social revolution. Even now, they can still find

Julia O'Faolain (b. 1932) was born in London and educated in Ireland and abroad. Since 1970 she has published five novels, four story collections, and several scholarly works and translations. The volumes of short fiction — *We Might See the Sights* (1968), *Man in the Cellar* (1974), *Melancholy Baby* (1978), and *Daughters of Passion* (1982) — have established her reputation in the genre. Ms. O'Faolain commutes between London and Los Angeles.

a frondeur's rage in the dregs of their third double whiskey. Of course, you might see that happen anywhere. I've caught flickers of it in the *bien-pensant* French families with which I've stayed *au pair*—we have, you see, all the habits. I've had the traditional advantages—but with us a whole class is prone. My mother's college-day memories are of raids, curfews, and dancing in mountain farmhouses with irregular soldiers who were sometimes shot a few hours after the goodnight kiss. She once carved up an ox and served it in sandwiches to a retreating procession of civil-war rebels. She has the track of a Black and Tan bullet in her thigh and spent a brief spell in prison. My father and all my friends' fathers have the same memories. Even the nuns in school had nonconformist quirks, traces of a deviated radicalism which crept with heady irrelevance into the conventional curriculum. We've never known what to do with it. When our parents sing their old marching songs and thrill to images they won't pass on to us—scenes from those haylofts, for instance, where the young men hid and their girl couriers rested after long bicycle rides—we, with our blood pumping to their tunes, neat and shy in the deep clasp of the armchairs, finger our cocktail glasses and feel faintly silly. They mock us. "Yerrah, ye missed it!" they say, their vowels broadening reminiscently. "I have to pity the young today. . . ." They return to the Eden of memory. It is as if sex, in Ireland, were the monopoly of the over-fifties.

And why should it be? an outsider might ask. Why *do* we sit there listening to them like envious paralytics? Why has it taken me this long to get to sex if that is what I want to talk about? If I knew, I wouldn't be telling this ridiculous story. It wouldn't have happened in the first place. If I were talking now instead of writing, the rush of my breath would be noticeable, a faint bravado at having taken even such a gingerly hold on the matter. I suppose it would be clear then that I am a virgin, a twenty-one-year-old virgin, which is something I usually try to conceal from foreigners. From the Irish I couldn't—and besides it's nothing to want to conceal here. *"Mon petit capital"* (as Robert, my disappointed French beau of last June, called it) is really just that in Holy Catholic Ireland. Though it's not that I wouldn't like to disperse it secretly, feed my cake to the pigeons and have it too. But? Oh, a lot of impalpables. For one thing, I'm mechanically very ignorant. I've read *Ulysses* carefully and the *Complete Rabelais* and *Fanny Hill* and a number of other promising and disappointing books, but I don't quite know how humans make love. In the convent we didn't study biology and my mother's explanations when my brother was born were unclear. When I add that contraceptives — *whatever* they are — are unavailable in Ireland and that *three* of my mother's maids ended in the Magdalene Homes with illegitimate babies, I think I've stated the most tangible reason for my hesitation.

I imagine the girls in my group are even more ignorant than I am. Of course, if one did emancipate herself she would conceal the fact with all her might, so it's hard to tell. Maeve may have "gone rather far" — our favorite euphemism — with her French escort in Paris last summer. I know I went further with mine than I'd been before. I would probably have trusted to his precautions and slept with him if I'd liked him better. But there's where the residual native romanticism — my grand-opera morality — hamstrings me like a mucky umbilical cord. And I abominate it!

For my degree, I chose all the periods and poets who worked with their eye on the object: brisk Gallic *gaillards* of the sixteenth century, late Latin sensualists whose tight rhythms leave no room for droll, eighteenth-century types like N. de Lenclos or Ch. de Laclos whose *Liaisons* I've studied as a chess player studies old strategies. And then after all that and hours defending Mme. de Merteuil to Maeve, who can't see that hers was the only response to a phony society like ours, I pull away from Robert when he moors the boat under a bush in the Bois — what more setting did I want anyway? — and asks: *"Eh bien, tu as envie ou pas?"* *"Non,"* I said. He was the most beautiful creature I'd ever seen — casual, well-tailored, amusing. *"Menteuse!"* The boat rocked under us as he slid his hands all over me and I felt liquids racing within me, tides quivering down my spine and along the soles of my feet, and I wondered when I must stop him before he got too excited to be stopped. This is one of our great anxieties which I discuss constantly with Maeve. Can they — men — really not control themselves? I don't mean Irish men, because they don't seem to have any needs at all. Or they're queer. Aidan is queer. And I need hardly add that I don't know precisely what that means, either. I wonder how much precision matters? I mean anatomical precision. It's curious how abstract the most reputedly bawdy French writers are when you get right down to trying to understand details from them. Maybe if I'd read classics instead I'd have learned more by now. Because I can't ask anyone. I'm twenty-one and it seems ridiculous. I'll probably learn in practice if someone I like enough to satisfy my disgusting romanticism ever does try to sleep with me. I go round in a constant state of excitement. I wonder does everybody? Maeve says she doesn't, but I think she's a liar. When I'm in a crowd, on the bus, say, and something touches me — often it turns out to be a shopping basket or a dog — I get violent sensations of liquids running inside me. Everywhere: the back of my knees, my breasts. Sometimes I can hardly stand up. Then if I see Aidan it becomes almost unbearable. Usually I do see him from a bus, and often, even if it's the rush hour and I've had to queue for forty minutes to get on it, I get off and dash round the block just so that I can pass him by casually and say, "Hullo, Aidan." "Hullo," he says with his furtive smile, and rushes off with his head bent. He has a long white face and has neither the poise nor the class, the looks or the taste of Robert. He's unsure of himself, bad-tempered, and with a chip on his shoulder. All that. I enjoy saying this about him. It's true, and I say it not so much to try and deceive people about my feelings for him — Maeve has probably told everyone anyway, so there wouldn't be much use — but simply because I like to talk about him. He seems tormented, and this — romanticism again — I'm afraid I enjoy. I know his torment comes from something quite ignoble like the fact that his family probably live in a slum. We've deduced this from his always insisting on being set down at Merrion Square when he gets a lift home, which is about a mile from his postal address.

It suddenly occurs to me, seeing the ingredients of my love set down on paper, that they look like the ingredients for hate, or as if I were insincere and didn't *want* sex at all and so chose to fall for a queer, or were masochistic, or reacting against my class or some such oddity. It would no doubt be easy for some dab to erect theories like this which it would be hard for me to deny. One can never prove things, anyway, which is what makes them rather dull. I only know that I am attracted where I sense tensions and dissatisfactions — I prefer the fat, panting Hamlet to Hotspur — and that it was the grace and *easiness* of Robert's approach that turned me away from him. This may seem to contradict what I said earlier about liking the eighteenth century; I would answer that one can choose one's intellectual polestar but not the way one's bowels jump.

I am usually rude to Aidan. It is the one form of intimacy open to me. I think he's aware of this. I also think he likes me and that the reason he doesn't invite me out is simply that he has no money. Though as a matter of fact he once did invite me. We met uncomfortably on the canal bridge where our bus routes cross. It was damp and we walked along the towpath while he talked allusively of Rimbaud. I don't know whether this is his technique with businessmen in pubs who like listening to a University boy, or whether it was intended as an oblique confession of queerness—though if he thought that necessary he underrates the grape-vine. He talked French the whole time, saying, *"C'est difficile, c'est difficile!"* and giving me the *vous.* Then suddenly he rushed me into Mooney's. "Jesus! A drink!" He paid, which must make me one of the only people ever to have got a drink out of him—hardly a consoling distinction. Still, I went home feeling less miserable than someone who doesn't know Dublin might think. I'm used to Irish dates. For one thing, he had given me to understand that he was not a virgin, and I had hopes of him—and had until this past Saturday.

I wish there were someone whose advice I could ask about *that.* Not Maeve's. And priests make me sad with their good-housekeeping morality. ("Now you wouldn't," says our PP on the subject of matrimony, "if you were giving someone a present, want it to be chipped or cracked?") So I am writing this down and maybe I shall send it to Aidan. Why not? Or to Robert, whom I shall probably be seeing at Easter. (Actually, I know I shall do neither, but one has to pretend if the writing is to be a vent. Besides, I might.)

Since Saturday I've been feeling like a shaken thundersheet. What is bad is not the hollow sensation itself but the importance I find myself attributing to it, the way the mind gets subordinated to the belly and I take my bloody blood throbs for telepathic messages: Morse tattoos from some friendly *deus ex machina*—Aidan? ha!—who is going to solve my troubles without my having to take any responsibility. This feeding on fancy must do something to the brain. (Do Irish women ever recover?) Even writing this I am ridiculously expectant. I *must* lay out the facts.

Saturday? Maeve and I went to Enda O'Hooey's. He was giving a party together with Simon FitzSimons and had asked the two of us to come early and help. We accepted. A party is a party, and I knew that Aidan was to come later. It was the usual thing. While we made sandwiches, the men talked and we giggled appropriately from time to time or said: "You're terrible!" or: "Don't make me laugh!" Half mechanical, half ironical. They talked about their families (Enda's was away for the weekend), pretending to deride them; boasting. Simon comes from a line of Castle-Catholics — pre-revolutionary collaborators, which gives his gentility seniority over ours — and he talked about *that*. Enda's father made his money in children's prayer books with pastel celluloid bindings. He got a monopoly from the Republican government in return for *his* father's having been hanged by the British — which is the bit of family past which Enda prefers to remember. The O'Hooeys own an enormous eighteenth-century house with a rather tarty nineteen-sixtyish bathroom on the ground floor, fitted, including the lavatory bowl, in bright baby-pink. It was while Enda was regaling us in the drawing-room with a doggerel ballad on his grandfather's death that Maeve broke this lavatory bowl. How she did I don't know, unless it was made from celluloid left over from the prayer-book bindings. Once broken, the ensuing fuss left us feeling flighty for the rest of the evening. It is not the sort of misdemeanor that a girl of our set feels comfortable about confessing to her host. If Maeve had broken a decanter or something of that sort she would have insisted on paying. We are sticklers about money. Unfortunately, we are sticklers too about taboo words, and "lavatory" tops the list. So Maeve, who couldn't think of an acceptable euphemism, was in a fix. She stayed for a while in the bathroom drinking whiskey and laughing at herself in the mirror, then dashed into the drawing room and began hissing at me in French: *"Ecoute, Sheila, j'ai cassé le cabinet, le water, la machin, le . . . enfin tu me comprends!"* This embarrassed me. I calculated quickly that (a) she would not confess; (b) Enda might suspect me of breaking the thing; (c) I might as well encourage her nervousness in the hope that this would give the men a clue as to where, eventually, to lay the blame. So I teased her, whipping her, and by the way myself, into a state of hilarious idiocy. *"N'y touchez pas,"* Maeve yelled, *"elle est brisée,"* and cackled untunefully — to the obvious annoyance of Simon, who had been trying to set the atmosphere for a little mild necking, before the arrival of other guests. When he tried to cuddle her, Maeve — she doesn't like him, anyway — let out a screech. "I'm mortified!" she called, and began to hop about waving a beer-glass full of whiskey, "Am I positively repulsive to her" Simon asked me in earnest distress.

By the time Aidan came we were so lightheaded that, with most unnatural aplomb, I kissed him on the cheek and told him what had happened. It charmed him since he rather dislikes Enda, and our amusement cut out the need we usually feel to spar. "Come into the kitchen," he said. Aidan always gravitates toward kitchens. I felt promoted and physically tranquil, which often happens when I am with someone who attracts me.

We went on talking French, which was a help. It gives one a feeling of detachment. We managed to laugh a lot, too, and were warming agreeably toward each other — I had always known he liked me really, else why would I like him? A half-hour later, as we began to talk of some place to which we could go on, the back door opened, letting in a stream of cold air and a crowd of gate-crashers to interrupt us. "Will yez look who's here — Aidan!" Red-faced from wind and drink they arrived like pantomime demons with jovial, fake brogues and gushes of pestilential breath. "A friendly face!" said the same crasher, although Aidan's face had actually relapsed to its driest and prissiest detachment; his furtive grin was back, stuck across it like sticking-plaster. Being queer, he has whole sets of acquaintances outside the college crowd, and he is at pains to keep each apart from the other. It occurred to me, too, that he might not like it to be thought in certain circles that he shows interest in women. "Who's giving this bloody party anyway" yelled the crashers, gargling their consonants, drunken and pretending to be more so. An older crowd than we, they had not bothered to bring the usual gift of liquor. Aidan appeared to be savoring a sedate interior joke. The old empty feeling had come over me. I have had such practice in controlling disappointment that I freeze it before it gets started, only recognizing it in the vacancy of my own grin. "Any drink?" a crasher asked the absent Aidan. "Remember what Whistler said? I drink to make my hosts seem witty." Feeling I must be embarrassing him, I turned away from Aidan. As I did so I noticed that among the arrivals, though in her containment very much apart from them, was Claudia Rain. She is a tall, bee-blonde creature with stemlike neck and wrists and immense, painted, Byzantine eyes. One of those slightly monstrous females whose beauty is disputable but, to those who recognize it, overwhelming. She had always impressed me, though I had only seen her before across streets — the exhalations from damp lounge bars. She is a fable round town: the sort who strikes young girls' mothers as "a common tart" and the girls themselves as a creature of daring, both gallant and *galante*. I lend her figure when I read Proust to Odette de Crécy and prefer her for peopling Yeats's poems to the fuzzy-haired photos of Maud Gonne. She manages to project an image that is both exotic and sedate. She is English but has, as they say, "been around." She arrived in town first with Rory MacMourragh — who met her when he was sculpting in Vienna — and is still officially with him, although she has picked and dropped half the emancipated males of Dublin in the eighteen months since she came.

"Aidan, my dear!" She dived on him with a swish of expensively eccentric clothes. "Your horrid little friend, the host, is threatening to throw us out. Come and restrain him. He's ringing the *gardaí*." She said *gardaí* in Gaelic as we never would, an English concession which might be mocking or punctilious. The artificial pipe of her voice surprised me at first, but after a second I decided it was not affected, merely strange. Aidan muttered some excuse, gave me a mean, little grin, and trotted after her. He had not introduced us. I was furious. Did he think her too strong meat for me? I stood sipping my drink, staring in sulky wonder at the sottish men with whom she had arrived. What did such a splendid creature want with them? In a second or two she was back. She had begun unknotting the vast nest of hair which she wears, wound like a family-sized brioche, on top of her head. Suddenly she poured it over the face of one of the sots who was sitting on a chair drinking stout — *not*, I noticed, Rory MacMourragh. The man laughed and grabbed at her. She evaded him.

"Will you look at that one?" said Maeve, who had staggered in without my noticing her, although she was easy enough to pick out with her royal blue taffeta and Coral Glow lipstick. She had become dishevelled and tarty to an extent to which I could not imagine the English girl ever being reduced.

"You *have* been drinking!" I observed. There was a bleary patina, a kind of sweaty bloom over her make-up which was dissolving her face in a pointillist glow. "My mirror," I thought sourly, looking at her; "the drunken, rat-tailed virgin."

Maeve took no notice of my remark. She was staring sagely at Claudia. "*They* say," she stated, "that she's nympho!"

"Well, a damn' good thing for *them* if she is!" I snapped. "Given what the rest of us are!"

Maeve giggled, swaying on her spike heels. "Enda has taken down his grandfather's gun," she confided excitedly. "The one hanging over the mirror. He keeps threatening Aidan with it and all the crashers."

"Are guns dangerous after three generations?" I asked. "Not that it would be loaded." But I was annoyed with myself for even listening to Maeve. She is like a maidservant, always trying to frighten and excite herself with stories. I stared at the gores in the English girl's tweed skirt. They limbered the flow of it until it achieved some of the swirl of a dancer's dress. She was moving off again now, supple inside it as a paper streamer.

"I've heard," Maeve muttered, "that Rory MacMourragh likes Aidan. They say," she went on with typical Dublin mime of lowered voice and furtive eye which advertizes to a room of twenty that you're saying something scandalous, "that *she* has him so tormented that he's taken to the men. . . ." Maeve's sour breath was so close now I could feel its warmth horribly on my cheek and upper lip. "They say," and she dug her angular elbow into me with the rough gesture of country grandparents (it will take the convent schools a few more generations to lay *those* ghosts), "that her mother was a kind of kept woman until the end when the father married her! *He's* a peer, you know."

I was beginning to feel mortally tired. Standing and the issueless excitement of earlier in the evening had left me limp. "I'm going to see what *is* happening in front," I announced.

"That's right," Maeve said approvingly. "Keep an eye on Aidan!"

"Are you coming?" I asked with distaste.

"No," Maeve answered loudly. "I can't face Enda!" She raised her glass at me as I left. "I'm too mortified," she shouted, and smiled intriguingly at the men around her.

In the front room, among the usual Dublin mixture of Georgian antiques bought by lot and Dunlopillo upholstering, Enda was still posturing with the gun. "My grandfather shot sixteen men with this!" he said. "Isn't that a poem by Willy Yeats?" someone inquired. Enda's mouth was drawn down, his movements heavy. "Don't provoke me now," he begged with ponderous politeness. "I might feel it my duty to shoot."

I saw Aidan standing in the listless little group of onlookers, drinking Enda's whiskey. I went into the library. Rory MacMourragh was lying on a couch. He got up.

"An apparition," he said.

"Yes," I agreed, "and as brief." I turned back.

"Do you hate this party?" he asked. "Will you come home with me?"

"No," I said. "I'm waiting for Aidan."

"Are you in love with Aidan?"

"Yes."

"He's no good for you," said MacMourragh—who is, I should add, disturbingly attractive with an eighteenth-century Irish face, black curls, square jaw, and a sculptor's heft.

"I suppose I know that," I admitted.

MacMourragh caught my arm, and fixed his black eyes lengthily on mine. It's a trick I've had played on me before by men, but it always disconcerts me. His ease was of a quality different from Robert's. I imagined that I could sense reserves of controlled violence here, but this may have been suggested by stories I'd heard of his fights over Claudia. He is Anglo-Irish, of a different *pâte* to the natives. "You're probably thinking that Claudia went off with that sot Hennessey," Rory went on. "And you're doing a division sum in your head. Stop it. I'm not offering you a fraction of anything. Besides, calculations are so dreary!" He was still fixing me with both eyes. I did not want to flinch, but was aware that if anyone came in we would look rather absurd, and laughed to give myself a countenance. I did not want to break away from him, either, and the tides within me which had ebbed and curdled earlier in the evening were back, hammering at my temples and impeding my usual spate of words. I tried to laugh as unconsentingly as possible. "Come," said Rory, I stopped laughing. We faced each other in silence for several moments. It was then that I noticed someone watching us. Aidan was slouching in the door, whiskey glass still in hand, looking ridiculously censorious. The tides turned sickeningly. "Aidan!" Rory called easily. "You hide your friends from each other. But you're in time to make amends! I don't know this young lady's name yet."

"I shall *not* introduce you," said Aidan, loping toward us. "And I want you to keep away from this girl!" He straddled the fireplace, leaning back, surveying us down the slope of his nose. His absurdity was warming me to him until I remembered what Maeve had said about his liking Rory. Or was it Rory liking him? Which? Either way, *that* little element turned me into a piece of camouflage in the triangle, a fig-leaf, a *cache-sexe*. I sat dejectedly down in an armchair. Rage, despair, and my own fatal ignorance had me again by the groin. What an evening!

I was scarcely surprised, and anyway indifferent, when Enda came rushing in with his gun, yelling that he was giving no more parties. "Fine thanks I get!" He had got rid of the other guests, he told us, "before they did any more damage! They broke the bloody jakes!" he explained. "Bogmen! God knows what they're used to. I don't know what my mother will say!" He seemed near tears.

"I wouldn't be surprised," Rory suggested, "if it was that sot Hennessey."

"He's a gurrier," stated Enda. "Yez are all low-bred gurriers! Get out of my house!" I stood up. "You stay here, Sheila," Enda commanded. "I invited you out tonight and I'm responsible to your father."

"Oh, shut up, Enda!"

"I won't let you out of my sight," he bullied. "That pair of gurriers might take advantage of you. You don't know what you're up against. You're an innocent girl!"

This low cut roused me. "I'm going," I said. "I'm getting out of here." I went to look for my coat. It was the last one left in the bedroom except for Maeve's.

She herself had evidently passed out, for she was stretched across the bed, blowsier than ever, with powder spilled all down one side of her skirt. But even now she lay in a neat, convent-girl attitude, with clasped hands and crossed ankles.

When I left the bedroom the men were still threatening each other in the hall. I couldn't make out how drunk or serious they might be, so I skittered down the basement stairs and out the side door into the garden. By the time I reached the gate Aidan was with me. Then the other two appeared, and it looked as though Enda was not going to let us out. He stood with his back to the gate, waving the gun again and talking about his responsibilities.

"I'll shoot," he threatened. "I'll telephone your father, Sheila!"

"Enda, if you do that. . . ."

"They'll take advantage of you," he pleaded. "I can't stand by . . . Sheila, *I* asked you out this evening!"

This sad little appeal, coming after his rambunctious threats, might have moved me if he had been less drunk. But he was an unappetizing sight: mouth caked with the black lees of Guinness, sparse, pale stubble erupting on his chin, and a popped button on his chest revealing the confirmation medal underneath. Besides, I had never given Enda any reason to suppose I took him seriously. "Don't be childish, Enda," I said.

He lifted the gun as if to strike me. Rory snatched it. "Steady, now, fellow, steady! Remember that old Irish hero, Cuchulain, whose weapon used to get out of control and had to be put in a pot of soothing herbs? I think that's what *we* need here." And he planted the gun, barrel down, in one of Enda's mother's geranium pots. "Come on, now, good chap! Let us pass." He pushed Enda easily and gently out of the way, and the three of us went out the gate. The last I saw of Enda was through the railing. He was sitting on the ground weeping and muttering about "insensitivity" and his grandfather.

It was rather a miserable little incident, but in an odd way it made the three of us friendlier toward each other, which was a good thing as it turned out that neither Aidan nor I had the money to take taxis back to our opposite suburbs. Rory had no money either, and Claudia had taken their car.

"You'd better spend the night in my studio," he said. "That seems the best solution."

"What about Claudia?"

"She won't be back tonight!"

So we walked down Pembroke Road, Leeson Street, and the Green, singing the song about Enda's grandfather. There wasn't much for us to talk about and it hasn't a bad tune. When we got to the studio, Rory kicked over a milk bottle and began swearing, which diverted any embarrassment I might have felt. Who did seem embarrassed was Aidan. He kept whispering to me behind his hand that he was responsible for this and would never forgive himself and that I needn't be afraid. When Rory suggested that we all three get into the large and only bed, Aidan began twittering like a nun.

"Don't worry, don't worry," he kept telling me.

"I'm *not* worried," I said bitterly.

Rory yawned. "I'm sleepy. I'll sleep on the outside." He pulled off his trousers and climbed in. Aidan began pulling cushions about until he had a sort of barricade all down one side of the bed. Then he climbed in on Rory's side of this, fully dressed, and motioned me into the little furrow between the cushions and wall.

I took off my dress and climbed in in my slip. In the dark I tried to fix a couple of pin curls so that my hair wouldn't be straight as a stick in the morning. Then I lay staring at the light which was beginning to dilute the studio window and at the pattern formed by paper scraps pasted over broken panes. A rubber plant, which I remembered seeing in some of Rory's sketches of Claudia in the Grafton Gallery, complicated the design, giving it a live, animal, and foreign savor, reminding me that this was a studio: a place of freedom, alchemy, and secret intuitions. I almost expected the air to affect me as I lay there breathing it. The men had fallen silent and the only communication was when Rory passed across an egg-saucepan full of water. "Take a swig," he said. "The old malt dries the throat." Then there was more isolating silence. When Aidan's hand burrowed under the barricade toward mine, it was so obviously a fraternal grip that I couldn't presume on it. Besides, if I pressed or bit it, wouldn't he think this was from fear? And could I be sure that I wouldn't be afraid if one of them were to make a move?

In the middle of these wonderings the light snapped on. Aidan pulled the sheet over my head and the delicate, piping voice of Claudia Rain produced a four-letter word. "To think," she followed it up, "that I should come home to this! You have a virgin in my bed. A tight little virgin! And I could have had a passionate night with Louie Hennessey! I left him to come home to you," she called loudly to Rory, while Aidan's hand clamped over my mouth. "You clod! Get that virgin out of my bed! I won't have virgins in my bed! Damn you! Unblooded virgins!"

"Put a sock in it, Claudia!" Aidan growled. Rory said nothing and I, even if Aidan hadn't got both hands, like metal hooks, on me now, was too paralyzed with embarrassment to stir from under my sheet.

I could hear Claudia moving roughly around the room and lay in terror of a physical attack. "I could have had a passionate night," she repeated.

"Come and lie with me, then," Rory's voice coaxed. "Come on, sweetie!"

"I don't want *you!*" Claudia's accents were more and more cultured, British, and musical. "I want Aidan. I want to make love with Aidan. His virgin won't mind, will she?"

"Shut *up,*" yelled Aidan. "Can't you shut her up, Rory?"

"Come on," said Rory, "I'll give it to you, sweetie, let me give it to you."

"I want Aidan. You'll never get another chance, Aidan."

"Shut your filthy mouth, Claudia!" said Aidan, whose hands were kneading me ferociously in his rage.

"Well, make love with your virgin, then," Claudia suggested. "I won't have you lying there masturbating unhealthily in my bed."

Aidan nearly throttled me in his fury. Rory apparently got hold of Claudia, because the light went out and heavings of the mattress took the place of talk. After a while even that stopped and after another while Aidan cautiously released me, even uncovering my head so that I could breathe a bit and see the window, which had grown paler, and the rubber plant, which was grayer now and more three-dimensional than before. I must have been about 3 or 4 in the morning. Astonishing, I fell asleep.

I woke up to find sun streaming across my face and that it was 11 o'clock by my watch. The others were still asleep. I crept off the bed and dressed fast and furtively. I wanted to confront them from as poised a position as possible. In the bathroom I found pots of make-up with which I constructed for myself as understated and elegant a face as their tones permitted. Then I mooched about the studio, observing the odd appeal of things whose uses had got confused. I found food tangled up in some piles of scrap iron and the skeleton of a sheep. As there didn't seem to be much else to do, I got breakfast and brought it in on a tray. Claudia had been woken up by my clatter and had, to my relief, put on a very *Harper's Bazaar* dressing-gown.

"Good morning," she said. "How sweet of you. Let's eat it on the bed. There are bits of plaster and junk on the table."

We smiled at each other over cups of tea and boiled eggs and, when the men sat up, the four of us had a session as formal and sedate as any old county figures nodding their hats together in the Shelbourne Lounge. When he'd finished, Rory sprawled back on his pillow.

"Let's drive out to the country," he suggested. "Let's visit Crazy Shaughnessy, the bird-man in Glencree. You'll like him," he told me, "and I'm sure he'll like you. I'm going to do a bust of Sheila," he told Claudia. "She has a fine neck." Claudia agreed.

Were they being *too* sweet? I wondered. But they seemed spontaneous and I felt more relaxed than I ever do, almost as if I'd come to terms with my wretched state or as if its acknowledgment had in some way exorcised it. "I'd love to," I said. "But I'll have to ring my parents. They'll think I spent the night with Maeve, but even so they'll be expecting me back by now."

"The phone's broken," Rory told me. "But we can call in on them on our way to Glencree. Don't worry. We'll be out of here in a jiffy."

But it was another two hours before we managed to seat ourselves in Rory's ancient and elegant car. It was a tall, black, angular affair and Claudia, in unfashionably long hobble shirt and Ferragamo shoes, emphasized its antiquity. I wondered how consciously she planned her effects. The drive was convivial. The men sang, quoted, joked. Claudia smoked and I was happy in a way I never had been before and can't explain. It was as if their ease and freedom were communicable and everything was now going to be very simple for me. I was still careless as the wind when we turned in our drive and I saw my parents in their Sunday clothes, standing on the steps with their missals in their hands. "Wait a second," I told the others, "I'll just tell them I'm not lunching and be back."

My mother's outraged abuse was like a foreign language to me at first. I didn't understand. When I did I turned back to the others — I was still sufficiently attuned to them to know I needn't put a face on things — and asked them to go. "I can't come," I said. As they drove off my mother's words and sentiments began to assume impact.

"Consorting," I heard her say, "consorting with . . . bringing to the house . . . a filthy little whore like that! And where did you spend the night? Maeve's mother rang up. She's beside herself. Maeve hasn't been home all night. And you can imagine how we felt! Where is your self respect? Your values? . . ." And on and on.

I screamed at her, which was stupid as I like her a lot and she may be honest. I'm not sure. I don't, I realize, understand her at all, but she *does* get hurt. I think of the wild youth she had and the erotic books she enjoys and has let me read and I am utterly confused. Because of course I prefer not to think of my parents as consciously hypocritical. And, worst of all, I can feel the comfortable depression of my familiar groove ready to receive me again, and as nothing *actual* — goddamn it and damn me for being as vulgarly physical as they are — happened last night, maybe I am back where I began. Maybe nothing snapped—or mentally ever will. Maybe I am as unfree as ever. Maybe too I have ruined myself with Rory and Claudia and maybe Rory and Claudia are a mirage and next time I see them she will strike *me* as a "common little tart"? Or perhaps all this is irrelevant and I am just suffering from blood-pressure or something—though, my God, I am physically and mentally in a state and this bloody letter is doing me no good at all. . . .

Losing

KATE CRUISE O'BRIEN

Anne wobbled towards the kitchen and put the kettle on. She filled
a glass and crumpled two damp, fuzzy Alka Seltzer tablets into the
water. Her head throbbed. Her mouth felt as if it had been scrubbed
out with Vim so she lit herself a cigarette to justify the taste. She used
to enjoy Jonathan's parties so much. She never used to feel like this
the morning after them. In the early days he hadn't trusted her with
the cleaning up. He used to get a woman in, someone who could
handle his precious antiques. She'd been so young then and enchanted.
He'd been enchanted too by her youthful clumsiness.

"Funny little thing, aren't you. Wouldn't let you near a brass coal
scuttle, never mind a crystal decanter."

He used to deal in antiques and when the boom in antiques fal-
tered, the great carved furniture had settled uneasily in the large quiet
flat. It was an attic flat with low ceilings and a row of south facing
windows. The deep velvet plums and pinks and Wedgewood greens
seemed to absorb the light, and the Persian carpet, a bargain that no
one seemed to appreciate, obscured the wooden floor which used to
shine redly in the afternoon light.

Anne poured the boiling water over instant powder in her mug.
He'd never bothered much with the kitchen. It was a little dark hole
beside the bathroom with an ancient, sticky gas stove. She'd tried to
clean the stove once but black gunge stuck to her fingers and she'd

KATE CRUISE O'BRIEN (b. 1948) published *A Gift Horse and Other Stories* in
1978. She was born in Dublin and educated there and abroad. Her work
has appeared in *New Irish Writing* and *Best Irish Short Stories — 2*. Ms. O'Brien
won the Hennessy Literary Award in 1971.

given it up. She liked cooking but he was happier in restaurants. Restaurants were good for business. When he wasn't making contacts he liked to relax beside the coal effect electric fire with a Chinese takeaway and a fat American novel about cars, or hospitals, or hotels, but most of all about sex.

Anne staggered into the sitting room and groped her way through the antiques and empty glasses. She pulled back the heavy crushed velvet curtains and light filtered through the stale smoky air. She opened a window and leaned out. There was a soft rainy breeze and rushes of damp sunny air rustled the blossoms in the park beneath her. It was spring. It was a long time since she had noticed the seasons much. You noticed Christmas because it was the height of party time and parties were good for business. She'd noticed recently that the parties themselves didn't seen to be important. The important bit was meeting in the pub beforehand. There was a clutch of pubs in the narrow streets around Grafton Street. They were all very much the same. Comfortable, expensive and crowded. Full of loud voices and business deals.

It started to rain with gentle determination so Anne shut the window and went to see if there was any post. There was. She opened her letter with shaking fingers. She'd been accepted as English and History teacher in a small Protestant school.

She remembered the interview. "Why do you want this job, Miss Connell? I always ask, you know. I find it interesting to find out what you young girls are looking for in a place like this. It's a small school, you know, and when a teacher is ill we expect the others to rally around. Rather grueling sometimes. And you must know there's nothing glamorous about teaching." This with a look at Anne's leather embroidered coat.

"Oh I like teaching, and a small school, well, you can get to know the pupils better." Better than the jostling drinking crowds. A small school is a safe place. There's nothing as certain as quiet rows of desks, and the dusty smell of chalk.

Anne was writing the third copy of her letter of acceptance when Jonathan came home "to grab a sandwich."

"Still feel awful?"

"No, not now." It was true. She felt dazed and weak but better than she had felt for a long time.

"I've been accepted. I've got the job. I'm to start in September. Isn't it marvelous?"

She rarely had anything exciting to tell him, while his life was a continual explosion of events. Her excitement had made her careless.

"But what about the dating thing? I though you were going to help. You said you would. You know it starts in September."

Well, she *had* said she would help. She hadn't really thought she would be accepted and her life with Jonathan had seemed more real than the years at college — the scraped degree that she had managed to cling on long enough to achieve. The teaching diploma had been undertaken in the same spirit that some women do charity work. Just to pass the time when Jonathan was too busy to see much of her. To give her something to do when he was out on a deal. But somehow the quiet, necessary hours in the classroom and the soothing respect of the polite little Protestant girls had lured her into taking herself almost seriously at last.

"I know I said I'd help. But you don't really need me. You can get someone else."

That, though, made her hesitate. He *would* get someone else. Probably another girl and what would happen then. But after all, they'd been together now for five years. Surely their relationship would survive.

"But that's not the point, is it?" He took off his jacket and sat down on a green velvet wing chair. "The point is that you said you'd do it. You *committed* yourself to it."

"Oh Jonathan, really. You can't *commit* yourself to a computer dating business."

He was offended. "I don't see why not. It's a job. It provides a service for lonely people. It allows them to meet each other without embarrassment. You don't have to be snobbish about it."

One of the qualities Anne had always admired in Jonathan was his capacity for believing his own propaganda. If his ideas had been less ephemeral he might have been a rich man by now. As it was, he never lost money and usually made quite a bit.

"I'm not being snobbish. But you can find someone else." Again that stirring of fear. "And I'm really just hanging on the outside of your life. They're your ideas, your money, your friends you deal with. I want something of my own."

His light eyes flickered over her face.

"Look, I've always said you should have something of your own. God, I paid for your teaching course. I've seen you sitting there in the pub yawning and wishing it was closing time. That's not the point. You'll never be able to do anything properly until you learn to stop messing about. You committed yourself to one job. You've got to do it. Meet your first commitments first."

So that was it. The work ethic. Prior commitments first. Do a job well, however worthless the job.

"I can't. I've got to take this job. I'll help in the evenings."

"I'm warning you, Anne. If you let me down over this, then we're finished. Right now."

"Oh don't be silly."

She looked at him. He was leaning forward in his chair. His dark hair had just been cut but it still curled over his ears. His fingers gripped each other. He wasn't being silly. He meant it.

"You can't mean that. We've been together for five years."

"Oh I mean it all right. Look"— making it easier for her—"I need you for this. I can't pay someone. It would make the whole thing astronomical to set up. I need someone who'll work long hours for half nothing and who knows me and the way I work. You'll get money in the end of course. I've even been thinking of offering you a limited partnership."

She looked at him with suspicion. She knew that he could pay someone, easily, with the money he spent on her alone in a casual evening in a pub. He'd never offered her partnership, limited or otherwise, before. He knew how she'd longed to marry him. He'd joked about it. "Longing for domesticity in a semi, are you?" Now that she came to think of it, most of his friends' wives did live in far-flung semis. They never came to the pubs. They stayed at home, night after night, with their children, and waited for their wheeling, dealing husbands.

"Perhaps I wouldn't have liked to marry you after all."

"I told you you wouldn't." He leant back in his chair and stretched. "I can be right you know."

"You're not right about my job, you're right for you but not for me. I've got to do it."

He stood up and crossed to the cocktail cabinet, the one piece of modern furniture in the room.

"Well, you know where I stand." He didn't bother to plead with her any more. He was quite sure she'd give in. As Anne realized this, recognized this, she was almost sure that she *would* give in. She always had. Over marriage. Over the nights in the pubs. She'd learned to arrange herself like a chair for him to sit in. She began to wonder if he wasn't getting just a bit too heavy.

"Can I have a drink?"

"Sure."

As he poured it she looked down at her crumpled letter of acceptance. She'd squeezed it in her hand when he'd reminded her about the computer dating. Computer dating, indeed. It was terrifying really. How she'd almost believed in it, seen it as he saw it. Providing a service. A service for lonely people. He hadn't even cared when she'd woken in the night with a bad dream. She'd often woken him in her panic. "Ah, go back to sleep. It's only a bad dream." She had one particular very bad dream. It recurred. She dreamt she was about to be executed and that she was begging him not to let them do it. She knew, in the dream, that he could stop them. He'd take her arm and lead her to the sharp shining instrument that was going to remove her head. He'd put his arm around her to comfort her as he drew her nearer and nearer her doom. "It must happen," he'd say. "It's got to be done. The machine must be used today." Oh it was a ridiculous dream but it always left her drained and depressed the next day. As if there was something hideous that she'd forgotten about and would shortly remember. She'd never been able to tell him what the dream was. It was so ridiculous. But don't lonely people dream? How can you provide a service for them if you don't understand their dreams?

"Will you really finish it, Jonathan, if I take the job?"

He handed her a drink and lit himself a cheroot.

"Yes, I mean it."

"I've never let you down before." She sipped her drink. She felt numb, but pleasantly so.

"Every time you yawned in the pub you let me down. Every time you implied that my work had no value. Oh you let me down all right. You and your secret superiority. You *were* superior. You sneered at me and my job. I often thought you envied me. You'd never have the nerve to make money. You'd need to know that you had a degree in something and a certificate of moral worth from your intellectual friends before you'd even *earn* money."

"All right. I'm going to take the job." She waited. She already knew the answer.

"Take it then and get out." He ran into the bedroom and came back carrying her suitcase. "Here you are. Fill it yourself. Go on, pack. Just get out of here now." A fine hail of saliva misted the air. "You've let me down. You're getting out of here."

One of his oldest friends had once got a contract for supplying Georgian furniture to a hotel. It was a contract Jonathan had coveted. She'd come back from her lectures and found him lying, face downwards, on their bed.

"Jonathan, Jonathan what's wrong?" she'd asked. He'd looked up. His face was red. It shone and at first she thought he'd been crying.

"What's wrong?"

"That fucking bastard," he shouted, "he's taken my contract." He'd put his head back on the pillow and groaned.

He couldn't bear to lose.

The Sentimentalist

MAEVE KELLY

The Americans say that eccentricity is the norm in Ireland. I wish they were right. What after all is normality? Can it simply be equated with dullness? I ask the question because the only people I find interesting are those whom the dull people of my acquaintance call odd. And I am certain that behind my back I am called odd, with accompanying shakings of the head, which frequent shakings may account for the displacement of the few brains my charitable analysts possess. It does not worry me at all. But then I am not a lover of people. I find children irritating, the old irritable and the middle aged merely opinionated. And the young are so incredibly gauche. It pains me to have to acknowledge their familiarity. I do not care for animals, except for cows, who combine supreme usefulness with a rustic kind of beauty. I do not consider myself a misanthropist, but on the whole I find women silly and demanding, and men stupid and aggressive. Most people are dishonest. Worse, their dishonesty is contagious so that even I am occasionally infected and I find myself accepting their outrageous statements out of a false sense of good manners. Besides, it is wearying to be in disagreement all the time, and I confess I am a little lazy, which is why I live by myself in this three-roomed cottage in the middle of Martin Leahy's farm. I rent the house very cheaply because it has none of the inconveniences of so-called civilized living.

MAEVE KELLY (b. 1930) has published short fiction, a novel, and poetry. Her story collection, *A Life of Her Own,* was issued by Poolbeg in 1976; and her novel, *Necessary Treasons,* by Michael Joseph in 1985. A volume of poetry is soon to be released by Blackstaff. Ms. Kelly was born in Dundalk. She resides now near Limerick City. She received a Hennessy in 1972.

Its chief attraction for me is the lack of a roadway to my door and whenever my relations or acquaintances feel obliged to visit me they must do so on foot, along a muddy track of about three miles. I have an old ship's spyglass in my sittingroom and I occasionally scan the horizon to make sure I am not caught unawares. I cannot understand my relatives' need to visit me. I am sure they do not enjoy it, but they seem to take it on themselves as a painful duty and I am too considerate to deprive them of their sense of responsibility.

One visitor I welcomed was my cousin Liza. We knew each other since we were young girls. Her father and mother committed suicide in a romantic pact in 1915. They were pacifists, living in England, and refused, they said, to be embroiled in the folly of war. So they left their only child to the care of my parents, who, I think, fulfilled their obligation admirably. They gave her, and us, as much affection as was necessary for our survival. Very quickly Liza became one of the family. We loved her English accent and tried our best to copy her, with laughable results. Even more laughable were her attempts at acquiring Gaelic, which we were then just beginning to learn. It was quite beyond me. I have no flair for languages. Since English has been imposed on us, for historical reasons, I accept it and consider it adequate for my needs, a vehicle for communicating thought. I concede that I may have lost something, subtleties of expression more in keeping with my cultural background, not to mention the heritage of tradition which is difficult to translate adequately. However, I have always been a pragmatist and I accept the reality of conquest. The new nationalist fervor associated with the revival of the language was boring to me. I despise passion, wasted emotions. But not so Liza. Typical of the convert, she threw herself totally into the Gaelic revival. She joined the Gaelic League, attended the Abbey plays and became a member of *Cumann na mBan*. I could not approve. It has always seemed to me that organized groups, military or civilian or religious, are death to the individual and therefore retard human development. It can be argued that for the apathetic mass such groups are necessary, but I believe that one strong-minded individual can achieve more on her own if she is prepared to sacrifice her life for her cause. I do not mean by that the futile sacrifice of death, which simply perpetuates myths and has no logical value. Martyrdom is the ultimate folly, the self-indulgence of the sentimental. I mean that one person, standing alone, against the convention of her times, must, if she applies herself, learn wisdom, fortitude and knowledge, and provide the vital link between the generations which must lead to the ennoblement of all womankind. I use the term loosely to include men.

Liza was impulsive and sentimental in that charming way of the English. She scurried around the countryside in those early years waving flags and crying slogans. It saddened me to see her in her ridiculous uniform, allowing the uniformly foolish ideas of her group to take over. I do not deny that the history of this country has been a tragic one, but the worst tragedy of all has been the number and variety of its saviors—most of them with foreign or English blood—which it has attracted. Liza saw herself as one of those saviors.

In the course of her missionary work she married a young man from Waterford, a timid ordinary fellow whom she tried to indoctrinate. It was useless. She wept over his "dreadful tolerance" as she called it. He admitted the savagery of men, the injustices his countrymen had suffered, but he constantly saw the other side, and constantly made allowances. "I love him for it," she told me. "He is so gentle and kind, he can see no evil in anyone. I hate him for it too. He will not fight for anything. I know *you* won't fight, but somehow that is different. And father and mother were different too. They were committed and so are you. He is not committed to anything. He loves everyone." It was shocking that he died, shot down at their front door by the Black and Tans, before her eyes, probably because of her reputation as a nationalist. To me, it had a poetic justice, but I did not tell her what I thought.

I hoped the futility of his death could cure her. But no. She kept his hat and coat on the hall stand, left the bullet holes in the door and walls and the blood-stained rug where he fell, and carried on. But she was not political, not ambitious, not scheming, and she was not a man. So there was no place for her among the new policy makers born out of his blood and others like him. "I cannot give up my dream now," she said. "Poor Willie died for it. My house, his house, will be a memorial to him. It will be the glory of Ireland." Her grief and her innocence moved me. Against my better judgement I helped her to organize the house for students. It became the only summer school of its kind, open from April until September for young people from all over the world and from all over Ireland who came to imbibe

the old Gaelic culture and learn the language. For fifty years she kept
the school going. For fifty years she took only Irish produced food
and wore only Irish made clothes. She allowed herself tea and coffee,
confessing it a weakness, but grew her own vegetables and fruit. She
refused on principle to eat oranges or bananas because, she said, they
were the product of slave labor. She was always available for picket
duty, ban the bomb, anti-apartheid, women's rights. When the farmers were imprisoned after their marches she picketed the jail and was
booed by the town population. A city woman herself, she believed in
the nobility of working the land and declared the farmers were the
guardians of the country's traditions. Dedication of that sort is truly
admirable, and how rarely one finds it. But oh, the folly of it all. The
folly of living one's life for a useless dream.

Liza's house was in the center of a spreading suburb. All around
her walled gardens, hundreds of semi-detached homes sprouted the
inevitable television aerials. The view of the river which she used to
enjoy from her bedroom window became swallowed up in the new
hollow block landscape. When at the age of seventy she closed her
school, she was unprotected during the vulnerable months of fruiting
and had to fight to keep her apples growing. Hordes of boys challenged each other to climb her walls and rob her orchard, encouraged
to do so perhaps by the silliest of all aphorisms "Boys will be boys."
The bravery of these young fellows is typical of the spirit of our time.
One old lady became a formidable enemy to be challenged and de-
feated. To the socialists she was a property owner, a *fíor gael* crank to
the Language Freedom Movement, a rock in the path of progress to
the speculators who viewed her two acres with hungry eyes. Worst
of all, she was an embarrassing reminder to the few old nationalist
members of the government.

I visited her last autumn when the paths were slippy with the rotting leaves of her chestnut trees and the stone house seemed to fade
into the gray day. While we sat by the fire over tea I asked her would
she not think of settling in the Gaeltacht now that her work in the
school was over. "I am Gall to them," she said. Vinegary was not an
adjective I would have applied to Liza and I suppose I looked be-
wildered. "I mean Gall as opposed to Gael," she sighed. "Foreigner."

"Well, I suppose you are," I agreed.

"Not because I am half English," she said a little tartly. "*You* might be even more foreign to them."

I had to admit that I felt foreign whenever I visited such places. "Don't you think they are a little chauvinist in their separatism lately?" I asked.

"You don't understand," she said. "I don't mean to be harsh, but really Jo, have you ever felt deeply about anything? Have you no values at all? Don't you care what has happened to this country, or what is happening? What do you do with your life?"

"I think," I said. "What else is there to do?"

"You sit in that hut, reading and thinking. Is that a way to spend a life?"

"It's the only way for me," I said.

"But such a waste," she cried. "Don't you feel you have wasted your life?"

It seemed a strange thing for her to say.

But although she is only six months younger than I, she always seems much younger and I tend to indulge her. I did not tell her about my book, my life's work, which will, I hope, put all those foreign male philosophers to shame. It is time we had an Irish philosopher who does not come out of Maynooth tarred with the Roman brush, and it is past time we had a woman philosopher. But I could not discuss that with Liza. I am too old now to start exchanging confidences. It makes my life somewhat lonely, especially at my age, but I recognize that as being part of the price I must pay for my independence. Liza always said I was a cynic, but that was because she was a sentimentalist and only saw her own truth.

Last spring she visited me and accused me of deliberately torturing her by living in my isolated kingdom. "It is cruel to expect me to walk that distance to see you. Some day I will not come, and I suppose you will not care."

"But you know it is my only defense," I protested. "It's as good as a moat around a castle. Otherwise I would never have any peace. I am always glad to see you, Liza. But not too often. Not even you."

"Oh you hard heart," she sighed. "I don't know why I bother with you."

I could not reply. Silence on these occasions seems the best policy and is often more reproachful than words. And then she said, "Forgive me dear. What would I have done without you all these years? You so sensible, I with my foolish, foolish dreams. Such folly."

I was horrified. Here was a threat to my own integrity. If Liza became a cynic anything was possible. I might end my days guarding her orchard with her.

"Gaelic Ireland is dead," she announced, as if she just unveiled truth. "I and others like me prop up its corpse and pretend we are keeping it alive."

I was forced to lie. "Nonsense," I said. "You know you have lived your life in the fullest sense, believing in what you did. And you were right."

"My gods were all false," she said. "You knew it. I should have looked for political power. That's obvious to me now."

"Politics would have destroyed you," I said.

"I am destroyed anyway. They are going to knock down my house and build sixteen houses where I have kept my summer school."

"Be precise." I had to be stern in order to hide my fear. "Whom do you mean by they?"

"The Corporation has compulsorily acquired my house. They are right of course. I am taking up far too much space. I am old. There are young people with children waiting for houses. Think of all the children who could grow up in my two acres."

What could I do but fight for her, poor sentimental Liza. I left my book unfinished and marched with her, up and down the path in front of the house, armed with placards of protest. Of course we made wonderful headlines. The cub reporters made their names with us. "Two indomitable eighty year olds fight for their home. A husband's young blood spilled here for Ireland. Is the Corporation the new oppressor?" I expected some salvos from the Socialist Magazine, but age, I suppose, still arouses pity, if not respect. Liza's old pupils rallied. She became the heroine of the day, the integrity of the past standing against the hollow men of the present. They flocked around her, middle aged and young, grandparents and parents. There were some emotional scenes in the garden last summer when after the success of our campaign, a hundred or so of her pupils came to cheer her. She stood in the center crying happily. "You dear people, you dear wonderful people."

I attended her funeral when she died a few weeks later. I owed her that much. It amused me to watch the performance, since it finally vindicated my life style. Everyone spoke in Irish. I suppose they praised her work, her dedication. When I passed her house yesterday I saw the demolition notice on the wall. Beside it was a brass memorial plaque with an inscription in Irish. Fortunately I could not understand it. I have never had a flair for languages.

The Shaking Trees

LUCILE REDMOND

It was a year for death, and the card of rebirth showed often in her Tarot. The old man on the corner said, shifting on his crutches, that "happiness comes early or never," but the swan who had her nest at the bend of the river would say "he who implores the butterfly to rest lightly on him has had commerce only with falcons."

She walked by the river every day, by the pine groves and down to where the tannery effluent poured its heavy mass into the glittering water. She avoided her own kind and they avoided her. Since Jimmy's death they seemed masks of skin on bone, and the time she spent talking to them was filled with silences. On a Thursday when the moon was rising she performed the conjuration of Vassago, but the images were unclear and the information phrased in symbols whose forms were distasteful to her. His deadness was unreal, and she was always surprised not to find him in the places where they had met. She had taken from his room some of his talismans; two car keys and an Ace of Spades, and occasionally she would take them out and look at them to see if they had changed, or perhaps if he had.

One day, as she sat by the swans' nest, reading the Book of the Dead to the cygnets, a boat came by. The man in the boat had features rounded into hardness.

— How deep is the water here? he asked.

LUCILE REDMOND (b. 1949) was born in Dublin and educated in England, Ireland, and the United States. She has been awarded the Hennessy–New Irish Writing and the Allied Irish Banks awards. Her collection, *Who breaks up the old moons to make new stars,* was published by the Egotist Press in 1978. Ms. Redmond lives now in Dublin.

It took a while for the question to reach her, and then some time while it bounced around the levels of her mind and came to rest as a thing of meaning. She considered it for some time, and then realized that it or its source required an answer.

—Shallow.

—You see I want to kill myself, the young man said with some satisfaction, but I can't find it deep enough.

The swan had returned with some reeds in her beak to patch the side of the nest, which had almost been swept away by the current, and she said indistinctly through them, When it is time to go, the path will show itself without questioning. The man in the boat paid no attention.

—The water by the tannery is deep and foul, whispered a rowan tree.

She pointed downstream, as the man loosed the branch he had been holding. The boat floated off with the current. She watched it go and returned to her reading.

It was soon after this, or perhaps it was not, but to her it seemed quite soon, that they cut down the pine forest. As she came near the river she could hear the sharp, dark buzzing of the saws, and as she came closer she heard the trees screaming. She walked through the cloud of sap and sawdust and on down to the town where the high walls of the slaughter house reeked with fear. In the clear water of the river the reds and browns and greens made steamy patterns. There were some boats with men dragging the bottom.

A week later the forest was gone and the hill was bleak with bleeding stumps. The cygnets were swimming now, and the cob had returned. She took out the talismans and found that a key was gone.

She had not eaten since the day Jimmy died, but at first drank sips of water whenever she began to tremble. Now she trembled all the time. The old man spoke of circles and haloes and she listened with the outside of her mind, not from politeness, but because he spoke in patterns. When she walked she performed as necessary the rituals of three and the laying of the patterns on the path, and spoke courteously to the older trees, because this was the custom. She began to feel cold even when the fish were basking at the surface of the water, and the small birds would perch near her to sing. Her skin felt transparent and fragile and she walked slowly, with care.

An aunt of Jimmy's came by one day and screamed at her.

—You killed him. You and these filthy things. She flung a handful of multicolored tablets to the floor. The colors mingled and fused, flowing through each other, moving and changing. The woman was shaking her, and the sounds of her screams of rage and pain mixed and swirled like the colors on the floor. After a while she left, the tablets remaining as an offering.

She stooped and played with them, rolling them at each other like little skulls, running them through her fingers like pieces of eight, then she put them in her pocket with the remaining car key and the Ace of Spades and walked slowly down to the river. It was later than she usually came and there were men fishing. The swans hissed in a mannerly way as she sat in the hollow beside their nest, and a man turned, warning, and shouted at her. He lives on death and must die to live, the pen remarked sadly. The line of the fisherman's rod sprang taut and he began to fight, drawing in the line and loosing it with harsh grinding sounds, letting the fish run and drawing it back until he dragged it in and netted it. It whipped and writhed in agony while he watched it, smiling, then he grabbed its body and smashed the head against a rock, and tossed it into a pile of corpses on the grass. She watched for an hour as the silver of its scales dulled, then as the reflections of sunset filled the air with a red mist, she walked to the tannery, pausing often to breathe.

She discovered the aspens because she needed trees. She sat and trembled in the middle of the grove and did not feel she had to talk or listen. It was the first time in a long while that she had relaxed. Once in a while one of the trees would make a remark, and some time later one of the others might answer, or merely sigh.

The swans were cool when she next came by their nest.

—All is one in nothing, but everything has its right place, said the cob, looking closely at her. She was startled into answering, "why?" and at the strange sound of her voice rose to run, but at the sudden movement merged into nothingness. When she woke she found the pen looking at her with a strange expression, mixing awe, sorrow, disgust, other emotions she could no longer name. The cygnets were milling curiously around, but the pen held her body between them and her. She stretched her arm into the water and felt its goodness flow through her. The Ace of Spades which she had been holding fluttered off down the surface of the stream.

The old man on the corner would not speak to her any more, and clumped into a doorway, humping along hastily on his crutches when she passed. He crossed himself, too, and called on images whose meanings were clouded, and almost transparent in her mind.

But the aspens were always there, and now the wind ruffled her as it did them. She liked to kneel on the scanty grass between them and hear the draughts humming quietly among them. Alone, she felt a longing for their company, and with them she was nourished and befriended.

When she went to the swans' nest only the cob was there, the pen and cygnets always seeming to be up the river or over the falls. He stretched his neck and tweaked gingerly at the tender green hairs that had begun to sprout on her arms.

She found that houses did not seem to like her, and would drop stones near when she walked, or change their shape so that she became lost and confused easily. She walked so slowly now that the dimensions of places seemed completely changed. She did not like to lose contact with the growing earth. After staying out all through one starry night she found it impossible to enter a house again and took to sleeping in the aspen grove or down by the river, or just lying and watching the moon glide through the clouds, the edge of the sky. She learned the phases and humors of the moon and understood slowly how they affected the moods of the different trees.

That month she noticed that her blood had lost its color and was a faint, opaque green. She had come to spend a lot of her time kneeling on the bare earth with her fingers threaded through the flesh of the clay.

The earth swirled slowly about her hands and the wind danced in her unfurling hair. The aspens laughed easily as the wind swayed their trembling bodies.

The swans' nest was empty. The season had changed. She did not know whether swans change their homes with the seasons. She asked the rowan tree, but it only whispered — below the falls the stream is fouled.

Walking by the wooden bridge she thought something, and stopped to consider what it was somewhere she knew. But she could only find after long searching, that something had happened, or used to happen by this place, but whether to her or to somebody or something she knew, she had no idea.

She was reluctant now to leave the green light of the grove. She knelt, her long fingers reaching down to the hidden streams, learning, always now talking sweetly with the stones and other sleeping things that lived below the grass roots. The moon played with her hair and it came to crinkle and stretch when it felt the first rays. She felt the subtle currents of warmth and moisture in the passing air, and she breathed her nourishment out for the animals that came to graze or nest among the still and trembling trees.

The season grew colder and the trees talked less often. Gradually a yawning silence spread through the grove. Sometimes small animals scuttled through the trees with amazing rapidity. Then it came that they moved so fast that they were like irritating buzzing. She wondered vaguely whether this was a seasonal change. She was too sleepy to bother reasoning it out. Her leaves began to itch at about the same time as the wind became gusty and blew them off in molting tufts. She cradled the nests in her branchforks and hunched against the cutting gale. The snow blew to bank around her shivering trunk. She became warm and dozy. The aspens slept for the winter.

The Quibbler

UNA WOODS

"Like flogging a dead horse," he said.

"Sure I know. You've said it."

It didn't mean anything. It probably did to them but not to Malcolm. Nothing meant anything to Malcolm except that Sheila had not turned up and he was running short of money and drink. And his mother would be scurrying around getting the parlor ready, pretending to be uninterested, her glazed eyes staring across at the red brick opposite when they arrived. Not uttering a syllable, begrudging them the space in the doorway to get in. But you'd know by the cushions, their corners up. He never put the corners up. But that's the way they would find it, he and Sheila, and the fire set. Occasionally she would scuffle up the hall and sit opposite them, bolt upright on a straight chair, her hard eyes piercing the window. Never communicating, but talking, to no-one. "Them lads an' their ball. I'll soon tell thim. Hit this door it did las' night. An' the cheek o' thim, not an ounce o' respect. Git roun' te yer own street, I told thim, but sher ye may's well not waste yer breath."

He doubted if she would recognize Sheila on the street. Certainly he'd never seen her as much as glance at her. She would sit there until he told her to go back into the kitchen or out to the door again. She needed to be told. The thought irritated him.

Then Sheila's freshness and youth moved in him. Sheila had power.

UNA WOODS is a Belfast writer and an accomplished singer of traditional songs. Though she left Belfast for Hertfordshire, London, and Dublin, she has recently returned home. Her first collection—a novella and four stories entitled *The Dark Hole Days*—was published by Blackstaff in 1984.

The power to decide not to come, by the look of it, and he'd had four pints, four fat, black pints. Sheila wouldn't like it, not if she arrived now and saw his eyes. They looked perfectly normal to him in the toilet mirror a minute ago but as soon as she looked at him Sheila would say, "You've had a fair bit" and look away as though it disgusted her. They might spend the rest of the evening quarreling over the meaning of "a fair bit."

"The Quibbler," Sheila called him and said it was his hobby. But in a sense she had stunted it by perfecting the art of walking away. Leaving him, his words pouring like an over-topped pint onto the table. She took it so far, she liked to triumph, control the argument, but it didn't take her long to realize that you can never win with a quibbler. The first day she'd walked away was shattering. It was in the middle of a sentence in the middle of a public house. She threw the chair back in furious frustration and when he saw her swish through the door his mouth was still hanging open. He could remember the very sentence till this day. Had he managed to finish it this is how it would have gone: "What do you mean I never have any money? It's all relative. In terms of whom have I no money? The third world? [Exit] The down-and-outs in Castle Street? Or are you comparing me with Kevin Murphy?" He still regretted that she hadn't stayed to hear that last bit. In a detached way it could appear to be a reasonable enough retort. But the point was he knew what she meant and what she had said was valid, and instead of answering her in the terms in which she had introduced her point, the argument had raged in vicious circles for nearly half an hour.

Of course this was only one aspect of their relationship.

It was incredible that she bothered with him at all. The day he'd run down Camden Street, his big boots with their metal heel-tips echoing across the terraced street and back, finally catching up with her on the Lisburn Road, do you think he'd imagined she would answer in the affirmative to his request for a date? She said no, she was baby-sitting. She was craning her neck, not looking at him, watching for her bus. He was persistent. When he had caught sight of her walking down the street he knew nothing could stop him running like an idiot after her. Now at the bus stop she stood casual, unperturbed. Uninterested, with a hint of disdain.

"What about Tuesday night?"

"Oh, here's the bus."

"Look, can I go up with you?"

"What for?"

He didn't know what for. He did know what for. To be with her.

She glanced into her blue file. Was there something in there? A list? Names? She closed it. The bus had stopped and people were getting off. She stepped on, it was so carefree the way she stepped on. Then, and why still baffled him, she turned and said,

"Maybe Wednesday night."

That was a long time ago. Almost a year. It was a moment he would remember for the rest of his life. It was still the same, the element of suspense and then at the last minute she would give the word. Another date. But where was she now?

He looked around the bar with an expression of superior inferiority on his face. It was a result of the anomalies in his position. He had stepped outside his background when he had entered university. No, long before that. The lads around the East had howled and clutched at themselves hysterically every time he had mentioned the fact that he intended studying that night. Yet he had gone along to the dances with them and taken girls down the entries too. Usually scrubbers.

His mother had only the vaguest idea of what a university was. She knew it was something important because occasionally when he got home she was in a state of agitated excitement and would point at the television. "It was on the news," she would say. "I seen it. The university." "What was it about?" he might ask casually, but this had the effect of sending her into a mood of sullen confusion. "How would I know?" she would mutter, going into the scullery to get his dinner. "Some man talkin' about somethin'." She had, after a time, latched onto the term "economics," and would often repeat it to the neighbors, who had no more idea than she what it meant, but were all the more impressed by the mystery surrounding it.

A strange woman. They were never close, yet she did everything for him, running round for fresh bread and the paper before he was up. Bringing him his breakfast in bed every morning, and if he had a late lecture he slept on and it sat there and got cold. But you couldn't tell her not to bring it. You couldn't tell her anything. She never listened, just did, did, all the time. Relentlessly following her own pattern. Running here and there, carrying loads, poking in cubby holes for money that his father had hidden. Rather than ask for it.

He lived his life in the parlor, where he kept a collection of records which he played on his makeshift turntable. Here he studied as well, only going into the kitchen for meals, talking to no-one because there was no-one to talk to. When his father came in, usually under the influence, he would crack jokes which only he, himself, understood, and ate the meal set down before him. There were never harsh words, nor ill feeling because each one identified solely with him or herself. Except that Malcolm had grown increasingly aware, and the knowledge annoyed him, that his mother was a slave, and that in her non-communicative way, she idolized him.

He clinked some change in his pocket, then drew it out and examined the coins. Another half pint and that's it. She'd let him down this time. No more of her suburban brightness lifting the dreary street parlor, bringing a fresh atmosphere to the tired Dylan lyrics. Was it last night, Christ that was probably it, he had overdone it for certain.

He brought his half pint down to the table. What was it? There were a few of them in the Students' Union having a drink, and the usual so-called intellectual discussion developed. What it was about was irrelevant but the word he'd got caught up in was "normal." Yes, what was normal. Somebody had said something about "most normal people." And he'd wanted clarification on the use of the word "normal." That was it. "You know what he means," Sheila had said quietly to him, trying to nip it in the bud, but no, he was adamant. "I object to the use of this term 'normal people.' What is a normal person?" Someone tolerantly gave a definition — "You know, ordinary, the usual." "Ordinary? The usual?" he stormed. "Who is to judge what is ordinary?" Then Sheila, losing her cool, snapped, "You certainly aren't. Neither ordinary, nor normal." "Are you?" he'd retorted. "Most people would say I am," she said, but almost immediately realized she'd fallen in. "Is what most people say necessarily right?" he turned on her. At this point Sheila rose, lifted her bag; "What is right?" she said into his face. The others laughed. "See you downstairs," she said back. "That's if you and I agree on the meaning of the word 'downstairs.'" That was very smart of her, he thought now. He was remorseful when he met her at the door. But the night had been ruined. Sheila said that the discussion had been interesting but as usual he was only looking for an argument. He turned every discussion into an argument for the sake of arguing. He wasn't interested in airing points to find answers, or even in simply delving into topics with other people to establish your own viewpoint above theirs. No, it was a case of pick on a word, any word, and refuse to let people get past it. It was hopeless.

He agreed. He would really try the next time. She was to tell him when to stop. He would obey her. He would do anything for her.

The pub was filling up. It would soon be bunged, bodies everywhere, standing all around the bar and someone would ask for the chair beside him—"Is anyone using this chair?" "It depends on what you mean by using. I mean you can see that no-one is actually sitting on it." No, still, he wouldn't. He wouldn't say that at all. He would simply say "No," and the chair would be removed. He probably would not be here that long, in any case. He fidgeted with his half empty glass. Or was it half full? Whatever it was now, he would leave when it was empty. He could wander up to the Union, sure to be somebody around, or maybe just head for home, across the wet streets to the East. His mother would be standing at the door. She wouldn't ask any questions but she would look at the space beside him and know he was alone. He had done it this time, no doubt about that. How could a girl like Sheila put up with him? Why would she waste her time? She was probably laughing with her brothers up there in suburbia. Joking in the sitting room of her semidetached house, in the armchair with her cup of tea, and the rhododendron bush gently blowing and glistening in the rain outside the window. She might be listening to one of her Beethoven LPs, her shoes off, feet tucked up, and wait a minute, who was that in the chair opposite her?

He sank the last mouthful, flung back his chair—"Have them both" he snarled to an innocent bystander, and stormed out.

He hadn't even the bus fare left but who needed a bus when the motive was so strong? It was only four miles and the rain was soft, almost pleasant. Hands in his jacket pockets, with youth and determination backing him, he stamped the miles behind. Impervious to the elements, the passers-by, anything except his imagination, he crossed street after street and about halfway he was startled by a shout in his ear. "Hey, Maguire, what are you up to?" He didn't turn, but the owner of the voice was now walking beside him.

"You're in a bit of a hurry."

"I am."

"Hang on. Are ye goin' te yer girl up the road?"

"I might."

Macdonald had probably nothing better to do, never had, and seemed intent on accompanying him. His big splayed feet sprinkled wet to either side.

"How's the studyin' goin'?" he said and laughed up into the drizzle.

"It's going fine, just fine," Malcolm said, intensely irritated and quickening his step in the hope of shaking off the idiotic Macdonald. but Macdonald had long legs.

"Y'a a doctor yet?" he persisted.

"I am not going to be a doctor," Malcolm said. Then he stopped and looked up at Macdonald's hanging jaw. "Look, do you mind," he said, "I'm in a hurry. We can discuss my career at a later date. I'll call down some night. Okay?"

Macdonald looked downcast, but then Macdonald always looked downcast. He turned his collar up. "It's rainin'," he said, holding out his hand as though to catch some and prove it.

"Your acumen in matters meteorological leaves me stunned," Malcolm said, sighing sarcastically. "Goodnight."

He didn't look back but he sensed that Macdonald stood uncertain for some time before making his way down the road again.

Malcolm felt his nostrils reacting in an unhealthy manner as he steamed past the cemetery. The dead, unaware of the urgency of his mission, slept on. No skeleton rattled on the other side of the wall but a drunk across the road sang mournful songs as he battled with the laws of gravity and completed the double trick of drinking from a bottle while he sang. He lifted his leg high in an effort to cross the road when he spotted Malcolm. Probably with the intention of imparting some vital information, for he had his hand in the air, waving in a gesture of importance. But Malcolm hurried on, in no mood to be delayed. He pulled a crumpled handkerchief from his trouser pocket and wiped the whole of his face.

At the bottom of her street he slowed his pace and thought, "What am I doing?" The light was on in the front room and he had a crazy fear that her father would open the door and flatten him. Jesus, it must be around midnight now but the increasing sobriety he had felt

during his walk in the rain was now being overtaken by an intoxica-
tion of frustration, annoyance, nervousness and other feelings too complex to disentangle in his blurred brain.

He had his head down as he stood waiting at the door. A pathetic, soaked figure, breathing heavily through widening and narrow-
ing nostrils.

It was her.

"My God, Malcolm, what's wrong? What are you doing here?"

"Both — questions — warranting — the same — reply." He needed a
breath between each word.

"What is wrong — is that you did not turn up — to meet me. That
is — also what I am doing here."

"Meet you?" She had on little turquoise slippers. He had never
seen those before but then he rarely got his foot past the doorstep,
did he? "Why should I be treated like that?" he thought. "Have I not
earned my place in the world? Anybody's world? Am I not a university student?"

"Can I come in? I am rather wet." He shook his jacket and drips
fell onto the step.

"Come in," she said. He passed her, into the warmly-lit hall. The
kitchen door was open and he could see one of her brothers fidgeting
at the fridge. He had a flash of his mother sticking meat and things
into that old cupboard under the sink. "Keeps thim fresh," she would
say with pride.

"Hi," the brother said out.

"Hi," Malcolm scowled.

She opened the sitting room door. "Nobody in here," she said.
She closed the door after them. "Give me that jacket and I'll put it
at the fire."

He removed his jacket and handed it to her. She placed it over
a fire guard. Then she looked at him and said, "You've had a fair bit."

He sat in an armchair. "The bit that I've had was not fair at all,"
he said. He was smoothing back his wet hair. "The reason it was not
fair is that you were not there."

She sat on the arm of another armchair. Only on the arm, he
thought, because she wants me to go. She looked so lovely, nothing
would ever go wrong for her. Nothing would.

"Do you want to know why I was not there?" she said and an amused smile gently shaped her lips. Just gently. Her turquoise feet were crossed. He wanted to eat the slippers.

"I do," he said.

"I was not there because I was not supposed to be there. Not until tomorrow night."

He was suspicious. She was laughing.

"Wednesday night we said," he said firmly.

"This is Tuesday." She was laughing blatantly now and in danger of losing control.

"It can't be," he said weakly. "Yesterday was Tuesday."

"Monday." She sank into the chair.

"Sshh," he said leaning over. "You'll have them in. Look—" he attempted to clear his brain but now it could be Saturday for all he knew.

"Brian," she called.

"What are you doing?" Malcolm straightened himself in the chair. "Look, what are you doing?"

Brian, a tall schoolboy, stood looking in at them.

"What?" he said.

"Brian, what day is this?"

Brian looked bemused but answered unhesitatingly. "Tuesday."

"Thank you, Brian," she said. Brian shut the door.

Malcolm was overcome with embarrassment. The insult of it. He got up.

"I'm going," he said.

Sheila rose and came over. Protectively she said, "Sit down and get dried and I'll get a cup of tea." It was a tone he couldn't resist. It might have been "Come to bed." If only it was. When she was out of the room he looked into the fire and then took out his comb and combed his hair. He spat into the fire and said "Silly wee bastard" at the thought of Brian standing there in the doorway in his supercilious pose. "Tuesday." Tuesday indeed. If he'd even thought of saying something to him like, "Who taught you the days of the week? Was that this week's lesson in school?" What's the point, he would probably have had a smart answer ready.

The toast had heavy, melted, yellow cheese on it. It drooped in your hand when you lifted it. He didn't feel like eating but it was part of something she was offering him. He hoped it wasn't sympathy pure and simple, and his position at the moment was confused; sitting here on a night that had not been allocated to him, he was an intruder. There was an uneasiness in her manner. She left the room frequently — some unfinished business with the family, he supposed. Yet she was effusive in a way towards him. "Enough toast? More tea? And you sat there all night on your own. I can't believe it."

"Jesus, it's incredible," he kept repeating, shaking his head.

"And you walked all the way."

"All the way."

And all the way back. He was in no mood to scrounge for the taxi fare and the last thing he wanted was to go at all. The whole thing was ludicrous, farcical. There'd have to be a better arrangement than this.

He moved over onto the couch.

"Come over here," he said.

She got up but instead of going over to him she lifted the cup he had left on the hearth.

"You haven't finished your tea," she said.

"Damn the tea. Come over here."

Uneasily she sat on the edge of the couch beside him.

"You can be very gruff," she said, not looking at him, but staring at her knees.

"Gruff, now how was I gruff?" he demanded.

"Your tone of voice."

"My tone of voice? What about the night I've just spent? Waiting for you."

"That was your mistake."

"Oh, my mistake. My mistake. So you were not involved?"

"Stop it." Sheila got up. "I'll see if I can scrape together your fare home."

He relented and, getting up, held her back before she had reached the door.

"No, look, I'm sorry, sit down, just for a minute. I'm going in a minute."

She sighed and sat down.

"What's wrong with you?" he asked her. He was trying to look into her eyes. But it was difficult. She was pouting and determined to watch the dying embers and she was in bad form. He'd put her in bad form, cast a shadow over the carefree night she'd been having at home — her natural environment.

"Why don't you tell me to piss off," he said, glumly joining her in watching the flickering ashes. "Why don't you, for once and for all?"

"Sshh, keep your voice down," she said. Then she turned and her expression had lightened, for this was a mood with which she could deal. She kissed his mouth. "I'll see you for lunch in the snack bar tomorrow. And tomorrow night we'll go out." She was sorting it out. She was irresistible. She would never tell him to piss off. She would have him hovering but, when at his most fragile, would welcome him back.

"I need you," he said, holding her close to his chest.

She rested there for a moment, then looked at him, tipped his nose and shook her head. But she was smiling, treating him like a schoolboy who had erred but who was eminently lovable. When she left the room, just as she was closing the door she gave him a delightful wink and he sat there feeling like a favorite teddy bear until she returned.

She was holding a fistful of change.

"Here," she said, "I scraped around. Didn't want to make it obvious." He took it and put it in his pocket. He would have to get a grip on his situation. Stretch out his grant so that it lasted more than two weeks. But Sheila was a student too. She understood. Sheila understood him.

"Madam, it would give me boundless pleasure if tomorrow night culminated in a visit to our house," he said to her at the door.

"Go home," she laughed and teasingly pushed him off the step. He waved and trundled off down the street. Brian came to the door in time to see him disappear around the corner.

"What a walk," he said. "Is he going to lurch the whole way home?"

"Mind your own business," Sheila said and shut the door.

As the taxi drove down the road he saw the dripping Macdonald standing at a corner engrossed in conversation, if one could describe it as such, with two old men. What a bloody lout, Malcolm thought. He was worlds away from Macdonald, from them all, and as soon as he got his degree he would be leaving the city forever. It was bearable only because it was no longer a chain. He was tasting the wider world, at university, and with Sheila, on the outward route, and these dank streets were prickles of his past. A few couples waited gloomily for taxis in Shaftesbury Square. He regarded the straggly queue. They weren't like him and Sheila. They were going and coming on a small, depressed scale. They were riveted to their roots. You'd know to look at them.

"This'll do," Malcolm said just over the bridge.

"Right son." You were always "son" in Belfast and girls were "daughters." They wouldn't even grant you your right to have grown up.

A girl in very high heels and a tight coat approached him. Her hair, swept up into a bun, was fair and wet. She glanced at him as he passed. Something made him turn and look after her and when he did so he found that she was looking back at him. She stopped. "Got a light?" she said, tentatively.

"Yes," he said, "I have." He took his lighter from his pocket and she came back and bent over to receive the flame. He shielded it from the rain with his hand, at the same time examining her face. She was very young and her hand shook. He couldn't help being struck by her features, pretty and perfect, and by her nearness to him.

"It's late to be walking on your own," he said to her.

"Had to get out. Them." She directed a glance towards the Newtownards Road. "I can't stand it."

Anything she said might or might not be true. In fact it almost certainly would not be true, but the face and body before him were not fictitious. She made no move to go. Malcolm's brain churned out several thoughts, like that his parents would be well in their beds, and that his metabolism had been aroused to expect something this night. Not that that something would be the same thing, but there was a young girl before him. In any case the least he could do was offer her a bit of heat and a cup of tea. It would be a good deed — if nothing else.

"Look," he said, "I live round here. Would you like to come in out of the rain for a while?"

She stared at him out of wide eyes, but made no response.

"Come on," he said.

She tripped along beside him and as they entered the street the fluttering inside him was fighting with itself. He fumbled for his key and she pressed in beside him. It could have been boldness or a desire for protection. He didn't know.

"Do you live on your own?" she asked him. In the lamplight her face was pale and winsome.

"No. They'll be in bed." If they heard voices they would assume it was Sheila with him. They knew not to interfere. He came and went as he pleased. His mother might shout down occasionally, "That you, Malcolm?" "Yes," he would respond and she would shuffle back into bed. Maybe she never slept until he came in, maybe worried constantly about his well being. But what could he do about that?

He drew the blinds and put on the light. The fire was set but it was too late for that now. He plugged in the electric one, and took off his jacket, self-conscious now in the brightness. He'd been meaning to buy a lamp for the parlor, he'd talked it over with Sheila but they hadn't got around to it. The crude light hung from the center of the ceiling, defying any subtle approach to the young girl he had brought home.

She was sitting on the couch, damp tights clinging to her legs, her eyes perusing the room. He was afraid suddenly that she was a child, a baby who had run away from home, that he should take her to the police station. Yet she had obviously spent some time preparing — red shaped lips, black mascara, some of which had smudged in the rain, or had she been crying?

"Look, what age are you?" he asked her, trying to sound casual. He was bending over, choosing a record.

"You've a cheek," she answered. "But I'm nearly nineteen."

She could be, she couldn't, but bar asking her to produce her birth certificate . . . He chose Bob Dylan. As soon as the words poured out he regretted it — "Shut the light, shut the shade, you don't have to be afraid" — and yet it helped him, a mood rippled, encouraged him. There was no contradiction, no shame. Sheila sitting there and this girl. He turned to her, kneeling on the floor in front of her — "Kick your shoes off . . ." the song went.

Color was rising in her cheeks with the heat from the bars and then she had her shoes off, she was peeling down her tights, unveiling slowly her statuesque legs. He knelt back and watched. What else could he do. She threw her coat to the other side of the room. Her dress was skimpy. Before him she rose and, going over, turned off the light so that the room was only lit with the red glow from the electric fire.

"You're a student," she said. She was leaning against him from behind, fingering his hair.

"How did you know?" He found it difficult to talk with the constriction in his throat.

"Books," she answered. She was massaging his neck now.

"And you?"

"Me?" she said. "I'm just a little girl who has problems at home." On the floor she clung to him. She cried into his body and he caressed her and told her it was alright. There was nothing to cry for. He rejoiced in kissing the tears and Bob Dylan sang on . . . She was no baby. She was a little fox and he was the innocent one, the chicken. But it didn't matter for in the end they were sighing together.

He was lying on the couch. She had turned the record over and was sitting beside him, dressing.

"I'd better go," she said. "It'll be alright now. He'll be out cold by now and she'll have stopped her whinin'. They'll leave me alone till the next time. Thank you."

"Thank you? No, look, lie down for a while. Have a rest. You can't go up there on your own at this time. And in the rain and all. As soon as it's dawn I'll walk you up. Look, stay."

She stopped what she was doing and stroked his forehead. Her hair was all down around her shoulders and Malcom thought she looked like a dreamy angel.

She lay down beside him.

"Alright," she whispered. "We'll sleep for a while. Just a wee while."

There were things to be worked out in the morning but for the moment it was nice, so bloody comfortable.

Malcolm woke and raised his head. It was the parlor he was in and there was a peculiar smell, an unfamiliar mixture of perfume and . . . good God where was she? He was alone. What time was it? My watch, where did I leave my watch? Christ. He frantically fumbled around the couch, crawled across the floor. The watch Sheila bought me for Christmas—no, the bitch, she didn't, she wouldn't. The bitch, after me taking her in out of the rain.

The only relief walking through the town and up towards the university was the cool breath from the autumn breeze. It blew away something. There was the watch, two of his favorite LPs, including the one he'd played for her last night, his mother's old clock, about the only valuable thing she owned, how under God was he going to explain that. There was no way, he'd pretend he knew nothing about it, and possibly a couple of brass candlesticks. He couldn't swear about those. He blushed at his stupidity and the thought of his sleeping simple face as she made off with the loot.

And Sheila, oh, Sheila. It was your fault. No, it was my fault. No, it was the day's fault. It should have been Wednesday. Why was it not Wednesday?

The snack bar was normal. Chaotic, loud, gushing, intellectual, colorful, pseudo-everything, and normal.

"Sheila, I'm sorry. Sheila, will I get you something? Look, come on up with me Sheila."

The others looked at him. He didn't care who looked at him. He needed only Sheila to wash away his sins. They would go into the Botanic Gardens after and sit amongst the flowers. That's what they would do.

Sheila got up and gave her friends a knowing look. Up at the counter she said, "What's wrong, Malcolm? You're in a state. Did you get home alright last night? What's wrong with you?"

"Nothing, look nothing. Look, forget your two o'clock lecture, will you? We'll go out. We'll celebrate."

"I don't mind about the lecture. I hardly ever go anyway. But celebrate what?" She put a scone onto a plate and lifted another one for him.

"Tea?"

"Yes."

"Celebrate what?" she repeated.

"I don't know. Anything. Today, tomorrow. Anything."

"Okay," she said. "I don't mind."

Sheila sat on the grass and sucked a blade. She had her shoes off and she was relaxed. She had a healthy attitude towards lectures, towards the whole damn thing. He kissed her on the cheek several times. She didn't change her position. She was demure, not the demonstrative type in public, nor in private come to think of it. But she had her way. Sheila had her way.

"Look, Sheila, I scrounged a few bob, we'll go down to the Club after a while and have a drink." He needed a drink, but only if Sheila came too.

"Maybe so," she said.

Sheila don't commit yourself. Never commit yourself whatever you do.

"Sheila, do you know what it is to love somebody?"

Sheila turned sharply, reacting quickly to the inferred accusation.

"Love somebody? Of course I do."

"Then who do you love, Sheila. Tell me who you love."

"It depends on what you mean by love," Sheila said.

"You know what I mean by love. Everybody knows what it means."

"But each person may have a separate definition. Your idea of love may be different to mine."

"Sheila, do you know what you are doing? You're quibbling."

"Am I? Well isn't that a change."

"I love you." He was looking seriously into her face. Didn't he need reassurance, affection, after what he'd been through?

Sheila was fixing on her shoes. "Come on, we'll have that drink," she said. She got up and they walked together down the road.

"Let's have a discussion," Peter Robinson said as soon as Malcolm and Sheila walked into the lounge.

"Yes," Barry McCullough said. "Upon what academic topic should we ponder? What do you think, Maguire?"

"Give us a break," Malcolm said, selecting a table some way away. "What do you want Sheila?"

"A beer," Sheila said. She was smiling over at them. In a way she would have liked to have joined them.

"I know," Robinson persisted. "A word. We'll select a word. Discuss it, dissect it. What about it, Maguire?"

"Whatever you like," Malcolm said back from the bar. "Just so long as you don't expect me to buy you a pint."

"Do you see the name you've got for yourself?" Sheila said when he sat down beside her.

"Name," he said, lifting and sipping. "What's in a name?"

"There can be a lot," Sheila said. She was doing it again, looking past him. If he told her it could have the effect of shocking her into committing herself. He would know where he stood then. She was too sure of him, maybe that was it. So confident she didn't even find it necessary to look into his eyes. Well, he would tell her about it.

"Sheila?"

"Yes?" She looked at him, then away.

"Sheila . . . what color are my eyes?"

"What?" she laughed. "You're mad. What a question."

"What color are my eyes?"

"A sort of greeny-blue. More green in the sunlight." She still did not look at him but she was right.

"Do you like them?"

"What?"

"My eyes. Do you like them?"

"Malcolm—" She was on the point of laughing, being flippant, but the earnestness of his expression stopped her, in a way startled her.

"I like them," she said, leaning over and giving him her full concentration. "Yes, they're serious, and quite deep, really."

"Deep," he repeated. "Do you mean deep or deep?"

"I do," Sheila said. There was an enveloping quality about her reserved relaxation.

"Did you notice that our sense of humor is compatible?" Malcolm asked her.

"I noticed that mine is," she said. Then she got up. "Mind that file, I'll be back in a minute," she indicated her blue file with its various notes which rested on the table.

When she was gone Malcolm sat back and considered the fact that with Sheila there was an ambiguous clarity. You felt good, optimistic with her although her own intentions were obscure. And what was last night? There was only one thing to be said about last night. It was gone. The past.

When he walked home the autumn mist settled around his shoulders and he felt set in his time, a part of today. Comfortably moving along. When he entered the streets of the East he heard distant melodies of his childhood, saw himself in boys running past. It was all necessary really, he thought, and then, realizing that thought was superfluous, he smiled and kicked a can along before him.

She was scuttling around the house, muttering angrily into the dotted breast of her apron.

"I seen thim, think I didn't, bifore ma very eyes. The dirty black-guards, snakin' away with it up 'is coat, that big skinny rake was . . ."

He had an impulse to run back down the street. If he'd thought he should have foregone his dinner, grabbed a bite in Dirty Joe's. Saved himself the agony of this. The nuisance of listening. He knew he didn't have to say anything. She never expected him to say anything, but he would hear her problems, the trials of her day. And occasionally, despite himself, he offered half-hearted advice.

On this occasion it appeared to him that it would be advantageous to show some slight interest.

"What are you talking about, Mother?" he asked her as he rinsed his hands under the cold water.

"A'm talkin' about that clock," she said with renewed vigor. "That's what a'm talkin' about. That parlor clock yer Uncle John left me. An' them hoodlums that came up that hall an' stole it bifore ma very eyes."

"You saw them?" he asked. He was settling down to the dinner she had set out.

"Didn' a see thim runnin' down the street?" she said, standing back, her hand on her hip and regarding him incredulously.

"You saw the clock?" he asked, confident of his own position and merely testing her out.

"What?" she said by way of delaying her reply. "Didn' a see 'im with it up 'is coat?"

"How do you know it was the clock?" He felt there was a slight suggestion of meanness in his stance, but there was no other way, and she was getting a certain amount of satisfaction from the validity of her annoyance.

"An' what else would it be? Is the clock in the parlor? Go on, you see if it's still in the parlor."

"If you say it's not in the parlor, then it's not in the parlor," he said. He just wanted to be left alone now to enjoy the remainder of his dinner.

"Well, then," she said smugly. "That's proof enough, isn't it, an' if you were half a man you'd go down to the polis for me an' report it."

This jolted him and caused him to pause.

"Look, we'll leave it for tonight, maybe it'll turn up," he said.

"Turn up," she muttered in exasperation as she went off to her lookout post in the hall. "'E doesn't believe a word a'm just after tellin' 'im."

The clock faded. The whole incident faded. His mother got the most out of it. Played it and replayed it until the record scratched. Standing at the door, hurling abuse at the handball players, seeing the guilt in their faces, amazed at their boldness, continually demanding the return of the clock—"Now yous'ns have that clock back here by the 'morra night or yis'll be sorry." They were never sorry, and became convinced that she was mad. The neighbors, having been told the whole story, individually and in groups, clubbed together and bought her a new clock. The fact that they would do this, that they thought so much of her to do it, made up for the sentimental value of the clock she had lost, and it was with considerable pride that she pointed to her latest acquisition now occupying the center of the parlor mantelpiece.

Malcolm nursed more serious worries now. Sheila had seemed to draw him to her. In his parlor in the firelight she did not only allow him to hold her close. She held him close. She stood vulnerable by the window and playfully released her independence, and at night when he left her home she was loathe to leave him; she stood on, talking, allowing him to hold her hand, even kissing him on the street. And looking back when she left him. He had been led to muse on his good fortune as he tramped the few miles home or sat in the taxi. She wasn't putting it into words but anybody could see that she was giving in, accepting that love is stronger than superficial ideas concerning identity and situation. She wasn't putting it into words but her messages were brilliant. Who needed words?

But words, when they came, shattered his illusion. They were having a drink and she was uneasy. Not unfriendly, but guilty somehow.

One sentence separated them.

"I am going to England," she said. She couldn't be. Not going to England. Maybe going, but not *going*.

"Going?" he asked, trying to hide his weakness.

"Yes," she said. She was quiet, not triumphant. Simply stating and concerned. Yes, concerned.

"What do you mean, going?"

"To work."

"To work? But you're only in your first year. How can you? Look, be sensible."

"No, Malcolm, there is nothing you can say. I have to go. I can't stand this place, this university. I want to go away and work." There was a combination of nervousness and release in her voice.

Malcolm was sure of his position. He would do his best to talk her out of it. He had to. It was his duty as well as his desire.

"You are being flighty," he said.

"Well then, I want to be flighty," she answered. He put forward the line about throwing away her opportunity of a degree, and what if England didn't work, she wouldn't get back into university. But as he spoke the realization dawned on him that you can only influence someone who has not yet made their decision.

"What about me?" he asked her. He was looking into his beer. Sympathy at least he deserved.

"It doesn't affect my feelings for you," Sheila said.

"Probably not. Because it couldn't. You had none in the first place."

After this their meetings were a combination of tenderness and coolness, unworkable plans and silences.

He left her to the airport all the same. While they waited they had a couple of drinks and he watched her, glimpsing her confusion. Was it adventure? Escape? Sensible? Silly? But she was brave, he would grant her that. And he admired her. And loved her.

He kissed her at the barrier but she was strained. Then, just as she turned to go she whispered to him, "You know I do love you, Malcolm. See you."

He panicked. A combination of the couple of pints, the atmosphere, the words he had waited to hear for so long, whatever, resulted in him racing to a window. He saw her coming out onto the tarmac and walking across towards the plane, and with sweat on his forehead and inside his clothes, he began banging on the window. "That's not love," he shouted. "You can't call that love, Sheila. What is it? You tell me."

Amazed travelers stared at him as he rubbed his breath from the window.

Sheila turned on the steps and waved down, although she saw no-one.

"Do you know what I did one night, Sheila?" he shouted. "Do you know?"

He waited until the plane door closed and then, turning, he surged through his baffled audience, and saw only the glass door ahead.

Winter Break

EMMA COOKE

Connie had been a child bride—back in the early fifties when it really meant something. That was one of the reasons for her being here, with Tim in Tenerife, her mouth reeking of garlic soup while the rain lashed in torrents against the window. The trip was in the nature of a New Year treat to themselves to celebrate the start of their twenty-fifth year together. As well as that, they both needed the break.

In the other bed Tim slept and slept as if nailed to the mattress, his almost hairless head a pale disc on the pillow. It was too dark to look out at the sea but Connie could hear it, miles down, crashing and roaring and hurling itself against the rocks. At least she *was* here, still in command of her senses. The plane had made it without the captain going berserk or the shady character in dirty denim and steel rimmed glasses across the aisle running wild with a shotgun. The whole flight had gone off without a hitch, whatever about the delay at Tenerife airport during which they sat and sat on the bus, looking at nothing at all, while their courier fixed up the muddle caused by two drunks who had got themselves detached from the group that he was sending back to Dublin. It was not going to be that kind of holiday for herself and Tim! He had to get himself better. That was what Maurice said, stethoscope in hand, back beside the comfortable big bed in their bedroom at home. "Take your pick oul' sod, either check

EMMA COOKE (b. 1934) is a native of Portarlington, County Laois. Educated in Dublin, she lives now near Limerick. *Female Forms*, a story collection, was issued in 1980 by Poolbeg; and two novels—*A Single Sensation* in 1981 and *Eve's Apple* in 1985—by Blackstaff.

into the hospital or get away from it all. Otherwise it's the knacker's yard. I'm telling you straight."

It had not been a very auspicious beginning. Tim had taken his pills out and swallowed them without comment while they waited in the darkness that fell so rapidly—first for the courier and then for the driver who disappeared shouting curses as soon as the courier turned up. And unfortunately the restaurant in their apartment building smelt of cabbage. Reeked of it! It was not Connie's job to go around opening windows or squirting air freshener. On the other hand, nothing would make her eat in a restaurant cocooned in an aroma of boiled greens and worse. They had to eat elsewhere.

Elsewhere was a place up the road full of fat Germans. Elsewhere was garlic soup and tortilla for Connie with a mixed salad—the only ray of light—on the side. Elsewhere was tunny fish and most of the jug of wine, the far too large jug of wine, for Tim. Afterwards they splashed their way back to their apartment with its balcony and room-divider, its twin beds and the sea roaring so indifferently beneath them. Now Tim snored as he slept on the other side of the bedroom mat, too far away from Connie for her to shake him into silence. Instead she said a rosary and tried to ignore the snores and the rain; tried to pray that Tim would be much better by the time they got home, even prayed that her recalcitrant children, whatever they were up to, would survive reasonably unscathed.

In the morning they saw the steps. Steps which even for a child bride of seventeen would have been a long climb down at nine o'clock in the morning without any breakfast inside her. Steps which left Connie, at forty-two, flapping along in web-footed fashion when they eventually got to level ground. Steps which landed Tim outside the *bureau d'exchange* clutching his left side while rasping noises came from his gullet. He felt so bad that Connie had to take over the financial transactions although she never handled money. Tim understood these things so much better than she did. Connie had to pay for their breakfast— one hundred and seventy-five pesetas—for tea and rolls and jam— which seemed to be more notes than was reasonable.

Afterwards, walking through the streets on Tim's arm, looking at all the fat men—much fatter than Tim—she found herself thinking it would be nice to walk a bit quicker, or to understand foreign languages, or even to have come with friends, although most of their friends were nearer to Tim's age than hers. Some of them were even over sixty. As it was, she and Tim sauntered along, staring blankly at French-looking people with berets and handbags, German-looking people with big backsides and expensive cameras, and elderly olive skinned men in business suits who stared back impassively through their sunglasses as they brushed past with brief cases under their arms. And then Tim's tongue was hanging out so they had to sit under the trees, where Connie passed over the rest of the money and sipped a beer, while Tim bought himself a Manhattan and then another and then another, and what had seemed like a small gathering of friends on the pavement beside them unwound and stretched itself into a queue for taxis.

They could not possibly have known that there was a bus strike on. But their courier seemed to think differently back at the apartment building when they arrived too late for the champagne welcome.

"But yes! Two months old. The bus strike is two months old. And the taxis? Impossible!" He snapped his fingers and showed his gold fillings when he laughed. However, when Connie protested, he shook his head and said "Not *mea culpa*, Mrs. Lynch. Not *mea culpa*." And he refused to be *mea culpa* because it was now two o'clock and so the supermarket up the road was naturally closed until four. And even Connie felt that he could not be expected to be *mea culpa* for the state Tim was in, with his bloodshot eyes and sports shirt open to the navel.

When she had got Tim up to the apartment and he had passed into oblivion on his twin bed, she went out and sat on one of the chairs on the balcony. There was another chair and a table and a cactus plant in the corner. It occurred to Connie that it would be pleasant to have someone sitting in the other empty chair. A companion. The weather was fine today and even though the balcony faced North it was warm. The sea was calm and the waves made a lullaby. Way down in the direction of the town she could see the scrap of black, sandy beach. It was crowded with people and two swimmers were plunging through the breakers. Connie always used to swim on holidays with the children in Kilkee, fair weather or foul. Not so much lately, of course, no one ever seemed to be around. Now she just sat here waiting for Tim to wake up. She began to feel restless. She began to wish that he was not in there asleep, then she could go in and attack the bathroom and kitchenette, the bedroom and sitting room. The place was only half-cleaned. The morning light had shown up all sorts of smears and smudges and dirt in the cracks in the kitchenette lino. Her premonitions about the cabbagey restaurant downstairs had been completely justified. And after she had cleaned up she could make omelettes — although eggs were not good for Tim — omelettes anyway and vegetable soup.

Tim's face gleamed dull pink across the restaurant table. He had pooh-poohed the idea of omelettes and vegetable soup. He had spotted a likely place downtown this morning. They were going to eat out. Connie stared at the lump of meat in front of her on a wooden platter. The waiter, immaculate in white — she granted him that — stood beside them with the wine list. She smiled at him and he looked back at her, blank-eyed. She played with her meat while he and Tim, through some strange, pidgin Spanish managed to procure a bottle of wine which the waiter opened, making little kissing noises of delight and Tim sipped with a faraway look in his eyes before embracing the waiter like a brother. It tasted just like any other wine to Connie, even if it did cost as much as a weekful of breakfasts.

Nobody else there, except Tim and the waiter, seemed to be in good humor. Nobody else seemed to have anything to say except a young German couple with faces as wooden as their platters who exchanged occasional monosyllables. Even when one of the decorations left over from Christmas, a dinged opalescent ball, plopped from its hook onto the table where the young couple sat, no one laughed except Tim and the waiter. The young couple never even lifted their eyes, just studied their beef and sauerkraut and shoveled it into their mouths; studied and shoveled and said "Jah" and "Bitte" and "Jah" and "Danke."

Out in the street Tim wanted to let a photographer with a monkey in a cowboy suit on his shoulder take Connie's photograph, but Connie refused. She was the one with sense, she said. And so she felt herself to be as they sat in the taxi which Tim's waiter had managed to get for them and drove back up the hill past the villas, some of which were lit up so that you could see the profusion of trees and flowers in their tiny gardens. Lemon trees and banana trees, while at home, Connie knew, no one would remember to water the hyacinth bowls.

"Who loves you, baby?" Tim asked, squeezing her thigh.

Connie walked through the markets counting her blessings. She walked past stalls where shifty pedlars pushed belts, shawls, embroidered table-cloths, zebra skins, leopard skins, shells, necklaces, handbags, Indian blouses, etcetera, etcetera. She numbered off the things she had to be thankful for. Her healthy children, her fond mother, their spacious red brick home, their summer lodge in Kilkee, the way her stomach had escaped stretch marks, her deep-freeze and fox fur coat, her good husband. She was going to buy a pair of crocodile shoes before she went home.

Her good husband . . . She made her way back between the stalls, up the steps past the black old woman who took the money at the fish stall, up onto the next floor with its rows of spinach and figs, apples, oranges, lemons, pineapples, aubergines, avocados, all laid out in neat, colorful rows, like edible counting frames. She climbed the stairs to the top level. Tim was there, waiting on the roughly finished terrace outside the rude market restaurant, an empty bottle on the table in front of him, an empty glass in his hand.

"Please, Tim," Connie said.

He just stared out across the panorama of tiled roofs and people and cars. She sat down opposite him and stared herself—at a string of nappies across the way, hanging outside the window of an apart-ment. The nappies were snow white. As white as the waiter's coat had been last night As white as the nappies that Connie had pinned on her clothes line long ago.

Her biggest and boldest daughter did not believe in nappies. She said that they were out of date. She said that marriage was out of date, as she bounced her baby on her knee and stuck him into a sort of quilted pouch which she hung from her shoulders when she wanted to go and drink coffee with her friends.

"Please, Tim," Connie said. He reached for her hand and they went to try and solve the taxi problem.

The weather was intermittently horrible. They had to dash from the door of the tour bus into the nearest shop and buy an umbrella. Even so, it was too wet to do much sightseeing. Far too wet for strolling about. And the shops! Connie and Tim went in to look for socks because Connie had forgotten to pack Tim's. Such a depressing place. Its high counters, bales of cloth, wooden drawers, large dim mirror, high wobbly chairs for customers, made Connie remember the shops of her girlhood. Shops where their bill was always overdue and stockinette gloves had to do instead of leather. "Buy the best ones," she said to Tim, even though the silk socks were a ridiculous price and drab enough for an undertaker, and the counter-hand bowed and clicked his heels when he handed them over, as if he was serving the Generalissimo.

The archaeological museum was worse. A room with steel-rimmed, polished wooden cases crammed full of skulls. Skull after skull, row upon row, ticketed and numbered up to one thousand and something. It gave Tim the horrors—and the armbones and leg bones and mounds of teeth. They ran past the showpiece—the mummy and the reconstructed burial cavern—ran out into the street and walked and walked, oblivious of the pouring rain. Oblivious of the fact that it had stopped until they saw two check-trousered Americans posing in Laurel and Hardy hats outside a masks and novelties shop, while their wives took photographs.

"No more day tours," Tim said back at the apartment. He had bought a bottle of whisky on the way back. "Unless you want to go on your own," he added. He poured out a glass for Connie as well as himself. She felt too feeble to argue. She felt that nothing was left in life except a series of unpleasant surprises—such as waking up tomorrow and finding herself a twin of one of the black-garbed creatures who hobbled in the shadows of the city they had just visited. A sister skull with a lookalike grin and empty eye sockets.

Tim had found a drinking companion. A solitary Dutchman who spoke excellent English. An embarrassing fellow. He launched into diatribes at the bar counter in the apartment building. He blinked his eyes across a dusty sunbeam that poked through the window and lit up the bottles behind the barman. He banged the counter. The Germans had robbed him personally of the best years of his life. The Germans had ruined his country. The Germans were all dirty bastards and he would trust the meanest Arab first. He had only been eighteen when the Germans came. Eighteen!

"One of our sons is eighteen," Tim said, pulling a long face over his brandy. "It's difficult."

Connie plucked the edge of her stool and looked around for an escape route. She thought of her eighteen year old son sitting in his room. His listless hands, the way he stared at her seeing nothing, not even minding the insect that crawled across his cheek. The way he flinched when she reached over to brush it away. She thought of his old dufflecoat rotting on a hanger and the way he screamed when she offered to take it to the cleaners. She thought of her younger children and all the robbers and dirty bastards in the world. She heard a German woman beside them say in English to her husband, "You do not hear him, Helmut. You do not hear him." The woman sent quick, pleading glances over his shoulder to Connie. She reminded Connie of her mother—the same tired hump, the same startled look on her face. The man was huge, with huge red hands and small lonely eyes.

"It's great to meet someone who speaks the lingo," Tim was saying to the Dutchman as Connie left the bar. She was not going to get mixed up in it. It had not been her war.

Connie prided herself that she looked a woman of the world. This morning, in the apartment, she had spoken quietly and emphatically to Tim. She had been dressed as she was now, in her new-length cream skirt and nylon tights. Tim had eventually lifted his head from the pillow, rooted through his pockets and shelled out all the cash he could find. As much as she wanted. Tim was not feeling himself. Connie remained neutral. He must go to Maurice for another diagnosis when they got home. In the meantime, she was going to shop. She let him keep some money for his most urgent needs. As to where they would eat lunch—she was completely indifferent. She would not be hungry. She was going to have coffee and cakes in that nice place downtown. Now Connie sat in the Café Columbus behind a big pot of coffee, afraid to go back to the apartment, imagining Tim and the Dutchman already sloshed and insulting more Germans at the bar. She bent her head and admired her new sling-back shoes. When she looked up a man was sitting opposite her.

The man observed the blue and green decor with a melancholy air. He was a dark man with a fixed look about him. He carried a guide book and a pipe and pulled a tobacco pouch out of his pocket. Connie noted his American accent when he spoke to the waiter. He was not her idea of an American. He was too subdued. He looked over and grinned at Connie as the waiter came back with hot water in a brandy glass which he swirled around and emptied into a slop bowl before pouring out the man's drink.

"To the good old days," said the American, raising his glass to Connie before he drank. Connie dropped her eyes, conscious of her cream skirt and good blouse. She did not want him to think that she was a woman on the loose.

"What would you recommend, lady?" the American said when the trolley of gateaux was wheeled over.

Connie did not intend to get involved and yet she found herself recommending one of the tiered cakes, the strawberry and cream and chocolate mixture on a layer of thin pastry. And when he had his strawberry confection in front of him, and the trolley had moved on, Connie found herself babbling away about how nicely they served things in the café and how they wrapped their cakes so daintily if you wanted to take them away, sticking a toothpick into the creamy tops to prop up the wrapping paper, and so on. It seemed like ages since she had had a proper conversation with anybody. "My husband adores them," she said, although it was not true, but she did not want the man to misunderstand her motives.

And later, when they knew each other's names, and Sid—for that was his name—asked Connie to have lunch with him she thought, Why not? and It serves Tim right, as she said "Well, that would be nice and I do think my husband would be just as well off left on his own. Sleep and starvation is the only cure for these touristy bugs."

They went to the markets and up to the roof restaurant where she and Tim had sat on the terrace. It was a warm day. The place looked more finished than the last time. The nappies were gone from outside the apartment across the way. Instead a pitiably thin old woman was there cleaning the windows. Connie sat across the table from Sid, both of them tucking into shrimps and garlic, and when he said "I admire a woman who can eat" she felt warmed by his sympathy although she had not told him any of her troubles. Indeed, they seemed to have shrunk.

"Life," Sid said. "Life is full of surprises." He lit his pipe and over the last of their wine he told her about why he was here and why he was walking around by himself. It was his day off. He pulled a comic face. He was worn out. He was sales manager of a firm in Illinois that made haysheds. He explained about his firm's incentive program. He described the young men who had qualified as prize-winners for this trip. Big hefty young men with muscles. Sid shrugged his thin shoulders. Eager young giants who had erected more haysheds than any of the other young giants who worked for Sid's firm in Illinois. "And they sent me along as baby-sitter," Sid said. Yesterday he had flown with them to Marrakesh in Africa and back. Tomorrow they were taking a trip up to the thin breezy top of Mt. Teide where Sid would probably have a heart attack. Tomorrow night they were hiring djellabas and letting it all hang out at a Moorish evening in their hotel. Today, he slumped across the table, looking quizzically at her, today was his day off.

It was Connie's day off too! It was odd, she thought, as she and Sid leaped on a bus that was going to the parrot park, she had never traveled anywhere for the last twenty five years with any other escort but Tim.

Connie and Sid strolled through the botanical gardens out at the parrot park. Connie knew that monkeys, toucans, cockatoos and flamingoes were not Tim's idea of a day out. She knew that monkeys gave Tim the creeps. She knew that the red beaks of the black swans would make him yawn or remind him of his thrist. It now seemed that he was the one who was out of step, he was the one who was peculiar.

Sid and she had the same set of rules. They were determined to miss nothing. They sat in a big airy café where a man wearing a nifty pink suit served them cocktails. Big glasses of green stuff studded with pineapple and cherries. Then, so fast it was amazing, the man was back with a collection of tropical birds. Birds so clever that they were almost human. One, a gleaming white parrot with pink undersides to her feathers, was the star. A balloon pump, roller skates, a miniscule scooter, rings to be thrown with the beak, colors to be matched, a parachute that ejected her out of a toy rocket—nothing fazed her. "She's killing me," Sid said, mopping his eyes as the white parrot pedalled up and down, braking at the end of the table, on a teeny parrot tricycle. "She's killing me," he said again in a different tone, as if he was referring to something much more lethal than a pretty parrot whose feathers were tinged with pink.

It was raining when the bus brought them back to town. In a state of wonderment Connie said "Yes" when Sid suggested a drink to seal their outing. Maybe it was the parrot, a green one this time, that swung in a cage outside the hotel at the bus stop. Maybe it was the ennui etched deep on the face of a woman pattering by as she scolded the lap-dog with the ribbon on its head that she carried. Connie would have been mystified if any of her friends had confessed to such a truancy. The scenes shifted so quickly from then until the final moment that she had difficulty afterwards remembering them in sequence.

The evening stroll through the markets. The daughter of the ancient cashier at the fish stall all business with plucked eyebrows and rubber gloves. Watching dodgems down by the harbor with salt from the poke of shrimps on her tongue. Pedlars tucking goods away into plastic bags and a bunch of roses from a flower girl in a stripy skirt and lace edged pinny. The ribbon threaded so delicately through the edging of the pinny. An attempt to part. A young man in a wheelchair, the legs of his jeans folded under his poor stumps. Tears on Connie's cheeks. The hag who guarded the entrance to the "Senors" screaming imprecations at the sleeping drunk who blocked Sid's way. Herself in a place with a hole in the middle of some filthy broken tiles and a smell—she could never have believed it. Surviving! An almost silent walk back by the church. That was the first part.

Then the scene changed. The café. The musical bar. The small circular floor and nostalgic records. "They tried to tell us we're too young." "Too old!" Sid caroled. Forgetting to stop when the music stopped—no, pretending to forget to stop. The missing button on the plush fawn seat. In the corner of the picture the carved ship's figurehead of a girl with a sheaf of flowers covering her bosom. The melodies still making them hum when they came out into the pearly evening.

And it was so early. They walked easily, quickly, racing over the pavements, not needing to stop for breath.

And then the mandatory scene. She tried to skim over it but there it was. The room. Its armchairs. Sid's blazer hanging from the wardrobe and Sid's transistor on the bedside table. A bottle of bourbon untouched beside some neat packages on the wooden chest. Her new shoes toppled in the corner. Her cream skirt in a pool on the floor. The flatness of Sid's stomach. The fact of her tickles. She always got tickles. Tim took it for granted. Sid's scratchy toenails. The fact that she didn't give a damn.

And the walk up the steps. She and Sid standing by the sea wall listening to the rhythmic roar of the sea. Connie feeling every spike of every palm tree incised on her brain. The wonderful spicy smell from all the growth spiraling through her nostrils.

"There she is," Sid said. He had been fumbling in his pocket. The girl in the picture had a baffled look. She lay in a languorous attitude on a scrap of grass in what seemed a very suburban landscape. A suburb in brightest America. She had a foam of silvery hair and wore a pink sort of lounging pyjamas. She was very young.

"Your wife?" Connie said. She held the piece of pasteboard as if it was a razor blade.

"My wife," Sid said. He put his arm around Connie's shoulders. "That's why it has been so — such a real pleasure, Connie. I want to thank you." He spoke slowly as if to a child being taught the alphabet. "She is young, you know. She is very young."

Connie folded her arms against disappointment and hurt. She saw the silvery siren with her lush young face being carried off by one of the Illinois giants while Sid stood wringing his hands. She saw her own daughter coming down the street towards her with the baby joggling over her back. Her daughter was laughing her head off. She saw a capacious bed and Tim and herself in it. The big hump that was Tim and the little hump that was her. She saw her son standing at the door of their room staring at them. He was trembling like a leaf.

"A child bride!" Connie said, giving back the girl's photograph to Sid.

He laughed in a relieved way and said, "You know how it is."

Back in the hotel was the last scene of all. No scene at all in fact. Tim had found his way back to bed — that was if he had ever left it. Connie took off her tights. She sat out in the living part of the room, glad to feel the cold tiles beneath her aching feet. There did not seem much point in getting her rosary beads. She sat in the darkness, letting the day's events run through her mind. What had she expected? What had been expected of her? She did not know. She never had known.

The Wall-Reader

FIONA BARR

"Shall only our rivers run free?" The question jumped out from the cobbled wall in huge white letters, as The People's taxi swung round the corner at Beechmount. "Looks like paint is running freely enough down here," she thought to herself, as other slogans glided past in rapid succession. Reading Belfast's grim graffiti had become an entertaining hobby for her, and she often wondered, was it in the dead of night that groups of boys huddled round a paint tin daubing walls and gables with tired political slogans and clichés. Did anyone ever see them? Was the guilty brush ever found? The brush is mightier than the bomb, she declared inwardly, as she thought of how celebrated among journalists some lines had become. "Is there a life before death?" Well, no one had answered that one yet, at least, not in this city.

The shapes of Belfast crowded in on her as the taxi rattled over the ramps outside the fortressed police barracks. Dilapidated houses, bricked-up terraces. Rosy-cheeked soldiers, barely out of school, and quivering with high-pitched fear. She thought of the thick-lipped youth who came to hijack the car, making his point by showing his revolver under his anorak, and of the others, jigging and taunting every July, almost sexual in their arrogance and hatred. Meanwhile, passengers climbed in and out at various points along the road, maneuvering between legs, bags of shopping and umbrellas. The taxi swerved blindly into the road. No Highway Code here. As the wom-

FIONA BARR (b. 1952) is a television critic for the *Irish News*. A native of Derry, she has had stories broadcast on Radio Four and adapted for BBC television. Her collection *Sisters* was published by Blackstaff in 1980.

an's stop approached, the taxi swung up to the pavement, and she stepped out.

She thought of how she read walls—like tea-cups, she smiled to herself. Pushing her baby in the pram to the supermarket, she had to pass under a motorway bridge that was peppered with lines, some in irregular lettering with the paint dribbling down the concrete, others written with felt-tip pen in minute secretive hand. A whole range of human emotions splayed itself with persistent anarchy on the walls. "One could do worse than be a reader of walls," she thought, twisting Frost's words. Instead, though, the pram was rushed past the intriguing mural with much gusto. Respectable housewives don't read walls!

The "Troubles," as they were euphemistically named, remained for this couple as a remote, vaguely irritating wart on their life. They were simply ordinary (she often groaned at the oppressive banality of the word), middle-class, and hoping the baby would marry a doctor, thereby raising them in their autumn days to the select legions of the upper class. Each day their lives followed the same routine—no harm in that sordid little detail, she thought. It helps structure one's existence. He went to the office, she fed the baby, washed the rapidly growing mound of nappies, prepared the dinner and looked forward to the afternoon walk. She had convinced herself she was happy with her lot, and yet felt disappointed at the pangs of jealousy endured on hearing of a friend's glamorous job or another's academic and erudite husband. If only someone noticed her from time to time, or even wrote her name on a wall declaring her existence worthwhile; "A fine mind" or "I was once her lover." That way, at least, she would have evidence she was having impact on others. As it was, she was perpetually bombarded with it. Marital successes, even marital failures evoked a response from her. All one-way traffic.

That afternoon she dressed the baby and started out for her walk. "Fantasy time" her husband called it. "Wall-reading time" she knew it to be. On this occasion, however, she decided to avoid those concrete temptations and, instead, visit the park. Out along the main road she trundled, pushing the pram, pausing to gaze into the hardware store's window, hearing the whine of the Saracen as it thundered by, waking the baby and making her feel uneasy. A foot patrol of soldiers strolled past, their rifles, lethal even in the brittle sunlight of this March day, lounged lovingly and relaxed in the arms of their men.

One soldier stood nonchalantly, almost impertinent, against a corrugated railing and stared at her. She always blushed on passing troops.

The park is ugly, stark and hostile. Even in summer, when courting couples seek out secluded spots like mating cats, they reject Musgrave. There are a few trees, clustered together, standing like skeletons, ashamed of their nakedness. The rest is grass, a green wasteland speckled with puddles of gulls squawking over a worm patch. The park is bordered by a hospital with a military wing which is guarded by an army billet. The beauty of the place, it has only this, is its silence.

The hill up to the park bench was not the precipice it seemed, but the baby and pram were heavy. Ante-natal self-indulgence had taken its toll — her midriff was now most definitely a bulge. With one final push, pram, baby and mother reached the green wooden seat, and came to rest. The baby slept soundly with the soother touching her velvet pink cheeks, hand on pillow, a picture of purity. The woman heard a coughing noise coming from the nearby gun turret, and managed to see the tip of a rifle and a face peering out from the darkness. Smells of cabbage and burnt potatoes wafted over from behind the slanting sheets of protective steel.

"Is that your baby?" an English voice called out. She could barely see the face belonging to the voice. She replied yes, and smiled. The situation reminded her of the confessional. Dark and supposedly anonymous, "Is that you, my child?" She knew the priest personally. Did he identify her sins with his "Good morning, Mary," and think to himself, "and I know what you were up to last night!" She blushed at the secrets given away during the ceremony. Yes, she nervously answered again, it was her baby, a little girl. First-time mothers rarely resist the temptation to talk about their offspring. Forgetting her initial shyness, she told the voice of when the baby was born, the early problems of all-night crying, now teething, how she could crawl backwards and gurgle.

The voice responded. It too had a son, a few months older than her child, away in Germany at the army base at Munster. Factory pipes, chimney tops, church spires, domes all listened impassively to the Englishman's declaration of paternal love. The scene was strange, for although Belfast's sterile geography slipped into classical forms with dusk and heavy rain-clouds, the voice and the woman knew the folly of such innocent communication. They politely finished their conversation, said goodbye, and the woman pushed her pram homewards. The voice remained in the turret, watchful and anxious. Home she went, past vanloads of workers leering out at the pavement, past the uneasy presence of foot patrols, past the church. "Let us give each other the sign of peace," they said at Mass. The only sign Belfast knew was two fingers pointing towards Heaven. Life was self-contained, the couple often declared, just like flats. No need to go outside.

She did go outside, however. Each week the voice and the woman learned more of each other. No physical contact was needed, no face-to-face encounter to judge reaction, no touching to confirm amity, no threat of dangerous intimacy. It was a meeting of minds, as she explained later to her husband, a new opinion, a common bond, an opening of vistas. He disclosed his ambitions to become a pilot, to watching the land, fields and horizons spread out beneath him—a patchwork quilt of dappled colors and textures. She wanted to be re-membered by writing on walls, about them that is, a world-shattering thesis on their psychological complexities, their essential truths, their witticisms and intellectual genius. And all this time the city's skyline and distant buildings watched and listened.

It was April now. More slogans had appeared, white and drip-ping, on the city walls. "Brits out. Peace in." A simple equation for the writer. "Loose talk claims lives," another shouted menacingly. The messages, the woman decided, had acquired a more ominous tone. The baby had grown and could sit up without support. New political solutions had been proposed and rejected, inter-paramilitary feuding had broken out and subsided, four soldiers and two policemen had been blown to smithereens in separate incidents, and a building a day had been bombed by the Provos. It had been a fairly normal month by Belfast's standards. The level of violence was no more or less ac-ceptable than at other times.

One day—it was, perhaps, the last day in April—her husband re-turned home panting and trembling a little. He asked had she been to the park, and she replied she had. Taking her by the hand, he led her to the wall on the left of their driveway. She felt her heart sink and thud against her. She felt her face redden. Her mouth was sud-denly dry. She could not speak. In huge angry letters the message spat itself out,

"TOUT."

The four-letter word covered the whole wall. It clanged in her brain, its venom rushed through her body. Suspicion was enough to condemn. The job itself was not well done, she had seen better. The letters were uneven, paint splattered down from the cross T, the U looked a misshapen O. The workmanship was poor, the impact perfect.

Her husband led her back into the kitchen. The baby was crying loudly in the livingroom but the woman did not seem to hear. Like sleepwalkers, they sat down on the settee. The woman began to sob. Her shoulders heaved in bursts as she gasped hysterically. Her husband took her in his arms gently and tried to make her sorrow his. Already he shared her fear.

"What did you talk about? Did you not realize how dangerous it was? We must leave." He spoke quickly, making plans. Selling the house and car, finding a job in London or Dublin, far away from Belfast, mortgages, removals, savings, the tawdry affairs of normal living stunned her, making her more confused. "I told him nothing," she sobbed, "what could I tell? We talked about life, everything, but not about here." She trembled, trying to control herself. "We just chatted about reading walls, families, anything at all. Oh Sean, it was as innocent as that. A meeting of minds we called it, for it was little else."

She looked into her husband's face and saw he did not fully understand. There was a hint of jealousy, of resentment at not being part of their communication. Her hands fell on her lap, resting in resignation. What was the point of explanation? She lifted her baby from the floor. Pressing the tiny face and body to her breast, she felt all her hopes and desires for a better life become one with the child's struggle for freedom. The child's hands wandered over her face, their eyes met. At once that moment of maternal and filial love eclipsed her fear, gave her the impetus to escape.

For nine months she had been unable to accept the reality of her condition. Absurd, for the massive bump daily shifted position and thumped against her. When her daughter was born, she had been overwhelmed by love for her and amazed at her own ability to give life. By nature she was a dreamy person, given to moments of fancy.

She wondered at her competence in fulfilling the role of mother. Could it be measured? This time she knew it could. She really did not care if they maimed her or even murdered her. She did care about her daughter. She was her touchstone, her anchor to virtue. Not for her child a legacy of fear, revulsion or hatred. With the few hours respite the painters had left between judgment and sentence she determined to leave Belfast's walls behind.

The next few nights were spent in troubled, restless sleep. The message remained on the wall outside. The neighbors pretended not to notice and refused to discuss the matter. She and the baby remained indoors despite the refreshing May breezes and blue skies. Her husband had given in his notice at the office, for health reasons, he suggested to his colleagues. An aunt had been contacted in Dublin. The couple did not answer knocks at the door. They carefully examined the shape and size of mail delivered and always paused when they answered the telephone.

The mini-van was to call at eleven on Monday night, when it would be dark enough to park, and pack their belongings and themselves without too much suspicion being aroused. The firm had been very understanding when the nature of their work had been explained. They were Protestant so there was no conflict of loyalties involved in the exercise. They agreed to drive them to Dublin at extra cost, changing drivers at Newry on the way down.

Monday finally arrived. The couple nervously laughed about how smoothly everything had gone. Privately, they each expected something to go wrong. The baby was fed, and played with, the radio listened to and the clock watched. They listened to the news at nine. Huddled together in their anxiety, they kept vigil in the darkening room. Rain had begun to pour from black thunderclouds. Everywhere it was quiet and still. Hushed and cold they waited. Ten o'clock, and it was now dark. A blustery wind had risen, making the lattice separation next door bang and clatter. At ten to eleven, her husband went into the sitting-room to watch for the mini-van. His footsteps clamped noisily on the floorboards as he paced back and forth. The baby slept.

A black shape glided slowly up the street and backed into the driveway. It was eleven. The van had arrived. Her husband asked to see their identification and then they began to load up the couple's belongings. Settee, chairs, television, washing machine—all were dumped hastily, it was no time to worry about breakages. She stood holding the sleeping baby in the living-room as the men worked anxiously between van and house. The scene was so unreal, the circumstances absolutely incredible. She thought, "What have I done?" Recollections of her naivety, her insensibility to historical fact and political climate were stupefying. She had seen women who had been tarred and feathered, heard of people who had been shot in the head, boys who had been knee-capped, all for suspected fraternizing with troops. The catalog of violence spilled out before her as she realized the gravity and possible repercussions of her alleged misdemeanor.

A voice called her, "Mary, come on now. We have to go. Don't worry, we're all together." Her husband led her to the locked and waiting van. Handing the baby to him, she climbed up beside the driver, took back the baby as her husband sat down beside her and waited for the engine to start. The van slowly maneuvered out onto the street and down the main road. They felt more cheerful now, a little like refugees seeking safety and freedom not too far away. As they approached the motorway bridge, two figures with something clutched in their hands stood side by side in the darkness. She closed her eyes tightly, expecting bursts of gunfire. The van shot past. Relieved, she asked her husband what they were doing at this time of night. "Writing slogans on the wall," he replied.

The furtiveness of the painters seemed ludicrous and petty as she recalled the heroic and literary characteristics with which she had endowed them. What did they matter? The travelers sat in silence as the van sped past the city suburbs, the glare of police and army barracks, on out and further out into the countryside. Past sleeping villages and silent fields, past whitewashed farmhouses and barking dogs. On to Newry where they said goodbye to their driver as the new one stepped in. Far along the coast with Rostrevor's twinkling lights opposite the bay down to the Border check and a drowsy soldier waving them through. Out of the North, safe, relieved and heading for Dublin.

Some days later in Belfast the neighbors discovered the house vacant, the people next door received a letter and a check from Dublin. Remarks about the peculiar couple were made over hedges and cups of coffee, the message on the wall was painted over by the couple who had bought the house when it went up for sale. They too were ordinary people, living a self-contained life, worrying over finance and babies, promotion and local gossip. He too had an office job, but his wife was merely a housekeeper for him. She was sensible, down to earth, and not in the least inclined to wall-reading.

A Scandalous Woman

EDNA O'BRIEN

Everyone in our village was unique and one or two of the girls were beautiful. There were others before and after but it was with Eily I was connected. Sometimes one finds oneself in the swim, one is wanted, one is favored, one is privy, and then it happens, the destiny, and then it is over and one sits back and knows alas that it is someone else's turn.

Hers was the face of a madonna. She had brown hair, a great crop of it, fair skin and eyes that were as big and as soft and as transparent as ripe gooseberries. She was always a little out of breath and gasped when one approached, then embraced, and said "darling." That was when we met in secret. In front of her parents and others she was somewhat stubborn and withdrawn, and there was a story that when young she always lived under the table to escape her father's thrashings. For one Advent she thought of being a nun but that fizzled out and her chief interest became clothes and needlework. She helped on the farm and used not to be let out much, in the summer, because of all the extra work. She loved the main road with the cars and the bicycles and the buses, and had no interest at all in the sidecar that her parents used for conveyance. She would work like a horse to get to the main road before dark to see the passers-by. She was swift as

EDNA O'BRIEN (b. 1932) is regarded the most successful of the Irish women writers. She was born in rural County Clare and worked in Dublin before moving to London in 1958. Since *The Country Girls Trilogy* (1960–64), Ms. O'Brien has produced more than a dozen works of fiction, two plays, a filmscript, and a women's history of Ireland, entitled *Mother Ireland.* The most widely known of the Irish women writers, she resides now in London.

a colt. My father never stopped praising this quality in her and put it down to muscle. It was well known that Eily and her family hid their shoes in a hedge near the road, so that they would have clean footwear when they went to mass, or to market, or later on, in Eily's case, to the dress dance.

The dress dance in aid of the new mosaic altar marked her debut. She wore a georgette dress and court shoes threaded with silver and gold. The dress had come from America long before but had been re-styled by Eily, and during the week before the dance she was never to be seen without a bunch of pins in her mouth as she tried out some different fitting. Peter the Master, one of the local tyrants, stood inside the door with two or three of his cronies both to count the money and to survey the couples and comment on their clumsiness or on their dancing "technique." When Eily arrived in her tweed coat and said "Evening gentlemen" no one passed any remark, but the moment she slipped off the coat and the transparency of the georgette plus her naked shoulders were revealed, Peter the Master spat into the palm of his hand and said didn't she strip a fine woman.

The locals were mesmerised. She was not off the floor once, and the more she danced the more fetching she became, and was saying "ooh" and "aah" as her partners spinned her round and round. Eventually one of the ladies in charge of the supper had to take her into the supper room and fan her with a bit of cardboard. I was let to look in the window, admiring the couples and the hanging streamers and the very handsome men in the orchestra with their sideburns and the striped suits. Then in the supper room where I had stolen to, Eily confided to me that something out of this world had taken place. Almost immediately after she was brought home by her sister Nuala.

Eily and Nuala always quarreled — issues such as who would milk, or who would separate the milk, or who would draw water from the well, or who would churn, or who would bake bread. Usually Eily got the lighter tasks because of her breathlessness and her accomplishments with the needle. She was wonderful at knitting and could copy any stitch just from seeing it in a magazine or in a knitting pattern. I used to go over there to play and though they were older than me they used to beg me to come and bribe me with empty spools or scraps of cloth for my dolls. Sometimes we played hide and seek, sometimes we played families and gave ourselves posh names and posh jobs, and we used to paint each other with the dye from plants or blue bags and treat each other's faces as if they were palettes, and then laugh and marvel at the blues and indigos and pretend to be natives and do hula hula and eat dock leaves. Once Nuala made me cry by saying I was adopted and that my mother was not my real mother at all. Eily had to pacify me by spitting on dock leaves and putting them all over my face as a mask.

Nuala was happiest when someone was upset and almost always she trumped for playing hospital. She was doctor and Eily was nurse. Nuala liked to operate with a big black carving knife, and long before she commenced, she gloated over the method and over what tumors she was going to remove. She used to say that there would be nothing but a shell left by the time she had finished, and that one wouldn't be able to have babies, or women's complaints ever. She had names for the female parts of one, Susies for the breasts, Florries for the stomach, and Matilda for lower down. She would sharpen and re-sharpen the knife on the steps, order Eily to get the hot water, the soap, to sterilize the utensils and to have to hand a big winding sheet.

Eily also had to don an apron, a white apron, that formerly she had worn at cookery classes. The kettle always took an age to boil on the open hearth, and very often Nuala threw sugar on it to encourage the flame. The two doors would be wide open, a bucket to one, and a stone to the other. Nuala would be sharpening the knife and humming "Waltzing Matilda," the birds would almost always be singing or chirruping, the dogs would be outside on their hind quarters, snapping at flies and I would be lying on the kitchen table terrified and in a state of undress. Now and then, when I caught Eily's eye she would raise hers to heaven as much as to say "you poor little mite" but she never contradicted Nuala or disobeyed orders. Nuala would don her mask. It was a bright red papier mâché mask that had been in the house from the time when some mummers came on the day of the Wren, got bitten by the dog, and lost some of their regalia including the mask and a legging. Before she commenced she let out a few dry, knowing coughs, exactly imitating the doctor's dry, knowing coughs. I shall never stop remembering those last few seconds as she snapped the elastic band around the back of her head, and said to Eily "All set Nurse?"

For some reason I always looked upwards and backwards and there-fore could see the dresser upside down, and the contents of it. There was a whole row of jugs, mostly white jugs with sepia design of corn, or cattle, or a couple toiling in the fields. The jugs hung on hooks at the edge of the dresser and behind them were the plates with ripe pears painted in the center of each one. But most beautiful of all were the little dessert dishes of carnival glass, with their orange tints and their scalloped edges. I used to say good-bye to them, and then it would be time to close eyes before the ordeal.

She never called it an operation, just an "op," the same as the doc-tor did. I would feel the point of the kinife like the point of a com-pass going around my scarcely formed breasts. My bodice would not be removed just lifted up. She would comment on what she saw and say "interesting," or "quite" or "oh dearie me" as the case may be, and then when she got at the stomach she would always say "tut tut tut" and "What nasty business have we got here." She would list the un-wholesome things I had been eating, such as sherbet or rainbow toffees, hit the stomach with the flat of the knife and order two spoons of tur-pentine and three spoons of castor oil before commencing. These po-tions had then to be downed. Meanwhile Eily, as the considerate nurse, would be mopping the doctor's brow, handing extra implements such as sugar tongs, spoon or fork. The spoon was to flatten the tongue and make the patient say "Aah." Scabs or cuts would be regarded as nasty devils, and elastic marks a sign of iniquity. I would also have to make a general confession. I used to lie there praying that their mother would come home unexpectedly. It was always a Tuesday, the day their mother went to the market to sell things, to buy commodi-ties and to draw her husband's pension. I used to wait for a sound from the dogs. They were vicious dogs and bit everyone except their owners, and on my arrival there I used to have to yell for Eily to come out and escort me past them.

All in all it was a woeful event but still I went each Tuesday, on the way home from school, and by the time their mother returned all would be over, and I would be sitting demurely by the fire, waiting to be offered a shop biscuit, which of course at first I made a great pretense of refusing.

Eily always conveyed me down the first field as far as the white gate, and though the dogs snarled and showed their teeth, they never tried biting once I was leaving. One evening, though it was nearly milking time, she came further and I thought it was to gather a few hazelnuts because there was a little tree between our boundary and theirs that was laden with them. You had only to shake the tree for the nuts to come tumbling down, and you had only to sit on the near-by wall, take one of the loose stones and crack away to your heart's content. They were just ripe, and they tasted young and clean, and helped as well to get all fur off the backs of the teeth. So we sat on the wall but Eily did not reach up and draw a branch and therefore a shower of nuts down. Instead she asked me what I thought of Romeo. He was a new bank clerk, a Protestant, and to me a right toff in his plus-fours with his white sports bicycle. The bicycle had a dynamo attached so that he was never without lights. He rode the bicycle with his body hunched forward so that as she mentioned him I could see his snout and his lock of falling hair coming towards me on the road. He also distinguished himself by riding the bicycle into shops or hallways. In fact he was scarcely ever off it. It seems he had danced with her the night she wore the green georgette, and next day left a note in the hedge where she and her family kept their shoes. She said it was the grace of God that she had gone there first thing that morning other-wise the note might have come into someone else's hand. He had made an assignation for the following Sunday, and she did not know how she was going to get out of her house and under what excuse. At least Nuala was gone, back to Technical School where she was learning to be a domestic economy instructress, and my sisters had returned to the convent so that we were able to hatch it without the bother of them eavesdropping on us. I said yes that I would be her accomplice, without knowing what I was letting myself in for. On the Sunday I told my parents that I was going with Eily to visit a cousin of theirs, in the hospital, and she in turn told her parents that we were visiting a cousin of mine. We met at the white gate and both of us were pep-pering. She had an old black dirndl skirt which she slipped out of, and underneath was her cerise dress with the slits at the side. It was a most compromising garment. She wore a brooch at the bosom. Her mother's brooch, a plain flat gold pin with a little star in the center, that shone feverishly. She took out her little gold flapjack and pro-ceeded to dab powder on. The puff was dry so she removed the little muslin cover, made me hold it delicately while she dipped into the powder proper. It was ocher stuff and completely wrecked her complexion. Then she applied lipstick, wet her kiss curl and made me kneel down in the field and promise never ever to split.

We went towards the hospital, but instead of going up that dark cedar-lined avenue, we crossed over a field, nearly drowning ourselves in the swamp, and permanently stooping so as not to be sighted. I said we were like soldiers in a war and she said we should have worn green or brown as camouflage. Her bright bottom, bobbing up and down, could easily have been spotted by anyone going along the road. When we got to the thick of the woods Romeo was there. He looked very indifferent, his face forward, his head almost as low as the handlebars of the bicycle, and he surveyed us carefully as we approached. Then he let out a couple of whistles to let her know how welcome she was. She stood beside him, and I faced them and we all remarked what a fine evening it was. I could hardly believe my eyes when I saw his hand go round her waist, and then her dress crumpled as it was being raised up from the back, and though the two of them stood perfectly still, they were both looking at each other intently and making signs with their lips. Her dress was above the back of her knees. Eily began to get very flushed and he studied her face most carefully, asking if it was nice, nice. I was told by him to run along: "Run along Junior," was what he said. I went and adhered to the bark of a tree, eyes closed, fists closed, and every bit of me in a clinch. Not long after, Eily hollered and on the way home and walking very smartly she and I discussed growing pains and she said there were no such things but that it was all rheumatism.

So it continued Sunday after Sunday, with one holy day, Ascension Thursday, thrown in. We got wizard in our excuses — once it was to practice with the school choir, another time it was to teach the younger children how to receive Holy Communion, and once — this was our riskiest ploy — it was to get gooseberries from an old crank called Miss MacNamara. That proved to be dangerous because both our mothers were hoping for some, either for eating or stewing, and we had to say that Miss MacNamara was not home, whereupon they said weren't the bushes there anyhow with the gooseberries hanging off. For a moment I imagined that I had actually been there, in the little choked garden, with the bantam hens and the small moldy bushes, weighed down with the big hairy gooseberries that were soft to the touch and that burst when you bit into them. We used to pray on the way home, say prayers and ejaculations, and very often when we leant against the grass bank while Eily donned her old skirt and her old canvas shoes, we said one or other of the mysteries of the Rosary. She had new shoes that were clogs really and that her mother had not seen. They were olive green and she bought them from a gypsy woman in return for a table cloth of her mother's, that she had stolen. It was a special cloth that had been sent all the way from Australia by a nun. She was a thief as well. One day all these sins would have to be reckoned with. I used to shudder at night when I went over the number of commandments we were both breaking, but I grieved more on her behalf, because she was breaking the worst one of all in those embraces and transactions with him. She never discussed him except to say that his middle name was Jack.

During those weeks my mother used to say I was pale and why wasn't I eating and why did I gargle so often with salt and water. These were forms of atonement to God. Even seeing her on Tuesdays was no longer the source of delight that it used to be. I was wracked. I used to say "Is this a dagger which I see before me," and recalled all the queer people around who had visions and suffered from delusions. The same would be our cruel cup. She flared up. "Marry, did I or did I not love her?" Of course I loved her and would hang for her but she was asking me to do the two hardest things on earth—to disobey God, and my own mother. Often she took huff, swore that she would get someone else—usually Una my greatest rival—to play gooseberry for her, and be her dogsbody in her whole secret life. But then she would make up, and be waiting for me on the road as I came from school, and we would climb in over the wall that led to their fields, and we would link and discuss the possible excuse for the following Sunday. Once she suggested wearing the green georgette, and even I, who also lacked restraint in matters of dress, thought it would draw untoward attention to her, since it was a dance dress and since as Peter the Master said "She looked stripped in it." I said Mrs. Bolan would smell a rat. Mrs. Bolan was one of the many women who were always prowling and turning up at graveyards, or in the slate quarry to see if there were courting couples. She always said she was looking for stray turkeys or turkey eggs but in fact she had no fowl, and was known to tell tales to be calumnious and as a result, one temporary school teacher had to leave the neighborhood, do a flit in the night, and not even have time to get her shoes back from the cobblers. But Eily said that we would never be found out, that the god Cupid was on our side, and while I was with her I believed it.

I had a surprise a few evenings later. Eily was lying in wait for me on the way home from school. She peeped up over the wall, said "yoo hoo" and then darted down again. I climbed over. She was wearing nothing under her dress since it was such a scorching day. We walked for a bit, then we flopped down against a cock of hay, the last one in the field, as the twenty-three other cocks had been brought in the day before. It looked a bit silly and was there only because of an accident, the mare had bolted, broke away from the hay cart and nearly strangled the driver, who was himself an idiot and whose chin was permanently smeared with spittle. She said to close my eyes, open my hand and see what God would give me. There are moments in life when the pleasure is more than one can bear, and one descends willy nilly into a wild tunnel of flounder and vertigo. It happens on swing boats and chairoplanes, it happens maybe at waterfalls, it is said to happen to some when they fall in love, but it happened to me that day, propped against the cock of hay, the sun shining, a breeze commencing, the clouds like cruisers in the heavens on their way to some distant port. I had closed my eyes, and then the cold thing hit the palm of my hand, fitting it exactly, and my fingers came over it to further the hold on it, and to guess what it was. I did not dare say in case I should be wrong. It was of course a little bottle, with a screw-on cap, and a label adhering to one side, but it was too much to hope that it would be my favorite perfume, the one called "Mischief." She was urging me to guess. I feared that it might be an empty bottle, though such a gift would not be wholly unwelcome, since the remains of the smell always lingered; or that it might be a cheaper perfume, a less mysterious one named after a carnation or a poppy, a perfume that did not send shivers of joy down my throat and through my swallow to my very heart. At last I opened my eyes, and there it was, my most prized thing, in a little dark blue bottle, with a silverish label and a little rubber stopper, and inside, the precious stuff itself. I unscrewed the cap, lifted off the little rubber top and a drop of the precious stuff was assigned to the flat of my finger and then conveyed to a particular spot in the hollow behind the left ear. She did exactly the same and we kissed each other and breathed in the rapturous smell. The smell of hay intervened so we ran to where there was no hay and kissed again. That moment had an air of mystery and sanctity about it, what with the surprise and our speechlessness, and a realization somewhere in the back of my mind that we were engaged in rotten business indeed, and that our larking days were over.

If things went well my mother had a saying that it was all too good to be true. It proved prophetic the following Saturday because as my hair was being washed at the kitchen table, Eily arrived and sat at the end of the table and kept snapping her fingers in my direction. When I looked up from my expanse of suds I saw that she was on the verge of tears and was blotchy all over. My mother almost scalded me, because in welcoming Eily she had forgotten to add the cold water to the pot of boiling water and I screamed and leapt about the kitchen shouting hellfire and purgatory. Afterwards Eily and I went around to the front of the house, sat on the step where she told me that all was U.P. She had gone to him as was her wont, under the bridge, where he did a spot of fishing each Friday and he told her to make herself scarce. She refused, whereupon he moved downstream and the moment she followed he waded into the water. He kept telling her to beat it, beat it. She sat on the little milk stool, where he in fact had been sitting, then he did a terrible thing which was to cast his rod in her direction and almost remove one of her eyes with the nasty hook. She burst into tears and I began to plait her hair for comfort's sake. She swore that she would throw herself in the selfsame river before the night was out, then said it was only a lovers' quarrel, then said that he would have to see her, and finally announced that her heart was utterly broken, in smithereens. I had the little bottle of perfume in my pocket, and I held it up to the light to show how sparing I had been with it, but she was interested in nothing only the ways and means of recovering him, or then again of taking her own life. Apart from drowning she considered hanging, the intake of a bottle of Jeyes Fluid, or a few of the grains of strychnine that her father had for foxes.

Her father was a very gruff man who never spoke to the family except to order his meals and to tell the girls to mind their books. He himself had never gone to school but had great acumen in the buying and selling of cattle and sheep, and put that down to the fact that he had met the scholars. He was an old man with an atrocious temper, and once on a fair day had ripped the clothing off an auctioneer who tried to diddle him over the price of an aladdin lamp.

My mother came to sit with us, and this alarmed me since my mother never took the time to sit, either indoors or outdoors. She began to talk to Eily about knitting, about a new tweedex wool, asking if she secured some would Eily help her knit a three-quarter length jacket. Eily had knitted lots of things for us including the dress I was wearing—a salmon pink, with scalloped edges and a border of white angora decorating those edges. At that very second as I had the angora to my face tickling it, my mother said to Eily that once she had gone to a fortune teller, had removed her wedding ring as a decoy, and when the fortune teller asked was she married, she had replied no, whereupon the fortune teller said "How come you have four children?" My mother said they were uncanny, those ladies, with their gypsy blood and their clairvoyant powers. I guessed exactly what Eily was thinking. Could we find a fortune teller or a witch who could predict her future?

There was a witch twenty miles away who ran a public house and who was notorious, but who only took people on a whim. When my mother ran off to see if it was a fox because of the racket in the henhouse I said to Eily that instead of consulting a witch we ought first to resort to other things, such as novenas, putting wedding cake under our pillows or gathering bottles of dew in the early morning and putting them in a certain fort to make a wish. Anyhow how could we get to a village twenty miles away, unless it was on foot or by bicycle, and neither of us had a machine. Nevertheless, the following Sunday, we were to be found setting off with a bottle of tea, a little puncture kit, and eight shillings, which was all the money we managed to scrape together.

We were not long started when Eily complained of feeling weak, and suddenly the bicycle was wobbling all over the road and she came a cropper as she tried to slow it down, by heading for a grass bank. Her brakes were non-existent as indeed were mine. They were borrowed bicycles. I had to use the same method to dismount, and the

two of us with our front wheels wedged into the bank, and our handlebars askew, caused a passing motorist to call out that we were a right
pair of Mohawks and a danger to the county council.

I gave her a sup of tea, and forced on her one of the eggs which
we had stolen from various nests, and which were intended as a bribe
for our witch. Along with the eggs we had a little flitch of home-cured
bacon. She cracked it on the handlebars, and with much persuasion
from me swallowed it whole, saying it was worse than castor oil. It
being Sunday, she recalled other Sundays and where she would be
at that exact moment and she prayed to St. Anthony to please bring
him back. We had heard that he went to Limerick most weekends
now, and there was rumor that he was going out with a bacon curer's
daughter, and that they were getting engaged.

The woman who opened the side door of the pub, said that the witch
did not live there any longer. She was very cross, had eyebrows that
met, and these as well as the hairs in her head were a yellowish grey.
She told us to leave her threshold at once, and how dare we intrude
upon her Sunday leisure. She closed the door in our faces. I said to
Eily "That's her." And just as we were screwing up our courage to
knock again, she re-opened the door and said who in the name of
Jacob had sent us. I said we'd come a long way, miles and miles, I
showed the eggs and the bacon in its dusting of saltpeter, and she said
she was extremely busy, seeing as it was her birthday and that sons
and daughters and cousins were coming for a high tea. She opened
and closed the door numerous times, and through it all we stood our
ground, until finally we were brought in, but it was my fortune she
wanted to tell. The kitchen was tiny and stuffy, and the same linoleum
was on the floor as on the little wobbling table. There was a little
wooden armchair for her, a form for visitors and a stove that was smoking. Two rhubarb tarts were cooling on top, and that plus a card were
the only indications of a birthday celebration. A small man, her husband, excused himself and wedged sideways through another door.
I pleaded with her to take Eily rather than me, and after much dither-
ing, and even going out to the garden to empty tea leaves, she said
that maybe she would, but that we were pests the pair of us. I was
sent to join her husband, in the little pantry, and was nearly smothered from the puffing of his pipe. There was also a strong smell of

flour, and no furniture except a sewing machine with a half-finished
garment, a shift, wedged in under the needle. He talked in a whisper,
said the Mau Mau would come to Ireland, and that St. Columbus
would rise from his grave, to make it once again the island of saints
and scholars. I was certain that I would suffocate. But it was worth
it. Eily was jubilant. Things could not have been better. The witch
had not only seen his initial, J., but seen it twice in a concoction that
she had done with the whites of one of the eggs and some gruel. Yes
things had been bad very bad, there had been grievous misunder-
standings, but all was to be changed, and leaning across the table she
said to Eily "Ah sure, you'll end your days with him."

Cycling home was a joy, we spinned downhill, saying to hell with
safety, to hell with brakes, saluted strangers, admired all the little cot-
tages and the outhouses and the milk tanks and the whining mon-
grels, and had no nerves passing the haunted house. In fact we would
have liked to see an apparition on that most buoyant of days. When
we got to the cross roads, that led to our own village, Eily had a strong
presentiment, as indeed had I, that he would be there waiting for us,
contrite, in a hair shirt, on bended knees. But he was not. There was
the usual crowd of lads playing pitch and toss. A couple of the younger
ones tried to impede us by standing in front of the bikes and Eily
blushed red. She was a favorite with everyone that summer, and she
had a different dress for every day of the week. She was called a fashion plate. We said goodnight and knew that it did not matter, that
though he had not been waiting for us, before long he and Eily would
be united. She resolved to be patient and be a little haughty and not
seek him out.

Three weeks later, on a Saturday night, my mother was soaking her
feet in a mixture of warm water and washing soda, when a rap came
on the scullery window. We both trembled. There was a madman who
had taken up residence in a bog-hole and we were certain that it must
be him. "Call your father," she said. My father had gone to bed in
a huff, because she had given him a boiled egg instead of a fry for
his tea. I didn't want to leave her alone and unattended so I yelled
up to my father, and at the same time a second assault was delivered
on the window pane. I heard the words "Sir, Sir."

It was Eily's father, since he was the only person who called my father Sir. When we opened the door to him the first thing I saw was the slash hook in his hand, and then the condition of his hair which was upstanding and wild. He said "I'll hang, draw, and quarter him," and my mother said "Come in Mr. Hogan," not knowing who this graphic fate was intended for. He said he had found his daughter in the lime kiln, with the bank clerk, in the most satanic position, with her belly showing.

My first thought was one of delight at their reunion, and then I felt piqued that Eily hadn't told me but had chosen instead to meet him at night in that disused kiln that reeked of damp. Better the woods I thought and the call of the cuckoo, and myself keeping some kind of watch, though invariably glued to the bark of a tree.

He said he had come to fetch a lantern, to follow them as they had scattered in different directions, and he did not know which of them to kill first. My father, whose good humor was restored by this sudden and unexpected intrusion, said to hold on for a moment, to step inside and that they would consider a plan of campaign. Mr. Hogan left his cap on the step, a thing he always did, and my mother begged of him to bring it in, since the new pup ate every article of clothing that it could find. Only that very morning my mother looked out on the field and thought it was flakes of snow, but in fact it was her line of washing, chewed to pieces. He refused to bring in his cap which to me was a perfect example of how stubborn he was, and how awkward things were going to be. At once, my father ordered my mother to make tea, and though still gruff, there was between them now an understanding, because of the worse tragedy that loomed. My mother seemed the most perturbed, made a hopeless cup of tea, cut the bread in agricultural hunks, and did everything wrong as if she herself had just been found out in some base transaction. After the men had gone out on their search party, she got me to go down on my knees to pray with her, and I found it hard to pray because I was already thinking of the flogging I would get for being implicated. She cross-examined me. Did I know anything about it? Had Eily ever met him? Why had she made herself so much style, especially that slit skirt.

I said no to everything. These noes were much too hastily delivered, and only that my mother was so busy cogitating and surmising, she would have suspected something for sure. Kneeling there I saw them trace every movement of ours, get bits of information from this one and that one, the so-called cousins, the woman who had promised us the gooseberries, and Mrs. Bolan. I knew we had no hope. Eily! Her most precious thing was gone, her jewel. The inside of one was like a little watch and once the jewel or jewels were gone the outside was nothing but a sham. I saw her die in the cold lime kiln and then again in a sick room, and then stretched out on an operating table the very way that I used to be. She had joined that small sodality of scandalous women who had conceived children without securing fathers and who were damned in body and soul. Had they convened they would have been a band of seven or eight, and might have sent up an unholy wail to their maker and their covert seducers. The one thing I could not endure was the thought of her stomach protuberant, and a baby coming out saying "ba ba." Had I had the chance to see her I should have suggested that we run away with gypsies.

Poor Eily, from then on she was kept under lock and key, and allowed out only to Mass, and then so concealed was she, with a mantilla over her face that she was not even able to make a lip sign to me. Never did she look so beautiful as those subsequent Sundays in chapel, her hair and her face veiled, her eyes like smoking tragedies peering through. I once sat directly in front of her, and when we stood up for the first gospel, I stared up into her face, and got such a dig in the ribs from my mother that I toppled over.

A mission commenced the following week, and a strange priest with a beautiful accent, and a strong sense of rhetoric, delivered the sermons each evening. It was better than a theater—the chapel in a state of hush, scores of candles like running stairways, all lit, extra flowers on the altar, a medley of smells, the white linen, and the place so packed that we youngsters had to sit on the altar steps and saw everything clearer, including the priest's adam's apple as it bobbed up and down. Always I could sight Eily, hemmed in by her mother, and some other old woman, pale and impassive, and I was certain that she was about to die. On the evening that the sermon centered on the sixth commandment, we youngsters were kept outside until Benediction time. We spent the time wandering through the stalls, looking at the tiers of rosary beads that were as dazzling as necklaces, all hanging side by side and quivering in the breeze, all colors, and of different stones, then of course the bright scapulars, and all kinds of little medals and beautiful crucifixes that were bigger than the girth of one's hand, and even some that had a little cavity within, where a relic was contained, and also beautiful prayer books and missals, some with gold edging and little holdalls made of filigree.

When we trooped in for the Benediction Eily slipped me a holy picture. It said "Remembrance is all I ask, but if Remembrance should prove a task Forget me." I was musing on it and swallowing back my tears at the very moment that Eily began to retch, and was hefted out by four of the men. They bore her aloft as if she was a corpse on a litter. I said to my mother that most likely Eily would die and my mother said if only such a solution could occur. My mother already knew. The next evening Eily was in our house, in the front room, and though I was not admitted, I listened at the door, and ran off only when there was a scream or a blow or a thud. She was being questioned about each and every event, and about the bank clerk and what exactly were her associations with him. She said no, over and over again, and at moments was quite defiant, and as they said an "upstart." One minute they were asking her kindly, another minute they were heckling, another minute her father swore that is was to the lunatic asylum that she would be sent, and then at once her mother was condemning her for not having milked for two weeks.

They were contrariness itself. How could she have milked since she was locked in the room off the kitchen, where they stowed the oats and which was teeming with mice. I knew for a fact that her meals—a hunk of bread and a mug of weak tea—were handed in to her, twice a day, and that she had nothing else to do only cry, and think, and sit herself upon the oats and run her fingers through it, and probably have to keep making noises to frighten off the mice. When they were examining her my mother was the most reasonable but also the most exacting. My mother would ask such things as "Where did you meet? How long were you together, were others present?" Eily denied ever having met him and was spry enough to say "What do you take me for, Mrs. Brady, a hussy?" But that incurred some sort of a belt from her father, because I heard my mother say that there was no need to resort to savagery. I almost swooned when on the glass panel of our hall door I saw a shadow, then knuckles, and through the glass the appearance of a brown habit, such as the missioner wore.

He saw Eily alone, and we all waited in the kitchen, the men supping tea, my mother segmenting a grapefruit to offer to the priest. It seemed odd fare to give him in the evening, but she was used to entertaining priests only at breakfast time, when one came every five or ten years to say mass in the house to re-bless it, and put pay to the handiwork of the devil. When he was leaving, the missioner shook hands with each of us, then patted my hair, and watching his sallow face and his rimless spectacles, and drinking in his beautiful speaking voice, thought that if I were Eily I would prefer him to the bank clerk, and would do anything to get to be in his company.

I had one second with Eily, while they all trooped out to open the gate for the priest, and to wave him off. She said for God's sake not to split on her. Then she was taken upstairs by my mother, and when they re-emerged Eily was wearing one of my mother's mackintoshes, a Mrs. Miniver hat, and a pair of old sunglasses. It was a form of disguise since they were setting out on a journey. Eily's father wanted to put a halter round her but my mother said it wasn't the Middle Ages. I was enjoined to wash cups and saucers, to empty the ashtray, and plump the cushions again, but once they were gone I was unable to move because of a dreadful pain that gripped the lower part of my back and stomach, and I was convinced that I too was having a baby and that if I were to move or part my legs some terrible thing would come ushering out.

The following morning Eily's father went to the bank, where he broke two glass panels, sent coins flying about the place, assaulted the bank manager, and tried to saw off part of the bank clerk's anatomy. The two customers—the butcher and the undertaker—had to intervene, and the lady clerk who was in the cloakroom managed to get to the telephone to call the barracks. When the Sergeant came on the scene, Eily's father was being held down, his hands tied with a skipping rope, but he was still trying to aim a kick at the blackguard who had ruined his daughter. Very quickly the Sergeant got the gist of things. It was agreed that Jack, that was the culprit's name, would come to their house that evening. Though the whole occasion was to be fraught with misfortune, my mother upon hearing of it, said some sort of buffet would have to be considered.

It proved to be an arduous day. The oats had to be shoveled out of the room and the women were left to do it, since my father was

busy seeing the solicitor and the priest, and Eily's father remained
in the town and boasting about what he wouldn't have done to the
bugger only for the Sergeant coming on the scene.

Eily was silence itself. She didn't even smile at me when I brought
the basket of groceries that her mother had sent me to fetch. Her
mother kept referring to the fact that they would never provide bricks
and mortar for the new house now. For years she and her husband
had been skimping and saving, intending to build a house, two fields
nearer the road. It was to be identical to their own house, that is to
say a cement two-storey house, but with the addition of a lavatory,
and a tiny hall inside the front door, so that, as she said, if company
came, they could be vetted there instead of plunging straight into the
kitchen. She was a backward woman and probably because of living
in the fields she had no friends, and had never stepped inside anyone
else's door. She always washed out of doors at the rain barrel, and
never called her husband anything but Mister. Unpacking the groceries she said that it was a pity to waste them on him, and the only
indulgence she permitted herself was to smell these things, especially
the packet of raspberry and custard biscuits. There was blackcurrant
jam, a Scribona swiss roll, a tin of herrings in tomato sauce, a loaf,
and a large tin of fruit cocktail.

Eily kept whitening and re-whitening her buckskin shoes. No
sooner were they out on the window than she would bring them in
and whiten again. The women were in the room putting the oats into
sacks. They didn't have much to say. My mother used always to laugh
because when they met Mrs. Hogan used to say "any newses" and
look up at her, with that wild stare, opening her mouth to show the
big gaps between her front teeth, but the "newses" had at last come
to her own door, and though she must have minded dreadfully she
seemed vexed more than ashamed, as if it was inconvenience rather
than disgrace that had hit her. But from that day on she almost stopped
calling Eily by her pet name which was Babbie.

I said to Eily that if she liked we could make toffee, because making
toffee always humored her. She pretended not to hear. Even to her
mother she refused to speak, and when asked a question she bared
her teeth like one of the dogs. She even wanted one of the dogs, Spot,
to bite me, and led him to me by the ear, but he was more interested

in a sheep's head that I had brought from the town. It was an arduous day, what with carting out the oats in cans and buckets, and refilling it into sacks, moving a table in there and tea chests, finding suitable covers for them, laying the table properly, getting rid of all the cob-webs in the corners, sweeping up the soot that had fallen down the chimney, and even running up a little curtain. Eily had to hem it and as she sat outside the back door I could see her face and her expres-sion and she looked very stubborn and not nearly so amenable as be-fore. My mother provided a roast chicken, some pickles and freshly boiled beets. She skinned the hot beets with her hands and said "Ah you've made your bed now" but Eily gave no evidence of having heard. She simply washed her face in the aluminum basin, combed her hair severely back, put on her whitened shoes, and then turned around to make sure that the seams of her stockings were straight. Her father came home drunk, and he looked like a younger man trotting up the fields in his oatmeal-colored socks—he'd lost his shoes. When he saw the sitting room that had up to then been the oats room, he exclaimed, took off his hat to it and said "Am I in my own house at all mister?" My father arrived full of important news which as he kept saying he would discuss later. We waited in a ring, seated around the fire, and the odd words said were said only by the men and then without any point. They discussed a beast that had had some ailment.

The dogs were the first to let us know. We all jumped up and looked through the window. The bank clerk was coming on foot, and my mother said to look at that swagger, and wasn't it the swagger of a hobo. Eily ran to look in the mirror that was fixed to the window ledge. For some extraordinary reason my father went out to meet him and straight away produced a packet of cigarettes. The two of them came in smoking, and he was shown to the sitting room which was directly inside the door to the left. There were no drinks on offer since the women decided that the men might only get obstreperous. Eily's father kept pointing to the glories of the room, and lifted up a bit of cretonne, to make sure that it was a tea chest underneath, and not a piece of pricey mahogany. My father said "Well Mr. Jacksie, you'll have to do your duty by her and make an honest woman of her." Eily was standing by the window looking out at the oncoming dark. The bank clerk said "Why so" and whistled in a way that I had heard him whistle in the past. He did not seem put out. I was afraid that on impulse he might rush over and put his hands somewhere on Eily's person. Eily's father mortified us all by saying she had a porker in her, and the bank clerk said so had many a lass, whereupon he got a slap across the face, and was told to sit down and behave himself.

From that moment on he must have realized he was lost. On all other occasions I had seen him wear a khaki jacket and plus fours, but that evening he wore a brown suit that gave him a certain air of reliability and dullness. He didn't say a word to Eily, or even look in her direction, as she sat on a little stool staring out the window and biting on the little lavalier that she wore around her neck. My father said he had been pup enough and the only thing to do was to own up to it, and marry her. The bank clerk put forward three objections — one that he had no house, two that he had no money, and three that he was not considering marrying. During the supper Eily's mother refused to sit down, and stayed in the kitchen nursing the big tin of fruit cocktail, and having feeble jabs at it with the old iron tin opener. She talked aloud to herself about the folks "hither" in the room and what a sorry pass things had come to. As usual my mother ate only the pope's nose, and served the men the breasts of chicken. Matters changed every other second, they were polite to him remembering his status as a bank clerk, then they were asking him what kind of crops grew in his part of the country, and then again they would refer to him as if he was not there saying "The pup likes his bit of meat." He was told that he would marry her on the Wednesday week, that he was being transferred from the bank, that he would go with his new wife and take rooms in a midland town. He just shrugged and I was thinking that he would probably vanish on the morrow but I didn't know that they had alerted everyone, and that when he did in fact try to leave at dawn the following morning, three strong men impeded him and brought him up the mountain for a drive in their lorry. For a week after he was indisposed, and it is said that his black eyes were as big as bubble gum. It left a permanent hole in his lower cheek as if a little pebble of flesh had been tweezed out of him.

Anyhow they discussed the practicalities of the wedding while they ate their fruit cocktail. It was served in the little carnival dishes and I thought of the numerous operations that Nuala had done, and how if it was left to Eily and me that things would not be nearly so crucial. I did not want her to have to marry him and I almost blurted that out. But the plans were going ahead, he was being told that it would cost him ten pounds, that it would be in the sacristy of the Catholic church, since he was a Protestant and there were to be no guests except those present, and Eily's former teacher a Miss Melody. Even her sister Nuala was not going to be told until after the event. They kept asking him was that clear, and he kept saying "Oh yeh," as if it were a simple matter of whether he would have more fruit cocktail or not. The number of cherries were few and far between, and for some reason had a faint mauve hue to them. I got one and my mother passed me hers. Eily ate well but listlessly, as if she weren't there at all. Towards the end my father sang "Master McGrath," a song about a greyhound, and Mr. Hogan told the ghost story about seeing the headless liveried man at a crossroads, when he was a boy.

Going down the field Eily was told to walk on ahead with her intended, probably so that she could discuss her trousseau or any last-minute things. The stars were never so bright or so numerous, and the moonlight cast as white a glow as if it were morning and the world was veiled with frost. Eily and he walked in utter silence. At last, she looked up at him, and said something, and all he did was to draw away from her, and there was such a distance between them as a cart or a car could pass through. She edged a little to the right to get nearer, and as she did he moved further away so that eventually she was on the edge of a path and he was right in by the hedge hitting the bushes with a bit of a stick he had picked up. We followed behind, the grown-ups discussing whether or not it would rain the next day, but no doubt wondering what Eily had tried to say to him.

They met twice more before the wedding, once in the sitting room of the hotel, when the traveling solicitor drew up the papers guaranteeing her a dowry of two hundred pounds, and once in the city when he was sent with her to the jewelers to buy a wedding ring. It was the same city as where he had been seeing the bacon curer's daughter and Eily said that in the jewelers he expressed the wish that she would drop dead. At the wedding breakfast itself there were only sighs and tears, and the teacher as was her wont stood in front of the fire, and mindless of the mixed company hitched up her dress behind, the better to warm the cheeks of her bottom. In his giving away speech my father said they had only to make the best of it. Eily sniveled, her mother wept and wept and said "Oh Babbie, Babbie," and the groom said "Once bitten twice shy." The reception was in their new lodgings, and my mother said that she thought it was bad form the way the landlady included herself in the proceedings. My mother also said that their household utensils were pathetic, two forks, two knives, two spoons, an old kettle, an egg saucepan, a primus, and as she said not even a nice enamel bin for the bread but a rusted biscuit tin. When they came to leave Eily tried to dart into the back of the car, tried it more than once, just like an animal trying to get back to its lair.

On returning home my mother let me put on her lipstick, and praised me untowardly for being such a good, such a pure little girl and never did I feel so guilty because of the leading part I had played in Eily's romance. The only thing that my mother had eaten at the wedding was a jelly made with milk. We tried it the following Sunday, a raspberry flavored jelly made with equal quantities of milk and water—and then whisked. It was like a beautiful pink tongue, dotted with spittle, and it tasted slippery. I had not been found out, had received no punishment, and life was getting back to normal again. I gargled with salt and water, on Sundays longed for visitors that never came, and on Monday mornings had all my books newly covered so that the teacher would praise me. Ever since the scandal she was enjoining us to go home in pairs, to speak Irish and not to walk with any sense of provocation.

Yet she herself stood by the fire grate, and after having hitched up her dress petted herself. When she lost her temper she threw chalk or implements at us, and used very bad language.

It was a wonderful year for lilac and the window sills used to be full of it, first the big moist bunches, with the lovely cool green leaves, and then a wilting display, and following that, the seeds in pools all over the sill and the purple itself much sadder and more dolorous than when first plucked off the trees.

When I daydreamed, which was often, it hinged on Eily. Did she have a friend, did her husband love her, was she homesick and above all was her body swelling up? She wrote to her mother every second week. Her mother used to come with her apron on, and the letter in one of those pockets, and sit on the back step and hesitate before reading it. She never came in, being too shy, but she would sit there while my mother fetched her a cup of raspberry cordial. We all had sweet tooths. The letters told next to nothing, only such things as that their chimney had caught fire, or a boy herding goats found an old coin in a field, or could her mother root out some old clothes from a trunk and send them to her as she hadn't got a stitch. "Tis style enough she has" her mother would say bitterly, and then advise that it was better to cut my hair and not have me go around in ringlets, because as she said "Fine feathers make fine birds." Now and then she would cry and then feed the birds the crumbs of the biscuit or shortbread that my mother had given her.

She liked the birds and in secret in her own yard made little perches for them, and if you please hung bits of colored rags, and the shaving mirror for them, to amuse themselves by. My mother had made a quilt for Eily and I believe that was the only wedding present she received. They parceled it together. It was a red flannel quilt, lined with white and had a herring-bone stitch around the edge. It was not like the big soft quilt that once occupied the entire window of the draper's, a pink satin onto which one's body could sink, then levitate. One day her mother looked right at me and said "Has she passed any more worms?" I had passed a big tapeworm and that was a talking point for a week or so after the furore of the wedding had died down. Then she gave me half a crown. It was some way of thanking me for being a friend of Eily's. When her son was born the family received a wire. He was given the name of Jack, the same as his father and I thought how the witch had been right when she had seen the initial twice, but how we had misconstrued it and took it to be glad tidings.

Eily began to grow odd, began talking to herself, and then her lovely hair began to fall out in clumps. I would hear her mother tell my mother these things. The news came in snatches, first from a family who had gone up there to rent grazing, and then from a private nurse who had to give Eily pills and potions. Eily's own letters were disconnected and she asked about dead people or people she'd hardly known. Her mother meant to go by bus one day and stay overnight, but she postponed it until her arthritis got too bad and she was not able to go out at all.

Four years later, at Christmas time Eily, her husband and their three children paid a visit home and she kept eyeing everything and asking people to please stop staring at her, and then she went round the house and looked under the beds, for some male spy whom she believed to be there. She was dressed in brown and had brown fur-backed gloves. Her husband was very suave, had let his hair grow long, and during the tea kept pressing his knee against mine, and asking me which did I like best, sweet or savory. The only moment of levity was when the three children, got in, clothes and all, to a pig trough and began to bask in it. Eily laughed her head off as they were being hosed down by her mother. Then they had to be put into the settle bed, alongside the sacks of flour, and the brooms, and the bric-à-brac, while their clothes were first washed and then put on a little wooden horse to dry before the fire. They were laughing but their teeth chattered. Eily didn't remember me very clearly and kept asking me if I was the eldest or the middle girl in the family. We heard later that her husband got promoted, and was running a little shop and had young girls working as his assistants.

I was pregnant, and walking up a street in a city, with my own mother, under not very happy circumstances, when we saw this wild creature coming towards us talking and debating to herself. Her hair was grey and frizzed, her costume was streelish, and she looked at us, and then peered, as if she were going to pounce on us, and then she started to laugh at us, or rather to sneer, and she stalked away and pounced on some other persons. My mother said "I think that was Eily," and warned me not to look back. We both walked on, in terror, and then ducked into the porch-way of a shop, so that we could follow her with our eyes, without ourselves being seen. She was being avoided by all sorts of people, and by now she was shouting something and brandishing her fist and struggling to get heard. I shook, as indeed the child within me was induced to shake, and for one moment I wanted to go down that street to her, but my mother held me back and said that she was dangerous, and that in my condition I must not go. I did not need much in the way of persuading. She moved on and by now several people were laughing, and looking after her and I was unable to move, and all the gladness of our summer day, and a little bottle of "Mischief," pressed itself into the palm of my hand again, and I saw her lithe and beautiful as she once was, and in the street a great flood of light pillared itself around a little cock of hay that was dancing about, on its own.

I did go in search of her years later. My husband waited up at the cross, and I went down the narrow steep road with my son, who was thrilled to be approaching a shop. Eily was inside the counter, her head bent over a pile of bills that she was attaching to a skewer. She looked up and smiled. The same face but much coarser. Her hair was permed and a newly-pared pencil protruded from it. She was pleased to see me and at once reached out and handed my son a fistful of rainbow toffees.

It was the very same as if we'd parted only a little while ago. She didn't shake hands, or make any special fuss, she simply said "Talk of an angel," because she had been thinking of me that very morning. Her children were helping, one was weighing sugar, the little girl was funneling castor oil into four-ouce bottles, and her eldest son was up on a ladder fixing a flex to a ceiling light. He said my name, said it with a sauciness as soon as she introduced me, but she told him to whist. For her own children she had no time, because they were already grown but for my son she was full of welcome and kept saying he was a cute little fellow. She weighed him on the big meal scales, and then let him scoop the grain with a little trowel, and let it slide down the length of his arm and made him gurgle.

People kept coming in and out and she went on talking to me while still serving them. She was complete mistress of her surround-ings and said what a pity that her husband was away, off on the lorry, doing the door-to-door orders. He had given up banking, found the business more profitable. She winked each time she hit the cash regis-ter, letting me see what an expert she was. Whenever there was a lull, I thought of saying something but my son's pranks commandeered the occasion. She was very keen to offer me something and ripped the glass paper off a two-pound box of chocolates and lay them before me, slantwise, propped against a can or something. They were emi-nently inviting, and when I refused she made some reference to the figure.

"You were always too generous," I said sounding like my mother or some stiff relation.

"Go on," she said and biffed me.

It seemed the right moment to broach it, but how?

"How are you," I said. She said that as I could see she was top-ping, getting on a bit, and the children were great sorts and the next time I came I'd have to give her notice so that we could have a sing-song. I didn't say that my husband was up at the road, and by now would be looking at his watch and saying "Damn" and maybe would have got out to polish or do some cosseting to the vintage motor car, that he loved so. I said and again it was lamentable, "Remember the old days Eily."

"Not much," she said.

"The good old days," I said.

"They're all much of a muchness," she said.

"Bad," I said.

"No, busy," she said. My first thought was that they must have drugged the feelings out of her, they must have given her strange brews and along with quelling her madness they had taken her spark away. There are times when the thing we are seeing changes before our very eyes, and if it is a landscape we praise nature, and if it is a specter we shudder or cross ourselves but if it is a loved one that defects, we excuse ourselves and say we have to be somewhere, and are already late for our next appointment.

She kissed me and put a little holy water on my forehead, delving it in deeply, as if I were dough. They waved to us and my son could not return those waves encumbered as he was with the various presents that both the children and Eily had showered on him. It was beginning to spot with rain, and what with that and the holy water and the red rowan tree bright and instinct with life, I thought that ours indeed was a land of shame, a land of murder and a land of strange sacrificial women.

STORIES BY CONTEMPORARY IRISH WOMEN

was composed in 11 on 13 Baskerville on Digital Compugraphic equipment
by Metricomp;
printed by sheet-fed offset on 50-pound, acid-free Glatfelter Natural Hi Bulk,
Smyth-sewn and bound over binder's boards in Holliston Roxite B,
and notch bound with paper covers,
with paper covers printed in 2 colors
by Braun-Brumfield, Inc.;
and published by

SYRACUSE UNIVERSITY PRESS

SYRACUSE, NEW YORK 13244-5160